*THE STORY
OF MY UNIVERSE*

THE STORY
OF MY
UNIVERSE

and other stories

*

CHRISTOPHER
GUERIN

First Edition   ISBN 13: 978-1-937484-81-1

AMIKA PRESS

466 Central AVE #23 Northfield IL 60093   847 920 8084

info@amikapress.com   Available for purchase on amikapress.com

Edited by John Manos. Cover photography by Christopher Guerin. Designed and typeset by Sarah Koz. Set in Ehrhardt, designed by Nicholas Kis in late 1600s, digitized by Monotype in 1991. Thanks to Nathan Matteson.

FOR
MICHAEL ANTMAN

CONTENTS

ACKNOWLEDGEMENTS

As always, my deepest appreciation to the love of my life, Ruth Diamond-Guerin, who has supported my writing and my career for almost fifty wonderful years. Herself an artist, as well as our two daughters, Julia and Alice, she has been my ever-present and untiring inspiration.

Special thanks to Michael Antman, whose taste, discernment, literary skill, and encouragement have been invaluable to me for decades.

Thanks also to Sarah Koz and John Manos of Amika Press for their professionalism and support.

In memory of James McNiece, who taught me that writing well is central to living well.

SHOOT ME

WHEN I was eighteen years old I almost killed a man. It would have been a "hunting accident," but looking back I can say it would have been less an accident than manslaughter. Though I'm as pro-gun-control as you can be, I happen to have a Sharpshooters badge from the NRA. When I was twelve, my Dad, who was a sergeant in the U.S. Army, used to take me to the rifle range. There, over the space of a few months, I worked myself up from a Marksman's badge in small-bore target rifle to Sharpshooter. God, I loved shooting. And when I was seventeen and could legally go out hunting on my own, I shot up everything in sight.

If you've read Flaubert's *Legend of Saint Julian the Hospitaller*, you'll know that in the first part, Julian is a maniacal hunter. He runs through the forest killing everything in sight. I was like that. My license might allow me to shoot only squirrels, pheasants, doves, or geese, but that didn't stop me from shooting muskrats, groundhogs, and even robins, bluejays, and every other bird in range. I seldom missed.

One day I was roaming through dense woods and saw a cardinal. I'd shot more than a few that year. I loved to see all those blood red feathers exploding. Only this time, no explosion. From behind a tree came a tall man in a red cap and military fatigues, carrying a hunter's bow. As he came straight for me, dropping his bow and lifting his quiver over his head and dropping it, his face was almost as red as

1

his cap. He punched me right in the nose, breaking it and decking me, then grabbed my .22/410 gauge over-under, broke it open and dumped out the shells, then flung it by the barrel against a big tree, shattering the stock. Then he leaned over me and took off his cap. He stuffed it in my face, his finger poking through the top. There was no button. Then he drew his finger across his scalp, showed it to me, then wiped the blood on my forehead. He reared back his right leg as if to kick me, then he stopped, said, "You stupid little fucker." I thought he was done; instead he got on his knees and straddled my chest, pinning my arms. As he pounded my face, I begged him to stop. I was totally helpless, but suddenly, after I said, "Please, mister, it was an accident," he stopped and asked my name. I told him, and he got off me and stood up, looking down at me and shaking his head. It was as if he'd worn himself out beating me. Then he charged off, picking up his weapons, as though looking for someone else to pummel. His bloodlust had been even worse than mine.

He had busted my right cheek, knocked out one of my front teeth, and fractured my collar bone. I passed out.

Of course, the guy knew my Dad, and as soon as he could reach a phone called the police, then Dad to warn him that the police would be there soon. He described exactly where I was probably still lying in the woods. Dad and the police found me still unconscious and took me to the hospital. I was released three hours later with a neck brace and my arm in a sling.

"You could have destroyed your entire family, you foolish bastard!" Dad yelled at me.

Instead of taking me home, Dad took me to the police station where I was arrested and charged with reckless endangerment. I spent the night in jail. The guy in the next cell had stabbed his girlfriend with a screwdriver. He kept humming the tune to Neil Young's "Down By the River". He scared the hell out of me.

The next day, while I was still in bed, an officer came in, yanked my blanket off and yelled, "Get the fuck up!" Then he took me into a room with a table, three chairs, and no windows. Expecting an officer or detective to come in, I was shocked when my Dad came in with my victim.

Dad sat down and said, "This is Fire Chief James Wiley. He's the man you shot yesterday."

"I'm sorry," I said in a whisper, as he sat down. "It was incredibly stupid and careless of me."

"Your father promises to have me arrested for assault and battery if I continue to press charges, so I'm letting it drop."

"I don't understand," I said, wondering why I was still there.

"I want you to say, 'With a razor in my hand,'" said the fire chief.

"What? Why?"

"We'll see. Go on."

I hesitated, looking at my Dad. He said, "Say it, damnit."

"With a razor in my hand."

"Again."

"With a razor in my hand."

"I think it was him," the fire chief said to my father. "When he was asking me to stop hitting him, I was pretty sure then."

"Go on," said my Dad, pointing at me.

"Did you call me this spring?"

"What?"

"Did you dial seven sevens in the middle of the night back in the spring?"

"Yes," I answered and put my head down on the table. He'd obviously told my Dad the whole story.

CLOSE CALL

I sit in my Dad's den, sneakered feet up on an ancient cobbler's table with shortened legs, sipping my fourteenth beer of the day. An hour earlier, I had been tackled in a driveway by a senior classman and kicked in the head by his young brother after I'd cursed at

their father in his own home after having crashed the party to cele-
brate the man's retirement from the Army Reserves. I had started a
shouting match because both boys thought themselves better than
me because my Dad was only an electrician and theirs was a lawyer.

It's one AM. I settle the bruise on the back of my head gently into
the corduroy sofa, pick up the phone and dial 777-7777. Someone
picks up after the first ring.

"Hello?" A man's voice.

I don't answer.

"Hello, who's there?"

I wait for the man to hang up.

"I know someone's there. I can hear your breathing. Is it you,
Clare? If it's you, Clare, I'm okay. You can talk to me now. Clare?"

I can tell he is getting increasingly emotional.

I still say nothing.

"Oh," he says, realizing it isn't Clare.

"Whoever this is, it's okay."

I can't believe the guy won't hang up.

"Are you in some kind of trouble?"

Finally, I say, "Why don't you just hang up?"

"Why didn't you?"

"Most people would have hung up."

"Probably." Now there is some exasperation. "Who is this?"

"Me. Sitting here with a razor in my hand."

"Yes?"

"I'm wondering whether I should use it on my wrists."

With my thumb, I work the softened label off the glass of the beer
bottle.

"Why would you even think of doing that?"

"Does that make any difference?" I say with a short laugh.

"I don't understand."

"Everybody's got reasons to do it, don't they? Doesn't everyone
have at least one damned good reason?"

"Reasons, maybe, but not one good enough. Tell me what's the problem."

"I've got this razor."

"You said that."

"I could draw a bath. They say it makes it easier. A nice hot bath and you don't feel much. And with the lights off."

"Messier, too."

I laugh again, briefly.

"Give me one reason, even a bad one, for not doing it."

"Let me ask you a couple questions, okay?"

"Sure."

"Are you sick?"

"No, but that's not…"

"Say just yes or no. Are you poor?"

"No, but we're not rich, if…"

"Please. Do you have parents?"

"A father."

"Do you like him?"

"Most of the time."

"Does he treat you badly?"

"I suppose not. What do you mean 'badly'?"

"Do you have friends?"

"Some."

"Do you have a girlfriend?"

"No!" I say, angrily.

"I see." His voice now gentle, thoughtful. "Now let me tell you something. Do you know what leukemia is?"

"I've heard of it."

"Do you know what it is?"

"Some kind of cancer, right?"

"It's my blood. It's rotten. It's turning bad like spilt milk."

Neither of us speaks for a minute.

"Who is Clare?"

"Clare is my wife. She doesn't want to be with me right now. She's at her mother's."

"Isn't there anybody there with you?"

"Just me. I'm still here. I say that to the mirror every morning. 'I'm still here.'"

Another pause.

I whisper, "I think I should go to bed. I'm really drunk."

"I could tell. I think sleep is a good plan."

"Were you asleep?" I have to ask.

"I don't sleep much anymore. I don't want to miss anything."

"Like this call."

"You got it."

"What's your name?"

"I'm Fire...no. On second thought, I don't think I should say."

"Do you want me to call again?"

"If you need to."

"You hang in there."

"You too."

"I hope your wife comes back soon."

"Me, too."

"I don't really have a razor," I add softly.

"I know. Maybe I don't really have leukemia."

I listen—his breathing is soft and measured, not a trace of excitement. I decide I don't want to know the truth that just one more question is likely to uncover. Then he hangs up.

I lifted my head up from the table and said, "So that was you."

"And that was you," he replied.

"What is wrong with you!" shouted my Dad.

The fire chief held up his hand. "It's okay."

"Are you still sick?" I asked.

"I'm in remission, for now."

"Did your wife come back?"

"The next day, actually, after I told her some crazy teenager had called me. I was very upset."

My Dad got up and said, "Let's go home."

The fire chief looked at him and said, "I would have dropped the charges anyway. It was an accident."

"A damned stupid accident," said my Dad, raising his voice.

"Can't argue with that," said the fire chief as both of us stood up.

I put out my hand and we shook, as I said, "Really, I am sorry. About everything."

"You're a strange one, I'll give you that," he said, turning toward the door.

"Not the word I'd use," said my Dad.

"Understood," he said, grinning at him.

I couldn't hold my tongue. "Can I ask you one question?"

He turned back and we looked at each other. "Did it make it better or worse that night?"

He turned to my Dad and said, "Believe it or not, it was a blessing."

BALL

"Ah, what a beautiful ball that is; red and round as an everywhere.
Good, that you created it. Wonder if it comes when one calls?"
                                                    —*Rainer Maria Rilke*

THE sheer fabric of physical impossibility billows like a blood-red balloon in the flickering dawn. We grow stupid and credulous in the hot, thick air, at the heights few riders reach. Under the obvious lamp of noon, we land with a bump and laugh at what was only an effect of lighting, after all.

What then gave more than it took? A gray ball the size of sponge rubber ball children toss about. It took my happiness—what there was of it—and nearly took my life.

And who was Randolph N. Domegas? He was nobody. He gave me the ball.

Any effective priest commands at will a demeanor of stern entreaty, to quell the dying man's blasphemies, to shame the drunkard's pummeling of his wife, or to chide his parish's neglect of the collection plate. Randolph N. Domegas was this way with everyone at our company. He drew apologies from people like juice from lemons.

In simple conversation he was unequalled by anyone I ever saw in a pulpit. Sin, taxes, politics, wages, the World Series, women's deodorants, all took on eschatological proportions. Nothing escaped his censure. One never took a stand in disagreement, and Heaven help the secretary who broached the subject of her boyfriend. Yet, in more ways than one, he held the lowest position in the company structure. Domegas was our record keeper.

Domegas wore the same chalk-streaked black wool suit summer

and winter and the same yellowed linen shirt every day. His huge, scarred face resembled a rumpled pillow and always bore razor cuts and tiny streaks of dark blood. His white hair flew in all directions. His black eyes glared from pinched watery sockets. The secretaries called him "the Deacon" behind his back, innocent of the irony. Through the wires of his record-keeper's cage he grimaced incessantly, puffed and blew, a gorilla performing for the Sunday crowd.

Why was he tolerated? In the basement, behind Domegas' screened counter, endless and labyrinthine rows of floor-to-ceiling steel shelving held every word, photograph, and bit of statistical data prepared for every client of our firm throughout its hundred-year history. Domegas knew where every piece of paper, cardboard and acetate lay. He knew, and no one else. His filing system was so hopelessly chaotic that without Domegas to decode it the contents of those myriad shelves were as accessible as the lost library of a dead culture with a forgotten language.

If Domegas didn't like you, if just the tone with which you asked for something was not to his liking, he would say, smiling stiffly, "That's not possible today. Come back when you can be more pleasant." There was nothing else one could do.

Watching all of this for several years with mounting fascination, I derived much satisfaction from the company's ongoing mistreatment of its workforce being in this one instance turned against itself. Even the company president was scared of Domegas. Unlike everyone else—everyone—Domegas was not expendable.

"Why don't you just fire him and have the files done properly?" I once asked a young vice president—bright red hair, ambitious, cutthroat.

"It's been proposed, of course," he explained, wincing so that I guessed he himself had made the suggestion. "We made a study of the difficulty of such a massive re-organization. Time, not money, is the problem. We calculated that it would take more than five years in total man-hours. Putting the entire clerical staff to the task, that amounted to roughly two months during which the files would be virtually useless. Lord help us the day that pompous old fart dies."

I assumed his having brought attention to the hopelessness of the situation—offering no workable solution—had done nothing to strengthen his position with the senior staff.

"Who let him run amok in the first place?"

"Nobody knows. It sure wasn't me!" he whined. "Most likely nobody let him. No one even knows how long he's been around, screwing things up. He won't let anyone see his employment records, and there's not a soul here who remembers when he was hired."

I was about to suggest that they offer him money when the vice president swore with exasperation and stomped off.

So what was Domegas' secret?

At first, I thought, an amazing example of applied mnemonics: a distribution of materials so cleverly devised that to Domegas, the immense jumble of information, appearing as so much confusion to anyone else, read like the pure logic of a recondite equation to an Einstein.

"How do you remember the whereabouts of everything so infallibly?" I asked him one day, poking my forefinger between the thin wires. "It is extraordinary. Some form of mnemonics, perhaps?"

I threw out the word, looking for the knowing smile.

"What's that?" the old man grumbled, "What are you jabbering about?"

"Recall by association," I defined.

"No!" he boomed his favorite word. But I thought I saw a twinkle in his eyes. Thinking I was close, I persisted.

"Then it must be photographic, or eidetic memory. Your mind takes a perfect or near perfect picture of that mess, such that it doesn't much matter where things are, your recall being total."

I was quoting from a book I'd been reading.

"No," he said again, more menacingly. "What in hell do you think this is, public entertainment? I just do my job the best I know how.

A feat you might try emulating as you've wasted the company's time for a full three minutes now."

"Then what?" I pleaded, aware of a certain risk in taking it further. Either he was lying, and these questions were a stupid waste of time, or his secret, like a magician's, was so clever and priceless that only a fool would expect him to divulge it. With an abrupt turn of his head, as though he'd just seen something in me he'd never seen before, he said, "If I tell you, do you promise to ask no more questions?"

I nodded eagerly.

"All right then. I bounce it in."

He said it without dramatic pause, without smiling. I walked off, shaking my head, forgetting the file I'd come for.

One day I betrayed Domegas. In private discussion with a superior, certain Domegas was invulnerable, I blamed him for something I had failed to do, which had cost the company a tidy sum. I'd seen it done before, even by the man to whom I betrayed Domegas.

I was later to learn that the record keeper had been severely reprimanded, docked a week's pay, and placed on supervisory probation. Had he sneezed in the wrong direction, labyrinth or no, they would have let him go. Or so they said.

I didn't see Domegas for more than a week, so I knew nothing of this at the time. I felt no guilt—ignorance has nothing to regret. I acted as though nothing had happened. Domegas, pale and sweaty, seemed sadly happy to see me.

"Would you like to know how I do it?" he asked breathlessly.

"Do what?"

"Remember. Remember everything. Everything!"

He was excited about something that might have excited me too, I supposed, but I had not only lost all curiosity in the subject of our previous discussion, I was hot on a new account with every opportunity of losing it without the proper effort right off. I began to explain my impatience when, amazingly, he stepped from behind his cage and held out his tightly-clenched fist. His right fist.

His knuckles were white. The arm trembled. He stooped, gracefully, to his knees and placed on the concrete floor with almost adoring care and gentleness a dull gray ball an inch and a half in diameter.

What's this nonsense, I thought.

He stood up and said, "Now, watch," and stamped his foot. He panted. This man is crazy, I thought, staring at the ball.

The ball lay there, motionless. I grunted. Then it began to tremble and dance as though the floor vibrated from a tremor. This mildly interested me. But when, without further encouragement, it quickly began to bounce inches off the floor, I was hopelessly enthralled. I watched the height of its bounce increase gradually with a soundless, accelerating rhythm that invigorated me like breaths of pure oxygen. When the ball bounced level with Domegas' waist he reached out and grabbed it with an exaggerated swooping of his right arm, which, I noticed for the first time, was muscular to the point of abnormality.

"Would you like to test me?" he asked with a gentle and genuine solicitude no less surprising than the ball's miraculous performance.

I stared at him, blinking idiotically.

"Test my memory?" he added with seeming illogic.

"What are you talking about?" I asked, but didn't wait for an answer. "Where did you get it? What's it made of?"

Ignoring this, Domegas took a ledger from under my arm and held it open in his left hand. He stared at the page and bounced the ball, catching it blind in his right hand with that same contorted swooping motion, as though he grabbed a bird in flight, trying not to hurt it. He handed me the report and said, "Ask anything."

I still didn't understand.

"Ask me anything from the list."

"Fourth line from the bottom," I said dully.

"Peteric Corporation. Six. Twelve. Forty-seven million, five hundred and two thousand, three hundred and seven dollars, and twelve cents. The double asterisk means the figure must be adjusted quarterly depending on accounts receivable."

Here's a genius making a fool of me, I decided.

"No, it's the ball." He seemed to read my mind. "You give it a try."

Shaking my head, I held out my palm. He grabbed it and put the ball there with a firm, gentle gesture that reminded me of a priest when he places the host on an extended tongue.

The ball was heavy, much more so than it had seemed by the old man's handling. I clenched it. Not giving, it seemed neither rubber nor plastic, but in hardness and texture more like steel, though steel would have made a ringing sound on the floor.

The ball was cold.

I tried to "bounce it in." Nothing happened. I remembered nothing of what I read, though there arose a faint sense of hope—the best word I can find—hope that what I was trying to do was after all not impossible. Twice I essayed the ledger's twin columns and twice failed. Just bouncing and catching the ball demanded total concentration.

"Of course it takes practice. And much discipline. Much practice and great discipline," Domegas said, "I can see that perhaps you may master it. You have great potential, but you must practice hard. You must learn to think!"

"I'm not so sure," I said and tried to hand it back to him.

"No, you keep it."

"I couldn't."

"Yes, you must. It is my gift. Yes, yes, I know. But do not worry. It's yours now. Happy you!" he concluded, enthused, pleased with his own generosity, gesturing reassurance as he disappeared behind the door to his labyrinth.

I never saw him again. It hadn't even occurred to me to thank him.

As I began to walk up the nine flights of stairs to my office, my bewilderment and an indescribably poignant anxiety gave way to excitement and wonder at the strange object I carried in my pants pocket. I understood, of course, that I now possessed a scientific phenomenon the discovery of which must be as momentous as that of gravity itself. Physics would be stood on its ear once again. Contemplating how I should make it known, to whom in the scientific community (where I had several business connections) I should reveal it first, I found myself leaping up the stairs, taking them two and three at a time. Upon reaching the sixth floor landing I'd reached no conclusions. I knew only that I wouldn't show the ball to anyone before I had the chance to play with it and explore its secrets for myself.

For the rest of the day it felt, deep in my pocket, like a small animal continuously turning in its sleep, or like a restless fetus ready to exit the womb. At times it grew quite active, forcing me to grab it. I became lost in thought of it, the ball's disciple.

That night, walking home, I smiled at everything. Strangers, friends, a chink in a red brick building, my unpolished black shoes. The ball slapped against my thigh in my loose trousers in time with my step, beating like a heart. I walked as Abraham must have walked, knowing he was chosen.

I arrived on my own block and had the fancy to take out the ball and with a properly angled bounce have it precede me like a pet dog. Just about to toss it, aiming, I glimpsed someone walking up the street. I jammed the ball back deep in my pocket and hurried in, thinking, Don't be a fool!

In my rooms, I discovered that I was exhausted. Intending to nap for an hour or so, I put the ball on the bedside table, steadying it against the clock radio until it was motionless. But it rolled off and began to bounce energetically around the room. I caught the ball up and stuck it in the dresser drawer among socks. Curled up in the blankets and on the verge of sleep I heard a thumping that grew and grew until I feared the dresser might be battered to pieces. I retrieved the ball. I went to sleep drained and irritated, with the ball quivering like a tiny generator in my clenched fist. I woke up at seven-thirty the next morning having all night dreamed the first of the dreams I suffer nightly:

Within a sphere, brighter, more reflective than chrome, smaller spheres travel randomly and collide with each other and the interior wall of the larger sphere with ever-increasing speed and violence.

A single ray of light illuminates the space like a comet ricocheting off the wall and the other spheres.

The smaller spheres number 332 and in aggregate take up exactly half the volume of the larger sphere. Each time they strike one another or the wall of the larger sphere they ricochet, moving twice the speed as before. With each collision the attendant sound, similar to the crack of two ball bearings when they percuss, increases in proportionate magnitude.

I am incarcerated within each of the smaller spheres. I am conscious and can see, touch, and hear. I cannot smell and I have no tongue. The three corporeal senses I do have are raw, keen, like three bare, tightly-woven nerves.

In seconds the din, the weird light, and the jarring have become excruciating. Not being able to scream becomes another sensation, strident and terrifying in itself.

Though to each sphere of me the others are moving too fast to be seen, when I collide head-on with another, there is an instantaneous stopping. Then, in the brilliant wall of the larger sphere I see, as though in a spoon, the fleeting apparition of my self-tormenting self.

The awareness of the multiplicity of self-torture becomes a fifth sensation—one of confusion, utter and perfect, which also grows at the doubling rate.

All the I's in each of the spheres are dreaming simultaneously. I am aware that this is a dream, but that does not lessen its horror. A sixth sensation, that of eternity, grows with the others as I struggle to awaken and cannot....

I took the ball with me to work, reconciled to the fact that only the resiliency of my body could contain it, that and concentration, attentiveness so constant that I could think of little else.

I had never before been so aware of my body.

At each moment I yearned to place the ball on the floor, to feel that almost sensual excitement as it rose higher and higher with each inexorable bounce.

I desired nothing but to be alone with it.

In a strategy meeting concerning my new account, the thought of showing the ball to someone, revealing it to scientists for research and, finally, the pronouncement to the world of something as improbable as the Philosopher's Stone or the Perpetual Motion Machine, lost its luster. I might become famous, rich. That seemed poor compensation for losing the ball forever.

Oblivious, I didn't hear a vice president's question. He stopped the meeting. "Damnit!" he yelled, "if you can't keep your mind on matters at hand, I'll pass the account to Jacobs here!" Jacobs looked at me hungrily. I was already halfway to the door when I said, "You don't know who you're talking to."

By day's end, I was talking to no one, keeping my distance. I had treated everyone, friends and enemies alike, with blunt and over-bearing patronization, not unlike Domegas. My behavior did not worry me. None of this seemed in the least bit important. That I had not been let go was a matter of indifference to me. I could make them toady to me with a phone call.

That night I kept a date with a girl from the accounting department. We'd been seeing each other for more than six months; she often hinted at marriage. I took her for drinks at a local pub, then dinner at a Greek restaurant around the corner. She talked about her job, a possible promotion, what she would do with the extra money. My sole contribution to the conversation was that she ought not count too much on anything the company promised.

"What's the matter with you tonight?" she cooed as we walked the four blocks to her apartment.

"Nothing."

"Well, there must be something wrong, honey. Did something happen at work? I heard that something happened," she ventured and took my arm—my hand, I knew, was white in my pocket, gripping the ball. "Why, you're tense as a tiger."

"Nothing happened. Nothing at all. I've just had a long day."

"Well, we'll just have to try to relax you a little bit," she crooned seductively and tugged my arm. I resisted the impulse to push her away.

In her bedroom, she excused herself and went into the bathroom. She could be a wild creature, but she never let me undress her. She'd say, with a wink, "This way you can be sure everything's just right."

I took off my jacket and began to unbuckle my pants. Then I thought twice about it and, with my fly still closed, I leaned back against the headboard.

She returned with a white towel wrapped around her thin body. She grasped the towel between her breasts. It barely covered her sex. She smiled and sat down next to me.

"You're not undressed, honey?"

"I'm not feeling too…," I began, but the sight of her breasts lifted tightly against the towel with the nipples peeking over excited me. "Let's try something different," I said. Her eyes darkened. "I'll keep my clothes on."

"If that's what you want," she sighed heavily, breathing faster, somehow spurred by the idea.

She let the towel drop and undressed me as little as necessary and climbed on top.

In the next few moments she moaned, I didn't. I clenched my secret in my right hand. My left hand gripped the bedstead. I decided not to see her again.

Later, back in my apartment, I had the same dream. It took up where the first left off.

The next morning I called in sick, and as I put the receiver on its hook, I knew that as long as I possessed the ball I would not go to work again.

I sat in a chair in my blind-darkened bedroom all morning. The hardwood floor perfect for bouncing the ball, I let it roll out of my hand, almost absentmindedly, watched it bounce high enough to drop back into my palm, and felt at once the most soothing and disquieting sensation, as though I was giving blood.

Again, I tried to prove the ball's power over memory. I failed in precisely the same way, except that now there was no feeling of hope for improvement. The drag on my concentration being even greater, I began to contemplate a possible weakness in my mind or character that might not exist in Domegas. I guessed that were I strong enough physically or mentally I might accomplish it, the remembering. But this came entirely from within. The ball no longer quivered as though trying to impart a secret. Instead, just holding it in my hand seemed to demand an inner strength I could only kid myself about having.

I left my apartment at noon totally ravenous. I couldn't remember ever being that hungry. For breakfast I devoured four eggs and a twelve-ounce steak. When that didn't satisfy me, I ordered a stack of waffles and ate that, too.

While gulping down the fifth cup of coffee, it came to me that the ball might have a use just as valuable as infallible memory.

It's common knowledge with pool players that a billiard ball, no matter how hard or how well it is stroked by the cue, cannot roll to hit the felt rails more than six times. It has nothing to do with strength or talent, but with the absorption by the rails of the ball's energy.

I soon found myself at the Cue and Cushion. The man I was looking for was practicing by himself at a corner table. We had played often, had gambled as much as a hundred dollars on a single game. Now I made a different bet.

After a few games of eight ball to soften him up, in which I lost forty dollars, I said, "Tell you what," producing the ball, "I'll bet whatever you like that I can make this ball go fifteen rails."

"You're crazy!" he laughed, "For one thing, it's too small to even hit the rail properly. It'll bury."

"Fifteen, easy."

"What is this, a trick?"

"No trick. Here," I said and handed it to him.

I couldn't believe I did it.

"Why, it's just a hunk of steel!"

I grabbed it back, thinking, Stupid! That was stupid!

"Tell you what. I'll bet you two hundred it won't go more than ten rails. For every one over ten I'll give you a hundred, and for every one under ten you give me two hundred."

"Bet," I said and made the shot.

The ball increased speed from rail to rail. I grabbed it at fifteen.

"Damn! What's it made of?"

"It's all in the stroke."

He kept asking to see it but I would only let him look as I turned it around with my fingers. I left with a grudgingly written check for five hundred dollars I vaguely hoped was good.

For the rest of the afternoon and halfway into the evening I sat in front of the television set, feeling the kind of enriched anxiety and nameless guilt that caffeine induces. Inert, I sat watching game shows and sitcoms, news programs and more sitcoms. Now and then I'd bounce the ball and feel its powerful shock run up and down my nearly numb arm. Sometimes, lost in contemplation of the ball, I would look up and realize that I'd missed half a program.

At nine-thirty I went out to find the whore I knew. Never before in my entire life had it even occurred to me to employ her services or those of any other. She was only the friend of a friend. He'd once introduced us in hopes of increasing her clientele, as a favor to her.

I took a taxi to where I knew she conducted her affairs, a clean little bar in a respectable neighborhood. When I asked the driver the fare, he turned to me, smiling ingratiatingly, and said "Four dollars, twenty centavos, por favor."

I gave him a five.

"Vaya con God," he said, nodding and grinning.

In the clean little bar, I didn't see her and ordered a drink. I sat alone for three hours, downing scotch and waters and thinking just one thought. The ball seemed lighter now, less demanding, easier to manipulate. I rolled it in my palm, thinking of what it might do to her.

When she walked in the door she saw me almost immediately, though I sat at a table near the back of the room. She looked less like a whore than I remembered.

"I never expected to run into you again," she said. "Have you come to meet a business friend? Is Panda coming?" she added, the thought just striking her. She sat down.

"Yes and no," I said and winked.

"Oh, really!" She laughed. "Well, that's fine with me. I always encourage Panda Bear's friends. I can trust his judgment. But I am a little surprised. Last time you acted like I carried some disease. "

"No, you're much mistaken," I said with lying exaggeration. "I thought you very nice from the beginning. I was just, well...."

"I hope it's been over for a while," she said, smiling suspiciously.

"No, not really. But don't worry."

"Good. Be nice and buy me a drink and I won't even charge you. How about that? At least not for the first time."

She winked and grabbed my leg under the table.

Her apartment reminded me of my own and I complimented her sense of taste. We applied ourselves to the usual grappling embraces on her purple satin bedspread. Soon weary of her, I said, "I want to file a complaint." I didn't say it jokingly.

The look in her mussed, flushed face was of blank, open-eyed curiosity.

"I don't like it when a woman has to fake it."

"Well, now...," she began, getting up.

I grabbed her shoulders and pushed her, gently, back down.

"Wait a minute. I'm not asking for much," I said, releasing her, patting her fleshy stomach. "I just want to try something that might make it a little more enjoyable."

She pushed my hand away and sat up.

"Panda Bear didn't say you were strange some way. I'm not..."

"I'm not," I pleaded gently, "Besides, how would he know? Don't worry. I've nothing the least bit dangerous in mind."

I reached into my pocket (my pants were still halfway on—she'd told me it was not unusual) and took out the ball.

"See? Just try it," I said, with two fingers spinning it before her mascara-smeared eyes.

She laughed. Then she spread her legs. "Is that all?" She laughed out loud and bawdily. "If it'll help make it better for you! Just don't put it in so far that you lose it!"

So, I put it there and pressed it in, sat back on my haunches, palms pressed between my knees, watching.

"Hey! What is it?" she asked, excitement growing almost against her will. "Is it electric? It feels great! God, what a ball! I think, I, I think I might after all!"

I thought I would too.

It worked like magic. Better than magic. Soon her cries were of no sort of joy at all. "God, get it out of me!" she screamed as I saw the blood on the satin.

We both groped for it. I pushed her flailing hands away. Safe again in my palm, the ball was clean, dull gray, as before.

The next morning, utterly exhausted from hours of pleading with and placating the hysterical woman with promises (I wrote her a check for five hundred dollars, though I knew she would never tell the police), and later, of sleepless tossing in my own bed, afraid to sleep again, afraid to dream, I retreated to my athletic club. Responsible for my actions in name only, I felt the need for enclosure and absolute geometric simplicity, to see what the ball could really do. I knew just the place: an old squash court with no gallery, just a simple, white cube with a door.

First, I did what Domegas had done. I placed the ball on the floor, stamped my foot and watched it rise. As it bounced steadily higher, a thought struck me: one hundred and one percent resiliency! So simple. So impossible.

I was lucid as space, as void.

When I grabbed the ball, it lifted me to my toes. Though the realization had been slowly growing, I now fully understood what Domegas had meant by discipline, that it involved much more than tricks of memory, more than huge, muscular arms.

If only I had thought more of Domegas.

Playing, I felt that even now, experiencing the ball in what I thought to be its purest manifestation, my enjoyment of it was somehow reprehensible, a violation of something I could not name. I threw the ball to the floor and grabbed it. My arm wrenched so that it sprung out straight, stretched to its fullest length; I whooped with depraved laughter. I rolled it and watched the roll turn into a loping bounce, off one wall, then the joining wall, and grabbed it shoulder high. What a marvelous sensation. Energy, pure and unfettered by any other law of nature.

Throughout all these experiments a fear doubled and doubled again in my chest, palpable, blood-thick, as though I were experiencing the slow, terrible revelation of a miracle, knowing that I was not strong enough to bear it.

Still, I persisted.

My next thought was to let it bounce to the ceiling. I expected the rapid increase in speed as the ball began to accelerate in both directions. With alarming rapidity, the ball slammed up and down, noiselessly. Then my understanding grew even deeper. Here, I knew, was the physical embodiment of infinity.

I became afraid that its speed might increase beyond my capacity to stop it.

By giving it just that much freedom, I'd already lost it.

I lunged for the ball. A massive arrow of pain shot from my hand to my shoulder. I fell to my knees, the arm limp at my side. Worse than shattering my arm, I'd deflected the ball. It now bounced all over the room, hitting all six planes, striking me repeatedly with ever increasing force.

Even more terrifying, the ball had become red. I screamed.

The ball exploded with a muffled boom and engulfed me in red particles that tickled. I was soon laughing hysterically, totally lost, the pain vanquished as by a powerful drug. Then, each particle shattered again; a cloud of hot dust laved me like a whirlpool—the sensation simple and complete purification.

I spent the next eight months in the hospital. The pain was unbearable, seeming to multiply when I remembered the exquisite sensation of that minute pelting, of that ecstasy I experienced when each mote shattered for the last time and vanished into the invisible pattern that runs through everything.

They tell me that I will never walk again, that my right arm might just as well have been taken off, that it may be years before I can wrench a sensible sound from the jumbled muscles in my face.

The police continue prodding me to write down the names or a description of the "maniacs" who did this to me. I tell them nothing.

A lawyer from the club sat on my bed and refused to go away until I'd signed his paper. He left a check for $500,000.

What do I do now?

Wait and think and dream.

Until the end (I think not soon to come), I'll be alone, as I was and am now. And after?

POET
TO POET

1

URING the '90s the resident poet at our Midwestern university had three wives: Clare (two years); Ellen (three years); and, finally, Marsha (three years).

Freddie Gault married poets, exclusively, which is the reason I'm writing this cautionary tale.

My university hired Freddie Gault after he published his first volume of poetry at the age of twenty-six. It was nominated for the National Book Award. His publishing credits—the book as well as dozens of book reviews and poems in literary magazines—made him a prime target for English departments across the country looking for poets for their burgeoning MFA writing programs.

A writer myself, primarily of short stories, I was already a tenure-track associate professor when Freddie arrived. We were tenured at the same time two years later.

I had little to boast of in the publishing world, except a slim volume of stories, which was kindly reviewed, and pretty much annual acceptance of a story by one of the upper-tier literary magazines. My primary value was as the director of our writing program and as a fiction writing teacher that my students liked, however little I was really able to help them.

I mention myself not only to explain how I know so much about Freddie's life, but also because I will become a part of the story. When it came to the writing program, I was technically his boss, but we were drinking buddies, so I heard just about everything.

To begin, Freddie was not built in the mold of poets like Lowell, Plath, Berryman, Sexton, or Thomas. He was not bi-polar, a dipsomaniac, a serial adulterer, suicidal, clinically depressed, or schizophrenic.

No, Freddie's problem was his ego, the gratification of which took many forms.

He married Clare a year out of graduate school at a state university where they had been classmates. They'd stayed on as adjunct faculty and could barely make ends meet.

Then we hired Freddie. We had no teaching position for Clare, but we needed a department secretary and, with a recent past of near poverty, she was happy to take the job.

As Clare was to tell me years later, she was, for a time, the more successful poet during their marriage. Even Freddie said so. In fact, her success with magazines, which resulted in two books of her own being published, outstripped his.

Then things changed. Each had been the other's "first reader." From unqualified praise, Freddie's criticism almost imperceptibly turned negative. She chose not to take offense and instead found herself praising his efforts more than they deserved. Then, having always offered his thoughts verbally over drinks, one day he took up a red pen and escaped to his study. The next day she found her poem in the living room virtually obscured with red ink.

What puzzled Clare most was that Freddie's own work was beginning to gain traction, including the appearance of his second book. Yes, some of the reviews accused Freddie's work of being difficult, often "impenetrable," and "deliberately obfuscatory." She thought that these judgments might have irritated Freddie, but there was nothing to be jealous about!

As this was only the first though worst incident of such brutal criticism, she kept quiet about it. Their relationship as "first readers" ended without it being mentioned. The poem he'd savaged was accepted for publication, as she had written it, a few months later. When she showed him the acceptance letter for her second book the following year, he took it into his study, returned half an hour later and dropped it—covered with red ink—into her lap.

"This jerk doesn't even know how to write a decent acceptance letter," he said.

"Men are jerks, not women," she said calmly. "The editor is a woman."

" 'Bitch' then."

"I'd say the equivalent for you would be 'prick.' "

Then it all blew up.

"I just want to know when you will acknowledge that everything you've written is far better than it would have been without my guidance."

"When it becomes true," she replied.

As she told it, she continued to stand her ground for the next two hours. The argument ended when he promised never to read even one more of her "miscreations."

"I consider you no more than a poetaster, a poet manqué, and a spiritual plagiarist, stealing the essence of my work and smudging it into your own scribblings."

They were divorced a few months later and, based on her two books, she found a teaching job at a top ten university, and, a year later, a husband.

She told me: "If he'd been screwing someone, it would have been less offensive, let alone forgivable."

2

As it turned out, he had been cheating on her, and with another poet.

This was Ellen, whom he'd met at one of his coffee shop readings that Clare had not attended. Ellen wrote sonnets. She was also the high school librarian. She was four years older than Freddie and had self-published two volumes of 200 sonnets each, based on the works of the great Renaissance painters and printmakers. They were married a year after his divorce came through. He went to the chancellor and suggested that the university library hiring Ellen would be an accommodation all parties should find agreeable.

They rented a rather dilapidated Victorian home not five minutes from campus.

Ellen was by far the most beautiful of Freddie's wives, even if she was past her dewy youth. This gratified his sexual ego, and her being a formalist poet was something he could safely look down upon.

Looking at those three years through the lens of numerous faculty cocktail parties and dinners, plus the many conversations Freddie and I had over drinks, it seemed that this marriage was made to last. Neither wanted children, and both spent enough time on their own writing that they didn't tend to get on each other's nerves. And, Freddie confided more than once, the sex was *sine qua non*.

Apparently that view was not equally shared.

After a few years Ellen found herself bored with him sexually and apparently rationalized her decision to find a lover at least partly on the assumption that he already had his own or eventually would, just as he'd found her.

But there were other things going on that contributed to her disaffection and to his lack of performance. He'd begun to drink too much. Not the come-home-late-drunk-as-hell variety. No, most of his drinking took place in his study as he wrote. Almost every night he'd drink two bottles of cabernet, no more and no less, and smoke a pack of cigarettes. All in two hours. The result was a new poem every night. The one time she complained that it made him surly or sleepy, he'd simply handed her the poem he'd written that night.

"Look, here's the reason. It's fuel! At this rate I'll write a book every six months!"

Now they'd made a pact early on *not* to read each other's work until it was published. So, she handed the poem back and let the subject drop.

Things went on this way until two things happened. At a cocktail party, she overheard a near-drunk Freddie say, "Formal poetry is like playing tennis with a bazooka; rhymes just blast through the net. Total overkill. And is there such a thing as a new rhyme? Nonsense! They were all exhausted by Byron, Keats and Shelley, Frost and Auden! The essential nature of rhyme is plagiarism!"

At first, she chuckled to herself at this reversal of Frost's famous dig at free verse (that writing it was "like playing tennis without a net"), then she realized he was talking about her sonnets. "With Ellen's," he continued, "every other line or so—Blam! Damn!— there goes a couplet! It gives me a headache, though I'd never tell her that to her face."

She stepped forward and shoved his arm, which held a glass of red wine, spilling it all over the rug. "No, you didn't have the balls to say something so ignorant and insulting to my face. And your *poetry*, dear one, is an utter crapitulation to ragged obscurantism."

Everyone howled with laughter, having merely giggled at Freddie's evisceration of his wife's efforts.

Yes, she had read and remembered those reviews of his second book.

The second event, which brought things to a head, was the night she stole into his study after he'd gone to bed early. Over the next hour, she read most of what he'd written under the influence. She kept this a secret until months later when this, his third book, was rejected by his publisher. By then she was on to her second lover and a real publisher had accepted her third 200 sonnets. Because each poem was meant to be accompanied by the famous image it was based on, a publisher of art books had taken it on.

After Freddie scoffed about her "coffee table book" to the entire English faculty, she told him about her love affairs, but not before revealing she'd read his latest poetry. She called it the worst shit since the confessional poetry of the '50s and '60s. When I asked Freddie what she meant, he told me that his entire book was about their marriage.

The book, called *Running Silk Stockings*, was eventually published and, except by feminist critics, praised for its candor, sexual frankness, and psychological insight.

Of course, Ellen saw it differently, and they were divorced later that year.

On the basis of the new book Ellen was hired by a private college to teach poetry writing for their MFA program; also, to Freddie's horror, a course for the Women's Studies program on male poets' abuse of women, with *Running Silk Stockings* as the primary text. She never remarried.

3

Freddie and I didn't see as much of each other outside the department for the next year. He was licking his wounds and writing poetry that had reverted to subject matter that he had only dabbled with in the past—politics.

His list of targets included everything from the current president's speech impediment to political correctness, from government bailouts to the National Endowment for the Arts, from the welfare state to tax loopholes for the super-rich. Nothing got a pass. He wrote from no political stance, left, right, or center, but from all possible angles. He'd created a voice he called "Mr. Privy," which came to mean "privilege," the state of being well-informed, and, of course, the toilet. Perhaps the most distinctive feature was the more than occasional use of "potty talk," like that of a naughty four-year-old boy.

Some of it was very funny, but the rest was a ranting bore. The magazines published a few of the shorter early poems, but eventually figured out where he was going. His publisher turned down the first book, as did five other publishers. Even his agent refused to spend time flogging his tantrums.

When it became clear that this was all self-defeating, he went silent. The drinking had moderated, replaced by sexual predation, his victim being my wife of seven years, Marsha.

Marsha was the first woman I hired for the writing program. She was a short story writer with publishing credits far better than mine. We started dating during her second year and didn't bother to hide the relationship; everyone seeming to approve gave it a sort of inevitability, of blessing.

Marsha and I were very happy, and our both being writers didn't figure into our relationship because we never talked shop. She gave me a beautiful boy, Devon, who, at five years of age, began to demonstrate real talent on the piano. Our evenings often found us in three different rooms, Marsha and I writing, and Devon practicing.

The first hint of something between Marsha and Freddie, which everyone ignored, me in particular, was a number of long, intense conversations at various faculty events. Of course, there was a lot to talk about: office politics, recruiting more staff, budget cuts, and the constant group evaluation of individual students. Did he or she have talent? Freddie was particularly good at this, the "discoveries," which he was so eager to take credit for.

Then these intense conversations took on the aura of being distinctly private. I didn't notice it because whenever I approached them they always welcomed my joining in.

One day, a colleague said in passing, "Hey, what's going on with Freddie and Marsha? Twice last night they gave me the brush when I tried to mingle their way."

I told him I had no idea.

He laughed and said, "Watch your back, buddy. They might be plotting your overthrow!"

I laughed and didn't give it another thought. Marsha was up for tenure and though I had to be excluded from the decision, Freddie was free to involve himself. That's what I assumed was going on.

One night after Devon was in bed, Marsha said, "I have a confession to make."

It took me a moment to look up from the novel I was reading to see her hesitant smile. She was smoking a Camel, a habit from her teens that she'd taken up again only a few months before, and a subject we'd argued about, with the compromise that she confine it to her study. I decided not to make an issue of it now.

"Sweetie?"

"I felt you should know," she began, "I've been writing different stuff for some time now."

"What does that mean?" I asked, slightly irritated by her mysterious way of speaking, which her smoking seemed to amplify.

"I mean poetry. I've been writing poetry."

"Well, okay, that's great. Why dramatize it? Write all the poetry you want."

Looking relieved, she said, "I thought you might have a problem with it because I teach fiction, not poetry."

"Why should that matter?"

"Well, in the sense that I'm not writing fiction at all. I'm done with it. I'm written out."

I put the novel aside and leaned toward her. Something else was going on here.

"I'm sure it's just a temporary block."

"I'm just going to blurt this out, okay? So don't be upset. But Freddie says I've always been a poet and he thinks I'm very good."

"So? Okay."

"I thought I was just going through a block too, but Freddie says I should never have been a fiction writer to begin with."

"Sorry, but that's nonsense. You've got a ton of publishing credits."

"And, well, he's been coaching me."

No, even this didn't make me suspicious.

"Well, he's the best," I said encouragingly.

"I wanted you to know because I have several poems coming out in the next month or two. Freddie's been recommending me everywhere."

"That's great!" I said, "I can't wait to see them."

"It's been funny. We just started spending an hour or so in his office or mine every few days and going over things. He's brilliant."

"I suppose you'd like to switch to teaching poetry."

"No, that's not necessary," she laughed. "I still know how to teach what I teach! But if you need another poet sometime, I'm more than willing to teach both."

"My Marsha, a poet."

She giggled girlishly, and then, again serious, "You don't think it will affect my tenure decision, do you?"

"You know I can't say anything," I began, then thought it would be innocent enough to add, "But I can't imagine why it would."

She tossed her cigarette into the fireplace, stood up and grabbed my hand, and dragged me from my chair.

"Yes, Marsha's a poet," she said, "right now a rather horny poet," and led me toward the stairs.

4

Maybe it was the distraction of her tenure decision (it was granted almost unanimously) or because I was working hard to finish a collection of short stories, but it wasn't until Marsha's poems were published that I was forced to wake up.

I'm getting a little ahead of myself, but it's time to confess my opinion of the state of poetry. With the exception of a few of our more famous poets, and they are a dwindling crew, contemporary poetry is execrable dross. Give a four-year-old child a pair of scissors, a copy of *Better Homes and Gardens* or *National Geographic,* some glue and paper, and the result would be about as compelling.

When I receive a magazine that has published one of my stories,

I feel obligated to at least glance at some of the poetry therein. I'm never disappointed: pages and pages of pointless, precious, pretentious Rorschach inkblots.

I do not include Freddie in my general criticism, even if his subject matter has never been to my taste. He has a genius for putting even a stupid thought into lovely, limpid, and intricately structured English.

Which leads me to the point of this aside—Marsha's "poetry"? Utter fail, as in a grade of "F," with only one comment in the margin: "toss this out, read some real poets, and start over."

Whereas her stories were always models of polished prose, with compelling characters and sharp, often shocking endings, her poetry was maundering mumbled muttering about her personal observations of the world around her, mostly nature.

There was even a feint at "originality"—each poem was entirely in caps, in HERCULANUM typeface, as though she was some sibyl speaking from Ancient Greece.

I received my copies at the office, with all my subscriptions, but somehow Freddie managed to intercept the first to arrive, *The Paris Review,* at the department's mailbox.

He knocked and came in and leaned back against the door with something behind his back.

His face was completely expressionless.

"Prepare yourself," he said.

"Okay," I said, pushing away from my desk where I'd been going through my students' latest short stories.

Then he smiled broadly, stepped forward, and handed me the magazine, which he'd already relieved of its wrapper.

"I can't look at that," I said, "I was going to savor the moment over a glass of wine with Marsha."

"She asked me to do it this way."

This would turn out to be only half true.

"What? Why?"

"She's scared you'll hate it. She doesn't want to see your expression when you've first seen it."

"Is it that bad?" I was joking, which he didn't get.

"Judge for yourself, but I think it's brilliant."

I put the magazine down without opening it. Something about his smirking interference had ticked me off.

"Before I look at it, I want to know why you're even here with this."

"You're upset that I delivered your mail," he scoffed.

Then it hit me.

"Is there something going on between you two?"

"What the hell?"

"Is there?"

"Marsha told me you know all about my helping her. Is that a problem?"

"It's one thing to sit with her and offer advice. This *intervention* —I can't find a better word for it—is a bit more than that."

"Well, yes," he laughed, "I suppose."

"Why? Did she suggest it?"

"Well, not exactly. She said she was anxious to see your reaction, but afraid as well, so I offered to do this."

I stood up and took a step toward him.

"What, what would you say if I told you it was inappropriate. Or, more accurately, it suggests that you two are a bit closer than I find understandable, given…"

"Now wait…" he began, but I quickly added:

"That she is my wife, and not some silly student of yours."

"You think she's silly?"

"That's not what I mean."

He took a deep breath, indicating to me that I was onto something.

"Freddie," I said, picking the magazine up and getting out my keys to the room, "the question I have to ask is better asked of Marsha, don't you think?"

The minute I got home I called to ask the babysitter if she'd be willing to have Devon at her home for a few hours. They left half an hour later.

Marsha had an afternoon class and got home about an hour after I did. By then I'd read her poems several times. There were three for a total of six pages. The only emotion they invoked in me was sadness and pity. If she hadn't been my wife, derision would have been my sole response.

The fact that she didn't shout "Hello," as she always did, enraged me. Freddie had already warned her.

She entered the living room with her coat already off. She didn't say anything, didn't look at me.

"Your *poetry* is not poetry," I began. "I don't know what it is. Unless, of course, it's a pretext." I thought about that a moment and laughed, a bit out of control. "A pretext! That's a good one."

"What are you babbling about?"

That got me out of my chair.

"Don't you dare!" I shouted. "Don't you pretend."

She sat down and took a cigarette pack from her purse.

"Only in your study."

She looked at me like a child told to stop crying, and put the cigarettes away.

"It's awfully easy isn't it?"

"What?"

"When he's got a big house all to himself with a two-car garage."

"Not easy enough, it seems."

"Then you admit it."

She nodded, then took the cigarettes out again. I let it go as she lit up.

"Remember your nineteenth century fiction?" she asked.

"And after all these years you have to be a fucking bitch about it as well?"

She flinched, but continued.

"You know, when the young innocent falls prey to an older, accomplished womanizer?"

"That's the silliest thing you could possibly have said."

"Sorry."

"Try again."

She took a deep pull on her cigarette.

"At first it was just a game. He praised and petted me like a prize puppy. Then I had to make a choice."

"Well, you chose wrong."

"That's not the choice I mean. It was about my poetry. Was it going to be any good or not? He made me believe it could be. At least that's how it was early on, until he made it clear what he really wanted."

"What? You whored yourself for a poet's help?"

"No," she sighed, "Or, yes, for a week or two, I guess. Then I fell in love with him, and the poetry really did become a pretext."

"And his little performance today?"

"I told him don't, that I could cope with whatever you thought of my poems."

"They suck, by the way."

"I'm not sure I care what you think."

I sat down and threw her magazine at her, knocking the cigarette on the floor. She stooped to pick it up, brushing away the ashes.

"So this was what he was trying to accomplish today. This."

"In hindsight, I'd say so."

"Divorce?"

"Yes."

"And with everything you know about him, you love him?"

She looked me in the eye and nodded.

I couldn't spare myself. I had to hear it. "And you don't love me?"

She shook her head, then looked at me, why I couldn't guess. I stared her down.

"I love Freddie."

"Well, I'll tell you this," I said as I got up and started for the stairs. "I'll ruin both of your careers if you fight my taking Devon."

I left her crying far less loudly than I expected. She didn't even give me that.

5

When everything was settled, I had custody of Devon, and they got married. Our lawyers managed it quietly, and their wedding was delayed long enough that most appearances of impropriety were avoided. They stayed on at the university, as did I. Tenure is like leg irons attached to a small tree. You can tear yourself free from the tree, but unlocking the leg irons to attach them to another tree is near impossible.

How is it then that Marsha and I were reunited two years later? Because Marsha committed adultery, her second adultery, with me. But there was plenty to lead up to it, which she told me about in detail the first time we betrayed Freddie in his own bed. It turns out there had been a duel of a kind.

MARSHA'S VICTORY

Later, I asked her to write down what happened, since it might make a good story. Here, while adding a few facts, is my faithful version:

Freddie eventually refused to continue coaching Marsha. She confessed that rather than being offended or angry at this reversal, she was relieved and told him so.

She said, "You stink as a mentor, Freddie."

"Look, I know you're upset," he began.

"No, really. I discovered not long after we got married that what you wanted me to write was pale imitations of your own work—all in that asinine typeface you forced on me."

"Nonsense. You'd think I was a lover trying to make you worthy of him."

"Dead on, lover!" she said, "I was never meant to be worthy of you. No, and not as good either. Or I should say especially."

"There was no threat of that happening, my love."

"Don't patronize me, damn you," she shouted. "I never once suggested I would or could be as brilliant as you. Never! All I wanted was to be publishable."

"And you have been. And that, darling, is why I'm cutting bait. It's time for the little bird to fly on her own."

She slapped his face.

"What was that for?" he asked, stumbling back a few steps.

"Your fucking mixed metaphors at my expense."

He laughed and took her in his arms.

"Sorry. Can we forget this?"

"Yes," she said, without kissing him, and retired to her study.

What Freddie hadn't counted on was Marsha's ability to spill ink like a pistol spills blood.

The duel was declared when one of her poems arrived in the mail only a month later. She'd written it without his knowing and before he'd stopped helping her. *The American Poetry Review* had immediately accepted it.

Over dinner that night she took up her wine glass and said, "Here's my challenge. Think of it as a matter of honor, rather than a bet. I believe I can publish more poems over the next two years than you can."

Predictably, he laughed and said, "Sure. I can't wait."

Then she handed him the magazine, open to her poem. The credit didn't make it clear that she was Freddie's wife, as she'd reverted to her maiden name when we were divorced. The poem, sans Herculanum, was a vicious and hilarious satire of Freddie's work—an almost word-for-word mimic of one of his more notorious anti-PC screeds, with many of his lines quoted verbatim.

The look on his face was somewhere between garroted and gut-shot.

"But this is plagiarism!" he exclaimed.

"Not according to my lawyer and to the magazine's editors. It's called 'fair use,' and I intend to use you a lot more."

No, my lovely Marsha did not play fair.

She paused to let this sink in, then started laughing.

"Freddie?!" she said, "I'm joking! I wrote that when I was pissed."

Marsha told me "he took the bait," and, after they both got drunk and fell into bed (and immediately to sleep), they acted like nothing had happened.

But that poem was quickly followed by half a dozen more over the next year. In these she made it clear that she was the wife of her victim. She even offered short introductions steering the reader to the originals. She spared no period of Freddie's output—his juvenilia, the confessional trash he'd written about his second wife, the political nonsense, or even his most recent work. One poem about a "grape arbor" she mocked with "rape ardor," referring to his attacks on women poets. And she turned "Mr. Privy" into "Mr. Plunger"— with all its several meanings fully made clear over time—and "Lord Genius," with the rhyme genius/Jesus indulged more than once.

"So this is real," he said one day, "this duel?"

"I'm at six and we're halfway there. Unless I'm mistaken you've only published four this year."

"You don't know how many have been accepted and not yet published."

"You don't know my backlog either."

"You might not have lied to me that it was all a joke."

"That was funny, wasn't it?"

"Fine. But why are you so angry?"

"I'm not in the least bit angry."

"Your poetry is."

"I am not angry. However, I do intend to get even."

"For what?

"You know what, and I have no intention of saying the obvious."

"I thought you loved me."

"I do love you. How could you question that?"

He was silent.

"What does stupid poetry have to do with that?"

That got him. With that garroted look, he left the room.

She enjoyed every moment of the few times they talked about their duel. Otherwise, they went about their family and professional lives as if nothing strained their relationship. The sex was tepid and infrequent. He professed a desire for a child, though he didn't try very often. She concluded that he just wanted to distract her. She hid them, but she never did go off the pill.

In the meantime, Marsha had discovered that an inexhaustible market existed for what one editor called her "revenge poetry," and that she was capable of churning out at least three poems a week. She kept the fact hidden and even hired a grad student to manage all of her submissions, preparing stamped, self-addressed envelopes, taking everything to the post office, and keeping track of all acceptances and the few rejections she received. At one point she had twenty-one poems in the publishing pipeline. It was book time!

The manuscript accepted by Farrar Straus included 107 poems, most of them between three and seven pages long. It was a hefty tome and one of the funniest things I've ever read. It wasn't for everyone, and if you didn't know anything about Freddie, it was just clever, without being acid. But to the thousands of poets and academics across the country who knew Freddie's work, every poem was delicious, both cruel and deserved.

As one feminist critic put it, "We've had fine poets as married couples, like the Plaths, and even marital attacks and plagiarism, such as Robert Lowell's outrageous lifting of lines from his own wife's letters, but I can't think of an instance when the wife so adroitly unmans her husband." Another wrote, "A few puns in poetry go a long way, but when the author writes, 'Mr. Privy is no Mr. Plunger,' I say, more, more, more!"

But what really struck the critics, and shocked Freddie, was the final section of the book. After an "Envoi" that seemed to say good-bye to the poetry of revenge, Marsha ended the book with a single meditative lyric, 500 lines about a young woman's painful arrival at maturity. It was taut blank verse written in the third person and contained nothing that I recognized as autobiographical. It read like a drama full of sex and betrayal, innocence, harassment, insult, pain, and redemption. It was glorious work—I thought it a masterpiece —and every critic said as much, with some saying it was better than anything Freddie had ever done.

In the end, things fell out this way. The night her copies arrived, she handed him one and left him alone to read it. An hour later she came back and found him pushing it around in the fireplace with a poker.

"You can burn the other copies too if you like," she said, refusing to show her anger.

"No, thanks." He looked up. "Go to bed. I have grading to catch up on."

In the morning, she found him on the couch fully clothed.

A week later, while Freddie was away on one of his tours, I called Marsha to congratulate her on the book.

She invited me over and we were in bed within minutes, much to my surprise and delight.

That night I heard the whole story so far.

Later, after Freddie returned, he'd come home drunk one after-noon and said, "You win."

"Yes?"

"The duel."

"Of course."

Then she told him about me.

"To the winner goes the soiled," he quipped.

"I think you've flipped your pun," she laughed.

He raised his hand as if to slap her. Instead, he sent her back to me that night.

6

I didn't see him in the department for a week. When he came into my office, he was slightly drunk.

"Thlee things," he slurred, holding up his fingers and folding them back, one by one, "Resignation. Lawsuit. Divorce."

"Are you alright, Freddie?" I said, actually concerned, though, selfishly, the only thing I regretted was losing him.

"I won't even fa-finish out the shemester," he said.

I could see it wasn't just the booze, so I didn't hesitate.

"Fine. I'll give Marsha your classes and I'll take hers. I have a light load this semester."

"You were my friend once," he said, flopping into a chair.

"And you were mine," I said, "but who screwed whose wife?"

"One of several mistakes," he mumbled.

"You can sue, but it won't go. You know what 'fair use' is, right?"

"Of course!" he shouted, "Damn, you're so superior."

"It's even more cut and dried when the use is for satire. Tons of case law. And imagine what the critics will make of it. Freddie can dish it out, but etc., etc."

"Fuck you! You let that harpy get away with it. She should be fired for harassing me! You should be fired!"

"I didn't do anything. I'm the cuckold, remember?

"You egged her on."

"Not a bit. Just stood in the wings and watched."

"You don't deserve her."

"I guess that's debatable, but that you do not is crystal clear."

"You probably have a point there," he conceded and started to cry.

"I'm just the injured party, happy to get a bit of my own back,"

I said. "Your resignation is accepted. Please be out of your office by the end of the week."

As he left I wondered if the chancellor would blame me for this mess.

7

When all the drama was over, Marsha and I were remarried and managed quickly to dispel the trauma the divorce had caused Devon. Freddie found a new job by the fall semester. His attorney convinced him that he'd lose any case of plagiarism he brought against Marsha.

Freddie wouldn't publish anything new for years. I didn't bother to read it, nor did Marsha. By then, Freddie was just a stale, distasteful memory. Apparently forgotten by his readers as well. I don't remember seeing any reviews, either.

As for the chancellor—who had always been proud that the university could boast such a distinguished author on its faculty—all he had to say was, "Marsha for Freddie? Seems like we got the better part of that deal."

Something in all this reawakened Marsha's maternal instinct, and a year later we had a daughter, Manon. Today, Manon is a successful poet, with twins, married to a rich insurance executive.

The last words I heard from Freddie arrived in 2020 on the title page of his *Selected Poems*, a thin volume published by his university's press. It was inscribed:

For [my name] and Marsha,
I hope you are happy and well.
I'm godly now—see you in hell.

MY
WATERFALL

I FELL in love with classical music in college and, though I couldn't read music, over the next few years I absorbed much of the standard repertoire and more, borrowing from the school library and buying cheap vinyl. Having grown up listening to rock and Top 40 radio, it was like going from the Sunday comics (and I still love comics) to reading Dostoevsky. From the ear candy of Mozart and the bombast of Beethoven, to the massive warm swimming pools of Mahler and Bruckner, to the thorny rose bushes of Schoenberg and Webern—I loved it all.

When I was twenty-four, having graduated with two degrees in English literature, I moved to a mid-size Midwestern city to take a job in public relations, which promptly fell through. While scanning the newspaper, I noticed an employment ad for a staff position with the local orchestra. I had always assumed that only people working for major orchestras were actually paid—that smaller orchestras were entirely volunteer organizations. The ad didn't even describe the position or list qualifications. I applied anyway, and though my background didn't qualify me for any job I could imagine, somehow I was granted an interview.

During the interview, I was asked, "Who are your favorite composers?" after I'd blurted out that I love classical music. I said Beethoven and Stravinsky and inexplicably threw in Josquin des

Prez. The manager smiled as though she couldn't quite believe what she'd just heard, got up and said, "Follow me."

She took me into the conductor's office, introduced us, and said, "Meet our new Operations Director. Do you have any questions for him?" He said, "Who are your favorite composers?" Looking back and forth between them as though this was a joke, I said, "Beethoven, Stravinsky, and I like Josquin des Prez a lot too."

The conductor stood up and shook my hand. "Welcome," he said, "We haven't had an Operations Manager who knew a damn thing about music in three years."

＊

In order to render comprehensible the behavior of the orchestra I intend to relate, a little context is necessary.

A symphony orchestra is a miniature city. Its eighty-odd players are men and women, young and old and every age in between, married to each other, partners, searching, sometimes cheating for love, or single for life. They have children, are childless, or behave like children, sometimes only in spirit, which can be fun sometimes, sometimes not at all. Some have money, some live from check to check. Some teach, some roof houses or flip burgers to pay the bills, and some have six figures worth of college debt. Some carry guns they leave in their instrument cases during rehearsal. Some drink to excess after every concert, but few do drugs. Wagner and cocaine don't co-habit well.

Imagine a large room with eighty desks. Behind each desk is a worker, let's say a programmer. Programmers are highly skilled. They are counted on to produce good work, working with others at times, sometimes alone. But, for the purpose of this analogy, imagine that at one end of the room, standing on a riser, is a man with a slide rule in his hand, waving his arms, and indicating to every worker what they need to be doing, at every moment. No room for independent thought, virtually no room for creativity. They can't even get up and go for a glass of water or to the bathroom unless the man with the slide rule puts his hands down and steps off the riser, which happens every seventy-five minutes almost to the second. There are only two professions I can think of that actually require this kind of strict obedience—soldiering and being a symphony orchestra musician.

Consequently, musicians can be peevish and mercilessly critical. I've never once seen a conductor survive a year's honeymoon as full-time "Music Director" still respected, let alone loved. By a series of chance circumstances, we had four conductors in the ten years I spent at this particular orchestra, and every one of them left with a smile of great relief on his face and a virtual kick in the breeches from the musicians as he walked off the stage for the last time.

✳

My name is Robert Brothers. Because I was part of the administration, also much disliked by the players, and was obliged to sit across the table from the players committee during union negotiations every few years, I earned the nickname Bother, a conflation of Bob and Brother. I didn't mind. On stage, before a rehearsal, it was "Hey, Bother, this," and "Hey, Bother, that." Of course, I could never do a thing to their satisfaction, put a chair or stand in the right place, or keep the stage temperature at the right level, whatever. It didn't matter. But, in my own area of authority, they did what I told them to. I was always polite and respectful, unless you jeopardized the performance—then I was on your case.

I was on my second conductor and in my fourth year on the job when I fell in love. I was twenty-eight and had never been in love before. I wasn't a virgin, though not by much, but I just hadn't yet found anyone who stirred me up like Kareen Baker, the orchestra's harpist. It wasn't just the instrument she played, with its dozens of "falling" strings, tipped back against her shoulder, and the way her hands passed over the strings ceaselessly, that caused me to think of her as the "waterfall," which would become my secret name for her. No, it was her long legs and lissome arms, even her fingers, all thin and graceful, her long blonde hair that she had to fling behind her before she started to play, her timid smile that hid luminescent teeth, and her large sky-blue eyes, which, all combined, reminded me of a thin rush of water in a forest falling six feet into a quiet pool.

It was only when I first saw her play that I actually took more than casual notice. There were other attractive women in the orchestra, and I hardly gave them a second look. But everything changed for me the first time Kareen started to play. The grace in her fingers was reflected in the slightly closed, slightly fluttering eyelids, the way she seemed to be looking up, as if she'd memorized the music and could ignore her sheet music, and that brilliant smile, which she saved just for playing. All this, combined with the slightly arched spine and the demure contact between her knees and the sound-board, plus the delicate movement of her feet from pedal to pedal, well, it was the sexiest thing I'd ever seen.

In spite of her beauty, she was, to everyone's astonishment, totally unattached. Yes, she was shy, would sit in her chair staring at her sheet music, looking neither right nor left, and respond to questions or comments with no more than a word or two, and never with a smile or a frown—without expressing any emotion whatever. The men in the orchestra soon learned to leave her alone. Once, when she felt a guy get one step too close, she turned and said, "Move off," as angrily as if someone had pinched her bottom. The few who tried to chat her up were met with a swift dismissal in the form of a flipped wrist. She wasn't specifically trying to be rude, I realized—she just wanted to be left alone.

I gained some admittance to her personal bubble on the day of her fourth rehearsal and her first not in the rehearsal hall but in the main concert hall. I was standing backstage as she walked in carrying her bench, when she said to me, "Will you help me?" I reached for the bench and she said, "Not with this!" rather sharply, putting the bench down. "Follow me."

We went outside where a blue-green Lexus station wagon waited with the hatch open. She dragged a dolly out and set it on the ground. Then she directed me how to help her oh-so-carefully lift the instrument out and set it on the ground, slide the dolly under it, and tip it back. "Thanks, I'll take it from here," she said and rolled it away. From then on, I kept my eyes open for the moment she arrived, so she wouldn't have to wait a second for my help.

It was at the beginning of her second season, with the hiring of contrabassoonist Joe De Razzi, that things took on just a hint of a circus atmosphere (though most of my colleagues in other orchestras described theirs as a "zoo").

A regional orchestra seldom needs a "contra" because the repertoire doesn't require it all that often. The one we'd had for years, who drove in from a major metropolis when we needed him, resigned, having won the chair with a major orchestra. We held auditions and had only three candidates. Joe quite literally blew the audition committee away.

Joe De Razzi, accent and all, was an Italian giant. He was six-foot-nine, but unlike the familiar tall basketball center, Joe had arms that in proportion looked like small branches, legs like only slightly thicker branches. He had ginger hair, red cheeks and was missing his left incisor. But the chest on him! He reminded me of the living trees in the Wizard of Oz movie—small limbs, enormous trunk! And could he play loud!

It's not universally understood that the contrabassoon, while a large instrument that looks like an anaconda double-folded over a branch, for loudness can't approach the decibel level of a clarinet or flute, let alone a trombone or tuba in the hands of a stout musician. In fact, its blats and rumblings are usually buried by the other woodwinds, which is why composers rarely give the instrument a solo to play. Not in the hands of Joe De Razzi, whose lungs could have blown the *Santa Maria* across the Atlantic.

"He'll have to bring that under control," was all the Music Director said after the audition committee voted to hire him.

*

The Music Director was, like most conductors at regional orchestras, precisely where he belonged. He was forty-five, trim, handsome, with a receding hairline, a scar on his chin and angry green eyes. Though once a student of the great Ozawa, he had jumped from small to slightly larger to slightly larger orchestras for his entire career. Any hope he had of conducting the Chicago or Boston Symphonies lay in a last-minute guest shot as a replacement, never as Music Director. (With rare exceptions, the players would never reach the big time either; another reason for their irritability.)

His name was Calvin Hoover, but the players secretly called him Hobbes, after the imaginary tiger from the newspaper comic strip. "Imaginary" being the point. As he waved his arms and bobbed his head, the players—their faces buried in their sheet music—generally acted as if he didn't exist. Once in a while, they'd look up and need him to re-establish tempo because someone had missed a cue and a train wreck might ensue. I could hear them after the concert say, with a rare display of respect, "Well, Calvin saved us that time." More often it was, "Hobbes phoned it in again," or "Hobbes has the baton technique of a lion-tamer."

*

There's a reason why orchestral musicians are unionized from coast to coast. In part, that reason has disappeared, though not completely. Back in the days of Toscanini and his ilk, conductors were dictators without any restraints on their abuse of a player's talent, emotions, or time. If they wanted a four-hour rehearsal, so be it. If they wanted to summarily dismiss a musician, they did it. Of course, wages and working conditions were important in the creation of a union, but the main purpose was to dethrone the imperial conductor.

Calvin was a diva and a dictator, but only within the limits set by the musicians' contract. He could go overtime by one minute if he chose to, but he would face the displeasure of his bosses (the orchestra's board of directors) for costing the organization the large sums of overtime pay required by the contract. If he wanted to fire a musician, the players could veto his decision with a super-majority vote of a review committee, which is usually what happened. All modern conductors know this, but it doesn't keep them from being assholes on the podium.

During his two-year tenure I saw Calvin glare, swear, and blare at the musicians, but only once did he truly, shamefully misbehave. The occasion was Joe De Razzi's first rehearsal. On the program was a totally forgettable slab of neo-romantic bombast written by one of Calvin's buddies from his conservatory days. Poor Joe. First he drowned out the violin solo, then he drowned out the oboes. Then, as the mæstro (he loved to be called "mæstro") kept waving his right hand downward at Joe, meaning "quieter," he blew so loud he seemed to be doing a duet with the trumpet! Calvin slammed his fist down on his stout wooden podium and shouted, "What the fuck, Joe, are you doing? Can't you see me up here trying to shut you the fuck up? And every note you're playing is sharp! Can't you hear that?"

I looked over at Joe, and he seemed to have shrunk to the size of a munchkin. Calvin stormed off the stage, and I called for the fifteen-minute break a half-hour early.

Two shocking events ensued. When break was over and Calvin returned to the podium, he apologized to the entire orchestra: "Please forgive my outburst. It was totally unprofessional, and it won't ever happen again." Of course, he hoped to mollify the players to prevent any possible grievance they might file complaining of his behavior—an effort that proved ineffectual, though the grievance, which was filed the next day, was soon dropped because profanity wasn't actually mentioned in the union contract. And the last thing poor Joe wanted was to antagonize his new boss further.

The second, even more shocking event, took place when rehearsal was over. Joe had packed up his instrument and was headed for the stage door when Kareen, pushing her dolly, set it upright in the wings and called to Joe. He turned and she motioned him over. For a moment, she stood on her tiptoes to speak to him, but—given that he stood almost a foot and a half taller than she—quickly gave that up and motioned him to bend down to her. He bent almost double and she whispered something in his ear. He turned toward her, nodded and smiled. He started to straighten up. She grabbed his shoulder and kept him at her level and, in front of at least a dozen gaping musicians, kissed him on the cheek. No little peck either, this was a lingering, heartfelt kiss of affection, or support, or whatever was needed to reinforce what she'd just told Joe.

That kiss would become legend.

*

The concert season progressed as they tend to do—the players got grumpier, the audiences thinner, because all the big hits were in the first two programs, or fidgety, because Calvin, like all responsible conductors, had programmed a couple of works composed in the latter twentieth century. Typically, the audience tolerates the new work, though the coughing increases, waiting patiently for the more familiar pieces to follow. But Calvin had to make matters worse. When, during the third concert of the season, one work of only eight minutes was over, receiving tepid, not even polite applause, he turned to the audience and said, "I'm not sure we did that piece justice. Let's try it again," to groans (and a few boos) from audience and players alike. The ensuing applause was appreciably louder, though a player quipped at intermission, "They just wanted to make sure he didn't play it again!"

*

It was a few days later that I got a call at the office from Kareen, inviting me to tea.

With my head ringing like a pair of crotales, I answered that I would be happy to come to tea.

"Where shall we meet?"

"At my house, of course."

I'll leave it to the reader's imagination what my imagination was putting me through at the moment. Of course, I accepted and a date and time were arranged for later that week.

"And please bring some flowers," she added, "anything you choose I'm sure will be fine." She gave me the address, said, "Bye now," and hung up.

Three days later, a bouquet of twelve red roses in hand, I rang the doorbell of a two-story white brick house. The neighborhood was one of the oldest and most exclusive in town. When Kareen opened the door, dressed in a white blouse and blue skirt, her hair in a ponytail—in other words, stunning—I proceeded to drop the roses and exclaimed, "Oh, I'm so sorry!" The flowers had come out of their paper wrapper and were strewn all over her welcome mat. I dropped to my knees and quickly gathered them up.

"Be careful," she warned me.

I stood up, clumsily rewrapped the flowers, and handed them to her with a slight bow, as though we were in a nineteenth century opera.

She stifled a laugh and motioned me in. I followed, sucking a not-quite-bloody scratch on my thumb. We passed through a short hallway and turned into a long rectangular room with floor-to-ceiling windows on three sides. In the center of the room was a harp and bench. The only other furniture, at the opposite end in front of a limestone fireplace, were two fancy settees facing each other and between them a small marble-top table on which lay a silver tray with a large teapot, food, and cups and saucers.

What I found most curious was the harp, which was not the one she brought to work. That one had a tapered black column and crown. This instrument looked as though every inch of it was made of sculpted gold.

As she motioned me to the other end of the room, I decided not to mention the harp just yet, but I was very curious where it had come from.

I sat quietly as she poured out the tea and offered me a biscuit. Finally, I said, "Ms. Baker, I was wondering…"

"Mrs. Baker, Bob. I'm married. It's one of the reasons I asked you here. I know everyone thinks I don't have a man in my life. For my own reasons, I'm happy to have them continue to think so. But, to be frank with you, I felt that you were beginning to feel a bit too attached to me. In other words, I like you and I'm happy we're friends, but I felt I owed it to you to let you know my situation. I'm sure I can count on your keeping it a secret."

She didn't have to ask me not to interrupt. I simply nodded.

"As you can see, I live in a lovely house that no mere harpist could afford. My husband, with the rather ordinary name of Baker, is a very successful consultant for the federal government. He spends half of his time in Washington, so my involvement in the orchestra is a great cure for loneliness."

"Yes, I see."

We ate and drank in silence until she said, "Tell me, do I have you to thank, at least in part, for my being included in every program this year? I really didn't expect that."

"I did make some suggestions to Calvin, which he seemed to appreciate," I lied. I assumed he liked having her on stage as much as I did.

"Thank you. I hope you'll continue to keep me busy. Now," she hurried on, "There's another reason I asked you to come by."

She turned and pointed at her harp, which stood like a Greek statue bathed in the afternoon sunlight slanting through all those windows.

"I am a composer. I've been one all my life, though I've never performed anything of my own publicly. I know you are somewhat knowledgeable about music," she said, standing and stepping toward the harp, "and I'd like to perform one of my works for you this afternoon."

It occurred to me that anything I might say at that moment would be either ridiculous or embarrassing, so I shut up.

Kareen quickly got comfortable on her bench, leaned the harp into her shoulder, plucked only a string or two (which told me she'd tuned the instruments moments before I'd arrived), and with a toss of her glorious hair began to play.

Everyone's seen Harpo Marx play the harp, particularly the scene when he breaks apart a grand piano and pulls out a harp and begins playing. The effect, beyond the humorous few seconds of the incongruity of it all, is quickly replaced by amazement and joy at Harpo's masterful performance. I went through a similar transition: first, astonishment that I was about to be serenaded; joy at this vision of a woman; and finally, serious appreciation of what she was playing. The music itself was, admittedly, derivative, with touches of Stravinsky's sprung rhythms and Strauss' rumbling in the lower register, but the overall effect was delightful, but serious. Not a cute "harp arpeggio" or musical cliché in the entire piece. I regretted only that it was just ten minutes long.

When she was done, she was visibly embarrassed, as I applauded heartily. Before I could say a word, she said, "Thank you so much, Robert, for coming. I appreciate your patience in listening, and I know I can trust you to keep my little secret—my two little secrets," she added, patting the sound board of the harp. She looked at her watch and rushed on. "Now I'm afraid I have to ask you to leave. I have a student arriving any minute."

The suddenness of all this caused me to rush to her side.

"I completely understand, and…"

She put her finger to her lips, winked, and said, "No words are necessary. Thank you for your kind response. I value your opinion, and I might need your help," she added, in a softer voice.

In seconds, I was standing on her porch as the door closed behind me. Two thoughts came to mind in quick succession. "Help," for what? And, what happened to the roses?

✳

Planning and programming for a symphony orchestra begins eight to ten months before the first concert of the next season in September; thus decisions for the entire season can affect concerts a year and a half away.

Calvin started early. We had our first session at his kitchen table in November. He was very methodical. There were seventeen classical music programs to be programmed, nine with full orchestra, eight with chamber orchestra. He went about it the same way for every concert. Overture or brief opening pieces first, for all seventeen. Then the main event, usually a symphony, for the second half. Lastly, he chose a concerto.

My role was scrivener. He'd complained to the executive director that he needed a secretary, but the budget would never support that. Instead, he got me. I had two jobs. First, I was to keep my mouth shut. I could ask a question if I wasn't sure about something, and it better not be irrelevant. Second, I was to write down his every work under consideration on one legal pad. These were his initial ideas, the product of much mumbling and stomping around the room looking at the ceiling.

Eventually, a reduced repertoire would be transferred to another legal pad, supposedly the final version. Of course, the final version was never final. I likened it to a chess game. We'd get to within a move of checkmate when Calvin would brush half the pieces on the floor. He didn't quite start all over, but he worried every concert for weeks, well into January.

I was to learn what Kareen meant by "help" when she called me in mid-December. There was an odd strain in her usually gentle voice.

"The mæstro is in the process of programming for next season, isn't he?"

"Yes. We've been meeting."

"I have something very important to ask you," she began.

"Would you like me to come over?" I blurted out. I couldn't help myself.

"No that's not needed," she said bluntly. She paused for a second, then said, "Remember the piece I played for you?"

"Of course."

"You liked it, right?"

"Of course. I loved it."

"I'm so glad." She paused again. "I have a confession to make about that. I should have said so at the time."

I waited. I could almost hear her frowning in self-disapproval. I had a fleeting vision of her playing the harp in the nude, which she extinguished quickly enough.

"Look, Robert. It's the first movement of my concerto for harp and chamber orchestra. I filled in some of the other parts around the solo part, so you'd get a better idea of it."

"I thought it was beautiful. You must be very happy with it to play it for someone, let alone me." What a stupid thing to say, I said to myself.

"Well, I am."

"You should ask Calvin over and play it for him."

"No! That's impossible. That's where I need your help. I need you to ask him for me. Tell him I have written a concerto, and I want him to consider letting me play it next season. I want to play it for him."

"I could probably do that, but I don't see the problem."

"It's my husband. He's incredibly jealous, and he dislikes Calvin. Violently. When he's in town, he sits in the back of the hall during our concerts and later, at home, all he does is complain about the man. The man, not the music. He can't stand the fact that Calvin seems to be deferential to me, though it's beyond me how he can think that. All he can see is his back!"

I couldn't quite stifle a laugh, though everyone knew she was Calvin's favorite. He'd even winked at her a couple of times.

"Go ahead. It *is* silly. But it's one of the reasons I have to keep my marriage quiet."

This made no sense to me at all.

"And why I can't ask Calvin over."

This I could understand.

"Then let me see if I can arrange something someplace else."

"Would you?"

"Yes, why not? I'd be happy to help. But I still don't know why you can't at least talk to Calvin first."

She mumbled something. I was clearly frustrating and upsetting her.

"I'm sorry," I went on, "I just think he'll be more receptive if you ask him. He's not my biggest fan, you know, and he hates it when I suggest repertoire to him."

"Yes, I see, but I can't ask him myself. I just can't. It's impossible!"

Then she began to cry. I couldn't believe it. And more than a few sniffles too.

"I'm sorry, Kareen, I didn't mean to upset you. Listen. I'll do it. After all, it's not like I'd be recommending some piece of ordinary music. This is written by a player in the orchestra. Besides, he likes you."

"Don't say that!" she cried.

I had no idea what to say next.

She finally got control of herself and said, "Thank you so much. Let me know what he says. Bye."

She hung up before I could say "Bye" too.

✳

Well, that was a dumb thing to do, I thought as I turned off my cell phone. It was five-thirty, and I was watching the news and drinking a beer when Kareen called. I turned off the TV and put some Stravinsky on the stereo.

Or was it dumb? I wondered. Of course, I had no illusions about the woman, especially given what she'd said about her husband. She was simply asking me to do her a favor. But what a favor!

"A no-win favor, you idiot," I said out loud. Calvin wasn't going to be angry with me for suggesting he should hear her play her concerto. Instead, he was likely to be furious that she hadn't asked him herself, and he might well bawl me out for it, as illogical as that would be.

There was some delicate calculation required before he could say yes. The players wouldn't need to know until he'd actually decided to put her on the season, but he knew that if he did they would see it as preferential treatment. She was only in her second season and getting a solo slot? Other principals had been in the orchestra for a decade without that privilege.

The fact that it was her own composition set her apart from them on that score, so to speak. Why shouldn't he say yes? I could hear him now if someone had the gumption to complain: "You write a concerto for yourself, and we'll play it—if it's any good, that is." Oh, what a snarl he'd put into that!

But, and here was the real potential problem—what if he said no? What if he heard what I heard: an earnest, tuneful, but derivative composition? What if he saw it as too risky—charming but without substance? Even worse, what if he said yes, and the players didn't like it? The potential for scorn for both him and Kareen was almost as frightening as feeding their suspicions that something might be going on between them.

Yes, the dilemma alone would endear our Music Director to me even less than he already was, and the likeliest outcome was that both he and Kareen would never speak to me again.

"You said 'yes,' you fool, so shut up," I said aloud. Nice, I thought, Stravinksy's *Pulcinella*. Did I choose that on purpose?

✳

It was now our third session at Calvin's kitchen table, and we seemed to be getting along okay. He hadn't barked at me once. Instead, his frustration resided with our executive director, Victoria (always "Victoria") Disch—a lovely woman with a brilliant laugh, ten years older than Calvin and something of a legend in the orchestra world for her financial acumen in running the same orchestra for more than thirty years with zero red ink. She'd given him what he called "a damned skimpy budget" for concerto soloists—significant, but less than the current season's. He had already had one argument with her about it, and there would be more. In the meantime, he struggled to balance name recognition with the talent for specific repertoire he'd come across over the years.

I knew he was swearing at her under his breath, though he wouldn't dare criticize her openly to anyone, let alone one of her staff members. He paced and mumbled, looking at his list every now and then. There were three slots left to fill and, though he hadn't told me the numbers, I knew he felt himself nowhere near being within budget.

This was my chance.

"I know a way to fill one slot, and it won't cost much at all," I said hurriedly.

He turned on me and growled, "What? Hell!"

"Kareen Baker has written a harp concerto and would like to play it. It would cost a fraction of the usual artist fees."

I was determined not to say another word unless he prompted me.

"Kareen, a composer? And how did you come across this information?"

"She played it for me."

"For you? What are you talking about?"

"She asked me to come by and help her with something," I lied, "and while I was there she offered to play it."

I had decided beforehand not to say a word of my opinion of the piece, and as hard as it was I stuck to that strategy.

"Help with what?" he said suspiciously.

"She had some furniture she needed help moving."

He could tell something wasn't quite right.

"In other words," he said, taking the bait, "she got you to come by on a pretext so she could play her concerto for you so you could mention it to me."

"Pretext? I almost broke my back moving her couch."

"And as a reward she plays her concerto for you."

"There was nothing devious about it. And it was me who offered to mention it to you."

"And she said 'go ahead.'"

"Sure, why not? So I have."

"I get it. *You* are the devious one."

I said nothing.

"Oĸ, young man. Set it up as soon as possible."

And that was it. Of course, he assumed his audience would be at her home, and he yelled at me when I arranged it for one afternoon in our rehearsal hall instead. But, wisely, he knew it was unseemly to insist on anything else.

✳

At the appointed time Kareen waited, tuning her harp, while I sat as far away as possible in the back of the second violins. We had positioned her instrument where it usually sat behind the cello section. I had suggested we put her in the usual soloist position to the left of the podium, but she said it seemed presumptuous. I set a chair for Calvin on the lip of the stage as close to her as possible.

When he arrived a few minutes late, he went straight to Kareen and shook her hand. She handed him the conductor's score. I was pretty sure that they hadn't spoken since he'd agreed to hear her work, and seeing the cordiality of that handshake, the slight stiffness in his demeanor, and the timidity in hers, confirmed it.

He turned and, seeing me, frowned.

"What are you thinking, Robert? Why isn't she up by the podium?"

Kareen spoke before I could reply. "I told him to put me here. It seemed forward of me to be up there," she said, pointing toward the podium. "I feel comfortable here."

"Yes, of course. There's plenty of time later to change things." He spoke so courteously, it was as though I wasn't there. "Let me sit over here and you begin whenever you're ready."

He took the chair I had set for him.

"Wait. One minute." He turned to me. "Robert, thank you very much for arranging this. You can go now."

Kareen was shaking her head "No!" which he couldn't see. But I had no choice. As he turned back, I held out my hands to her, palms up, and raised my shoulders—the traditional pathetic body language for "What can I do?" I mouthed "Good luck," then slipped away.

✳

That evening I got a phone call from the executive director.

"Hi, Victoria."

"Robert, what have you been up to?" She was mildly miffed. "Playing matchmaker?"

I didn't even bother to pretend I didn't understand.

"I'd hardly call it that," I said, unwittingly half-conceding her point. "I simply helped with an audition."

"You might have told me about it, Robert."

Whenever she started repeating my name, I knew I was in trouble.

"I'm sorry, Victoria. I didn't think it was anything out of the ordinary. I was just helping Calvin with repertoire."

She laughed, though it sounded mirthless and guarded. "Nice try, Robert. You're almost as sly as Calvin. You might at least have stuck around."

"He told me to leave. Why, did something happen?"

"Of course not. *Nothing happened.* Except you left Calvin alone with a vulnerable and attractive young woman with dreams of soloing with the orchestra and it ended up in tears of joy. And now you and I get to live with this arranged musical marriage for the next twelve months or so."

"How did you find out?"

"Robert, you sound like it was supposed to be a secret. Calvin told me. He's absolutely infatuated with her *concerto,*" she said with mild sarcasm, "which means Kareen herself, as you might have observed ever since she joined us."

"Oh, good. I'm so relieved."

"What the hell's that supposed to mean?" For Victoria, this was mild language when she was angry.

"I just mean I'm happy for her. I was afraid he wouldn't like it and tell her 'no.' She'd have been crushed."

"Hmm. Sounds like Calvin's not the only smitten one."

"We're just friends. She doesn't have hardly any and because I help her with her instrument she's begun to be friendly."

"Yes, so friendly, I'm told, that she invited you to her house to hear the piece and then asked you to mention it to Calvin. Yes?"

"That's right," I said, then, remembering (I'd gotten this much of the "story" straight with Kareen before the audition). "She also needed help with some furniture."

"Well, at least you didn't let him go to her damned house. If that got around…" She took a deep breath as if gathering the patience to explain things to a child. "You do understand that you should have told me at least before the audition, don't you? I would have handled it much differently. The audition isn't the problem; no harm in that. But I would have told him to forget it, at least for next season. Give her some encouragement, but ask her to wait 'til she's been around longer. That would have accomplished two things—keep the players from getting pissed that she's receiving special treatment, and, perhaps, would allow enough time for his, shall we say, *inclinations*, toward her to cool."

"I knew he liked her, but…. So, what did you say to him?"

"Don't be a dope. I didn't say anything. Not. One. Word. If he knows that I know he's got eyes for her, who knows what he'll do. He might even change his mind, just to prove he doesn't, and then poor Kareen will be crushed, when she should never have been in this position to begin with."

Oh, if only I could tell her that Kareen Baker was married.

"I was only trying…"

"I know what you were trying, Robert. Look, you're young, though not that young. What you've done is like arranging for them to go steady until performance night. And I get to be the fucking chaperone!" she nearly shouted and hung up.

✳

Now it was dilemma time for me. Should I tell Kareen about any of this? I couldn't act as though nothing had happened, but I would have to be so careful. If word of this little drama got to her husband, he could be furious with her. Would he actually confront Calvin, or, worse, refuse to allow her to perform? Even force her to quit? And what if she suspected Calvin's real motives had little to do with her concerto? She just might be that naïve. I hadn't imagined Calvin, from the sounds of it, talking like a lovesick dove to Victoria. And what did he say to Kareen? Probably went crazy with praise. Little did Calvin know how much Victoria had already noticed. She didn't think he was simply "deferential" to Kareen, like the rest of us. He was in love! And Kareen would now be impossibly happy, not realizing that a wrong word from her, Calvin, Victoria, or myself, would ruin everything!

I couldn't just be silent, either. She had to be warned. Unfortunately, I never got the chance.

✳

Programming for the following season ceases to be a secret the minute the board is asked to approve it, as it was that January. No one said a word about Kareen's concerto except one rich old crone who never failed to object to something. She always made discrete promises to other board members to give more money if she just got her way, and since she seldom did, she seldom gave much. Victoria loathed her.

With the mæstro sitting at the same table, she looked at Victoria and said, "I see our new harpist is programmed for a concerto."

"Yes, it's her own composition."

"I wouldn't call her 'new,'" added Calvin. "This is her second season."

"I see that. I know that." Never one to let go quickly once she'd begun, she added, "Still, it seems both premature and preferential."

Ignoring the implication, Calvin said, "It's a perfectly lovely concerto. It deserves to be heard."

"Yes, I'm sure it is *lovely.*" Her sarcasm like sour cheese. "That's what we pay you for, after all. To program *lovely* performances."

She sat back and crossed her arms. The question was called and the programming was approved with one abstention.

✳

That night was the first rehearsal for a full-orchestra program featuring Richard Strauss' (don't laugh) *Don Juan*. From the moment the first two musicians entered the rehearsal hall, the susurrus began about Kareen's "big score." Sometimes it was "Hobbes' big score." Among other less offensive complaints, I overheard the following: "She must have really pulled his harp strings," "It won't be a solo, if you know what I mean," "There must have been some *kissando*," "You've heard of the casting podium, haven't you?" "Do you think she thumbed his baton?" and in reply, "No, he plucked her."

By the time Kareen arrived, people realized I was listening in and had already shut up, or at least become more discrete. She summoned me at the stage door, as usual. I couldn't help but notice how differently she was dressed for a rehearsal. Ordinarily, she wore blue jeans and a print blouse. Very fetching, given her slender but rounded figure. Today she wore a mid-calf blue cotton dress that showed cleavage. It was more in keeping with what she wore for concerts, without being black. As we lifted her harp out of the car, she whispered, "My husband was furious when I told him."

"What for?"

She was almost in tears. "I think if I'd been just a little dismissive of Calvin that might have helped. I couldn't stop myself. I actually said a few nice things about the man!"

"He'll get over it. After all, it's a long way off," I said, wondering why, if her husband was angry, she'd left the house in such a dress. Maybe he was out of town, as she said he often was.

"I wish it was tonight!"

"Has he calmed down?"

"A little. For now," she said, with a hopeful grin.

"Good," I smiled back, but I couldn't leave it at that. "I hate to tell you this, but the players are being jerks. The room is buzzing with nasty comments."

"What do I care about *them?*"

I felt she wasn't ready to hear the worst of it, so I said nothing more as we rolled her harp through the stage entrance. After I got her settled, I wheeled her dolly off and parked it stage left. I noticed that there were more empty seats than usual twenty minutes before rehearsal would begin. I went into the green room and found it full of raucous laughter, which abruptly stopped when they all saw me. Joe De Razzi was sitting off by himself, in khakis and a light chocolate flannel shirt, holding his contrabassoon like a brown bear hugging a tree. Everyone quickly filed out past me, with smirks and giggles and more than a few adding "Hi, Bother."

"You sure know how to clear a room," Joe De Razzi joked rather pitiably, bringing up the rear. He stopped and whispered, "Why am I here? These are terrible people! They're animals!"

I shrugged and followed him onstage. I might have felt jealous if just Calvin, Joe and I were besotted with Kareen, but she was married, and we were all thwarted and inconsequential suitors. But I had to admit it—Joe had us both beat for the intensity of his devotion.

As he began to slip past the double-basses, I noticed on the floor the rubber tip to the spike that protruded from the bottom of his instrument. I picked it up and took it to Joe, who was seated by now. I handed it to him and he frowned slightly and thanked me, putting it in his pants pocket. I almost said something. There weren't rules about this, of course. The cellos and basses scarred up the floor all the time with their sharp endpins. I let it go.

Right on the half-hour, Calvin strode on stage and took the podium. *"Don Juan,* please," he said.

Don't you wish, I remember thinking as he raised his arms. And he hadn't brought his score. Every once in a while he pulled this stunt—conducting from memory. For some conductors, it isn't a stunt at all. They can remember every note, every marking, effortlessly. But I knew it didn't come naturally to Calvin. He did it very seldom, and only for shorter scores (*Don Juan* was under twenty minutes) that he'd conducted at least a dozen times before, and even then you sensed he'd spent hours memorizing it. No, he was show-ing off for his new girlfriend and challenging the players at the same time. His downbeat was met by at least five sour notes, five rasp-berries, including a loud "blat" from Joe that I could hear within the din of Strauss' opening bars, before the orchestra got down to serious rehearsing.

The break seventy-five minutes later was more of the same non-sense, so I didn't enter the green room until the last moment. As before, there was plenty of laughter until I entered, when it stopped immediately, and Joe, who again was the last to leave, seemed down-right disconsolate, like Emmett Kelly without the pancake makeup. He said nothing.

As I followed him out, we both saw what probably half the orches-tra had just seen, Calvin and Kareen whispering to each other near the back of the hall. They were not hiding, but their conversation was clearly confidential and somewhat impatient on Calvin's part, mildly beseeching on Kareen's.

When Calvin mounted the podium, he put down his baton and raised his arms for quiet.

"If you'll allow me a few moments, I think there's something we need to clear the air about."

I looked at Kareen and she was shaking her head vehemently "No!"

"No, I think it's best," he said, nodding to her. "You all know by now that I have programmed for next season a concerto by our fine harpist and now, we discover, an equally accomplished composer."

He rushed on through the silence, as if it were as tangible as fog.

"I'm not at all surprised that this should result in some chatter among you. But enough is enough. I chose Kareen's work because she's quite lovely and…." He checked himself. "I mean to say *it*, the concerto, the concerto, is quite lovely." The players, every man and woman, with two exceptions, burst out in helpless hilarity. I've never hear them play their instruments that loudly.

Calvin was so embarrassed he actually hung and shook his head, side to side.

Even paler than usual, Kareen stood up, walked off and seconds later returned, pushing her dolly. Exactly then, in what was her moment of greatest humiliation, soon to be surpassed, Joe stood up, shouted *"Bastardo!"* and, lifting his instrument—all fifteen pounds of it—with just his right arm, threw it, spike first, right at Calvin. This Ahabian missile—not the most reliable of weapons—might have struck a violist or cellist, even hit its mark and pierced Calvin through the heart. Maybe Joe meant it to. But no. The contrabassoon flew over everyone, the mæstro ducking, and hit the rehearsal hall's wooden front wall, about ten feet behind Calvin, where it stuck, quivered for a moment, then fell to the parquet floor, leaving the six-inch spike in the wall.

Kareen screamed, dropped the dolly, grabbed her harp by the soundboard with both hands, tipped it sideways and threw it to the stage floor as hard as her strong little arms could. She picked up her purse and ran through the orchestra—everyone leaning back to protect their own instruments—and out of the building, with Joe following her.

When I got outside, there was Joe, waving and shouting *"Ciao, bella!"* Calvin soon joined me and said, rather stunned, "She left her harp!"

"She has a much nicer one at home," I said, as the three of us watched my waterfall flowing away in her Lexus. She never came back.

RED

*T*HOUGH newly-married, Eliot often stopped off after work at
the Isle of White bar to play pool and bitch about work with
his colleagues. Usually, he was home by seven, but on this June
night in 1985 it was after nine and dark, but for a gibbous moon over
Lake Michigan. He'd run the table and was thoroughly drunk on
Guinness and Harp Lager black and tans.

Not long ago, he and his wife, Barbara Ann (a name she hated
and everyone used except Eliot, who called her Annie), had moved
into an apartment on the corner of Touhy and Sheridan. While he
applied his bachelor's degree in English Literature toward a career
in public relations and marketing, she taught middle school history.
Since she was always home much earlier, she usually cooked, but
when Eliot had begun his winning streak, he'd called her and said
not to bother. He would eat there at the bar.

Their apartment was right across the street from the beach, and
parking was always tough. He tried the lot across Sheridan and, as
he and Annie often joked, being born with great parking karma, he
found the last remaining spot. It was such a lovely, warm evening, he
headed first to the beach. He stood on the water's edge and watched
the moon slide across the calm water like the oldest idea in the universe. As he turned, he staggered and realized how drunk he really
was. He sat down and lay back, trying to find a star or two through
the city-lights-drenched sky. In seconds he was asleep.

He would later calculate he couldn't have been asleep for more than fifteen minutes when he awoke to the sound of a loud vehicle with a rough engine pulling into the parking lot. He got up on his left elbow and saw a black or dark green minivan pull up over a curb and onto the sand at the end of the lot closest to the water. Its front and sliding doors opened and from inside came an improbable number of young men and women dressed in a variety of casual clothing. It was, he thought, like the old movie joke when an impossibly large number of people come out of a phone booth or small car.

The driver left the headlights on.

The last person to exit the van was dressed in a brilliant white jumpsuit. He was very thin, almost frail, and tall, but he moved with a studied swinging of his arms as though he was on the verge of dancing. In the headlights, he had the brightest red hair Eliot had ever seen, like a big afro, though the young man was extremely pale.

Eliot tried to count how many there were, but they formed a circle around the redhead and began to move first clockwise then counter, confusing his count.

"Red! We are ready, Red!" they shouted as if on cue.

Red held up his arms and swayed as though conducting an orchestra. Then he clapped his hands, once, and they began to chant.

Eliot knew, of course, about cults and charismatic leaders—the Jonestown massacre had occurred only seven years before—and he had no doubt that this was what he was witnessing, though on a tiny scale. Expecting either a babble of prayers or praise to god, he was, even though drunk, profoundly shocked when he understood what they were actually saying:

"Lord, I'm worthless scum. I am shit, I am a stinking bowl of shit. I am disgusting because I disgust myself. How can you allow me to even exist —don't I make you puke, Lord? No one loves me and they'd be stupid motherfuckers to love me. Lord, hate me too! Lord, I am fuck. I deserve to be fucked by a baseball bat and burned in a car crash! Lord, kill me now and fling my filthy corpse in the lake. It's the only way!"

And on and on. It all became louder and more profane, with Red continuing to raise his arms up and up, demanding more and louder chanting. At least three times, he shouted, "LORD, PLEASE FUCK US!"

Eliot stood up. He couldn't be more than twenty feet away and since he'd been lying down, no one had noticed him. He couldn't help what happened next. He wasn't particularly religious. If he believed in anything it was in seeking rather than finding. He found Zen sympathetic, but had left the Catholic Church almost a decade ago. Still, this was too much.

"Hey!" he shouted, waving his arms. "Hey!"

Red must have heard him, since they stopped moving and chanting as though he'd flicked the off switch.

Then Eliot heard himself shouting as loudly as he could, "How dare you degrade yourself before your God?!"

Red came out of the circle, looked at Eliot, and with two fingers made a single high whistle sound, then turned away. Everyone turned as one and filed quickly into the minivan. Red climbed into the front passenger seat and closed the door. Not one word had been uttered since Eliot's interruption.

The minivan backed out over the curb and, gaining speed, rolled through the lot, and, seemingly without looking, the driver backed into the street, braked, then spun the van around and sped off down Touhy.

Whether from shame or disbelief, Eliot didn't tell Annie anything when he let himself in and found her reading in bed. He quickly got undressed and slipped under the covers. He could tell she was miffed and decided the best thing was to go right to sleep. His last thought that night was, What an idiot. They might have torn me to pieces.

Driving to work the next morning after a cold peck on the cheek and Annie's, "Please come straight home tonight, okay? You could barely walk last night," Eliot wondered if it had actually happened. He was only a few blocks away when he stopped and returned to the parking lot. He parked next to the beach and got out. The van's tracks over the curb and onto the sand were there. He could hardly believe it. As he got back into his car, he noticed that a young woman was sitting in a rather beat-up Mustang not far from where he'd parked overnight. He thought about that, as he drove away, and decided he wouldn't park in that lot again.

For some reason he couldn't quite explain to himself, he decided not to mention any of it to Annie, at all, except to tell her not to use the parking lot. He said he thought it was poorly lit and unsafe.

For the next few weeks, he'd scanned both Chicago papers, looking in vain for news of Red and his followers. He went to the library and found books that recounted the medieval (and in some countries modern) history of the flagellants, but they tended to focus on the "mortification of the flesh," through self-whipping, hair shirts and other perversions. Nothing about the mortification of the soul.

To expect that the experience would have no lasting meaning for Eliot other than a very strange and inexplicable memory, a great story to tell over drinks, is to misunderstand Eliot's opinion of his own behavior. The experience stuck with Eliot less as a strange and inexplicable memory than as an event that revealed something new about himself. He was not only proud of what he'd done, and quickly over his shock at how he might have endangered himself, but he began to think that he was a far braver and even, though marginally, more spiritual man than he'd ever considered himself before. And, most significantly, he soon convinced himself that his mysterious appearance in the dark and his addressing the cult members must have had a profound effect on them.

I might have seemed, I might have *been* a vision, he exulted one morning. Maybe I've become part of their theology? Was I their avenging angel? Their devil incarnate? Did what I say change them? Did I destroy Red's power over them, or strengthen it?

Countless times he went over the memory, what he'd heard, what he'd said, and, most of all, their reaction. That was the real mystery. Wouldn't the normal response have been to yell at him to go away, or to threaten him, or to ask him who the hell he thought he was interrupting their ceremony? Shouldn't Red have said or done something to neutralize the impact of Eliot's outburst as quickly as possible, either by saying something to Eliot or to his followers? Instead, not a word, just that single whistle, and they had filed, silent as spirits, into the van and sped away. And they *had* sped away, as if to escape as quickly as possible.

Though part of him knew it was laughable, the one consequence he couldn't accept was that nothing had come of his intervention in a blasphemous Walpurgisnacht.

That October, on a Monday, as he was driving to work, the morning radio news segment reported that a man with bright red hair in a white jumpsuit had been found washed up on the Morse Street beach, largely decomposed. No identification was expected any time soon.

Eliot spent the rest of the day in an unbelieving haze. It reminded him of the time his Dad, a doctor, had asked him to pee in a jar. Only four years old, he simply couldn't believe, in his innocence, that such a thing could be asked of him. Then, two days later his Dad yelled at him, and he realized he hadn't imagined it.

The next morning Eliot heard the same report, only to realize at the end that they were talking about a second death, again, white jumpsuit and red hair, near Lincoln Park. They repeated, "No identification is expected any time soon."

Knowing he should have done this yesterday, he turned around and headed home to look up the nearest precinct police station. He soon came upon a police car idling near a school bus stop. He parked and walked up to the officer behind the wheel.

"Excuse me, officer," he said, trembling a bit, "Can you tell me where the nearest precinct station is?"

"What's the matter, son? You look nervous."

"I need to tell someone in charge about a thing I saw a couple of months ago."

"What thing?" The officer smiled wider.

"You know about the two bodies washed up on the beach?"

"Hell, don't I?" he said, almost laughing, "I was the first guy there yesterday."

"I saw a young man with red hair and white overalls with some kind of cult…"

"Cult? What cult?"

"I'm not sure. That's what I need to talk to someone about."

"Come around," said the officer, pointing his thumb at the passenger's side. "Get in."

Once Eliot had slid beside the officer, he thought, What the hell have I done?

"Am I in trouble, officer?"

The officer ignored this.

Eliot told him everything he could remember, leaving out the fact that he was drunk.

"What were you doing on the beach in the dark?"

Eliot noticed a hint of suspicion behind the question.

"I got home late from work and it was beautiful night," he answered, as briefly as possible.

The officer paused for some time, thinking it through. Then he turned to Eliot and said, "We hear about cults all the time. Every little nut with a Bible and a big mouth and the hots for young girls, or boys, or both, tries to start one up. Some get lucky."

"You're not telling me everything."

"Of course not. Now get back in your car and forget all about it."

"Am I in danger?"

"I'd stay away from that beach if I were you. You're lucky they didn't beat the shit out of you, or worse.

"Now write down your name, address and phone number." He took out a pad and pen, shaking his head and handed it to Eliot. "I just wish to hell you'd kept your mouth shut that night. You might have seen something that would really help."

"I'm sorry." He handed back the pad and pen.

"Go on, Eliot."

"Goodbye," said Eliot as he got out of the car. He began to walk back to his car, then he turned and went back.

"There's one more thing."

Silence.

"It's probably nothing, but the next morning I left for work and then I just couldn't quite believe what had happened, so I turned around and went back."

"Back where?"

"To the parking lot. I drove right to where they'd driven over a curb and onto the sand. I got out just to see if there were tire tracks, which there were."

"So?"

"There was a young woman in an old Mustang sitting in the lot watching me."

"Watching you? How do you know that?"

"Maybe that's too strong a word. She was just sitting there, but she was backed into the parking space."

"So, big deal!"

"So I shouldn't worry about it?"

"Either they sent her there to find out who spoiled their party and she would have no other explanation for some dope getting out of his car to look at their tire tracks other than that you were the guy, or, more likely, it doesn't mean a damned thing."

Eliot turned and walked away. He had never felt so scared in his life.

That night Eliot told Annie all about it. She was just as frightened as he was. Later that night, they went out on the fire escape stairs, which looked out on the lake. They held hands, the apartment lights off, and watched the parking lot. She had him repeat the whole story, including everything the officer had said, and when he was done, she said, "We need to move."

But as the weeks went by and there were no more stories about red-haired men washed up on the beach, Eliot and Annie spoke less and less of what had occurred. The whole incident, even the deaths, seemed to take on the quality of a distant rumor that didn't concern them. Eliot soon rationalized his fear as totally unfounded, and Annie simply refused to talk about it, not that Eliot was eager to go over it again.

On a Saturday two weeks later, Annie was visiting her mother when he got home at two PM from playing tennis. When he unlocked the front door, it was chained. Somehow, he knew immediately that they had been robbed. He ran down the three floors of stairs to the lobby, outside and around to the fire escape stairs. When he reached the back door to his apartment, it was wide open, window broken. Enraged, he charged in without thinking. There was no one there. The robbery had taken place maybe hours before. Their small color TV was gone and his component stereo system as well. Eggshell clung to the corner of the frame of a large wedding photo, with a pool of yolk and white on the floor. In the bathroom, the toilet bowl was full, which he quickly flushed, thinking to himself it was necessary and maybe unwise. Could shit be evidence?

But as he reached for the phone to call the police, he saw that he wasn't alone after all. Though it was a spacious two-bedroom apartment, they didn't use the second bedroom except as storage. The door was always kept closed. It was now open. From where he stood in the living room, he could see a seated woman's crossed legs. His first impulse was to run from the apartment and find a phone, then the woman called to him sweetly, "Come here, Eliot."

"Who are you?" he demanded, thoroughly frightened, but taking several steps toward the bedroom door.

"Come here, honey. I'll tell you. No need to be afraid of a young lady, especially not me, Eliot."

"Are you alone?"

"What do you think? You're afraid, aren't you?"

Disliking the challenge, he stepped forward and through the doorway saw an attractive brunette dressed in a short denim skirt and a white t-shirt, shoeless, sitting in an old black beanbag chair they never used. Frowning, she raised a handgun and, before he could move or shout out, sent a stream of water at his feet.

"Sorry, I guess I lied." She giggled. "But that little squirt was all I have to make you afraid, as you can see," she said, shooting some water into her mouth and swallowing.

"You stole my stuff," he said, turning away, still afraid. "I'm calling the police."

He picked up the phone but saw the cord was cut.

"Come here, silly. Let's talk, Eliot."

He returned to the doorway. She re-crossed her legs suggestively.

"How do you know my name?"

"How else, the mail on your coffee table."

"You stole my stuff, damnit."

"You said that. Actually I didn't steal anything. I told the others to leave it, but as usual they said they don't take orders from a slut. The egg, though, that was me."

Now he was angry.

"Get the hell out of here!" he shouted, "I can't believe you're sitting there like you're a guest or something. You fucking robbed us."

"No, I didn't. I told you. But I am here to rob your wife."

"What?"

Within seconds she was standing in front of him stark naked. She'd pulled off her t-shirt and dropped her skirt, which must have already been unzipped. She wore nothing else.

"Now be a man, and Red will let you alone."

Then she had her arms around him and thrust her entire body at him. Her lips tasted like lip balm. Her body smelled slightly sour in a way Eliot didn't want to consider. He was human, after all, and aroused, but he felt far more fear than attraction for this little beauty. He struggled but she clung even harder, thrusting her hips into his. There was nothing else he could do; he punched her in the chest as hard as he could. She fell back, landing on the side of the chair, then slumped gracelessly to the floor. It took her only moments to recover.

"I'm sorry, but you wouldn't stop," he said, and extended his hand to help her up, which she took. "Did you say 'Red'?"

Standing, she rubbed her left breast where he'd struck her, then dressed quickly, stuck the squirt gun in her jeans pocket, and ran from the room.

"Don't call the police," she yelled from the kitchen, "They can't help. Only I can save you from becoming white!"

"Wait! What do you mean?"

She came back into the living room, stepping slowly.

"You must be consecrated. You saw us at prayer. That was you that night, laughing at us, wasn't it?"

Eliot almost denied it, but thought, What is the point?

"I wasn't laughing. I was shouting. I said, 'How dare…'"

"Stop!" she cried, "It was blasphemy!"

She calmed herself for a moment.

"You saw us at prayer, and you must be consecrated or you will become white."

"White? Unless I have you?"

Finally, Eliot understood.

"Yes. Fuck me and you'll never hear from us again."

Eliot looked at her more closely. She seemed tired, bruised, and weak. But she was all the more beautiful being so vulnerable. I just want it to be over, he thought.

"I just want it to be over," he said.

"This will end it."

"Come here," Eliot heard himself say. "Take those off."

Ten minutes later, he rolled off the couch, stood up, and said, "Please go now."

"Don't you want to know my name?" she said as she put on her clothes. She handed him the squirt gun. He took it without taking his eyes off of her.

"Okay."

"I don't have a name. None of us have names anymore."

"Fine."

"You don't either. You have only his gift. Red's gift."

"The consecration," Eliot mumbled. It had all been so extreme and sexy in a way he'd never experienced—he was stunned.

"Yes. What we all have. His gift."

She stroked his cheek and pecked him on the lips.

"His gift," he repeated.

As she left the room, she looked at him for the last time. "Yes, his sickness. His AIDS."

THE YORICK
OF YELLOW RIVER

*N*OT since his wife stuck the wooden end of a paintbrush in the droopy flesh beneath his left eye (it was an "accident") had Glaughte Blaugh winked. Such things can drain a guy of humor. Even puns now repulsed him. His universe shrunk to the insularity of withered tangerine pulp, he took up fly-fishing. Ducking the brightly-feathered hook each time it flew by was tedious, and more than once he'd worn the fabled "feather earrings."

He never caught anything larger than his middle finger, which, admittedly, was larger than most.

His wife Erma tagged along. The most famous female painter in the world, her work had made him rich. At least he had a decent allowance for his books, music, Japanese wood-block prints (loathed by Erma), and a gorgeous black whip of a graphite fly-rod that cost more than most foreign compact cars. Of her drippy, gooey, blotchy, sketchy oils, the critics said, "erotic!" "sensual!" "goatish!" "priapic!" "hot!" Camille Paglia called one canvas of an ovum being penetrated by a spermatozoa, "lickerish!" in an essay that placed Erma at the top of the entire history of female painters. "Big deal," was Erma's response.

No, she was no poacher in masculine disguise prowling the sacred hunting grounds of territorial males, like so many of her predecessors (Erma's opinion), but a lithe, strong, fast, and fearsome predator who, like any self-respecting lioness, brought home the bacon.

83

The river was wide, fast, clear, with a stone bottom. After Glaughte had pitched Erma's black beach umbrella and dropped her Pabst Blue Ribbon (in his useless creel) in the water; after he'd jammed the legs of her easel into the clayey riverbank and thoroughly massaged all ten of her horribly deformed toes (she loved tiny shoes), he escaped into the cool, thigh-deep water to stalk the stubborn trout.

Struggling against the stiff current, his waders slipping on the treacherous rocks made him think of his past life as a headliner on the comic circuit. His specialty was pratfalls, which made Chevy Chase look like Nik Wallenda, and the kind of jokes nobody understood, not even Glaughte himself, but laughed at like gut-shot hyenas because of his facial distortions, including outrageous winking. Just as he recalled his crowning moment, tipping over a podium to land in the lap of the brother of the President of the United States, he tripped on the dangling weave of his landing net and plunged headlong into a shallow pool. Thank goodness Erma was out of sight beyond a bend. As his waders filled with water, he sank, twisting and thrashing on the river bottom. He opened his eyes and tried to scream, or laugh, he wasn't sure which. Not two feet away, three huge trout—crimson-bellied, gold and silver spots flashing in the fractured sunlight—stared at him angrily from their left, champagne eyes. As though gripped by powerful and unseen forces, they swam slowly upstream, flicking their broad, dark green tail fins. As the air bubbled up from his tightening lungs, he thought not that he might drown but that he'd never seen fish as big as these. Their glaring at him made him feel like a naughty child who wants to steal a million dollars from his mommy's purse. As they passed beyond his peripheral vision, all three trout pooped. It's beneath this narrator to describe the desecration, but if you've ever seen a goldfish poop in his bowl, multiply that by 100 and you'll get the idea.

Before he blacked out, a muscular hand grabbed him by the hair and yanked his face out of the water. He gasped, coughed, gagged, and swore. Then he fainted.

He awakened to the familiar sound of his wife's singing from up-river (she always sang when she painted), a sound that resembled the shriek of wheel on rail when a locomotive brakes, which caused red-winged blackbirds to wheel and dive above Glaughte in silent confusion.

His clothes were almost dry. His hat, fly-rod, net, and Bowie knife lay in orderly arrangement beside him. Even the inside of his waders seemed dry, though his groin ached. He felt exactly as he would after Erma had unleashed upon his small frame the unsublimate portion of her enormous libido.

The intense July sun had not progressed perceptibly across the sky, but Glaughte felt, from the dull dry pain between his shoulders, that he'd been asleep on hard ground for hours. Limb by limb he thrust himself to his feet and gathered up his tackle. About to step back into the water, he remembered the three huge fish. He got excited. He pulled out the fly, still stuck in the cork handle of his fly-rod, and dangled it above the current.

The water exploded!

A long, crimson streak gashed the air, arcing two feet high, and disappeared in a fountain of water that splashed his face. The fish-line ran screaming off his reel. In seconds, all three hundred feet of floating and backing line was out, and Glaughte was running upstream, dodging tall weeds and thick tufts of scrub oak, chasing the tremendous fish.

He ran for miles, the line leading him on, taut as a violin string, twanging and singing as it caught upon a tree limb and sprang free, or cut through rapids at incredible speed.

Most fishermen would have lost the fish by now, his or her leader being no more than a sporting four- or six-pound test; taking no chances, Glaughte used a stout twenty-pound test that would take a shark to break.

As he ran, the sound of his wife's singing grew softer, less harsh. He heard an actual melody for the first time, a lyrical and lilting song of love that was new and strange to him. Maybe she knows what is happening, he wondered. Maybe she wants me to catch this fish! The song threaded the air, the waving grasses, and the swaying tree limbs with a golden mesh. As it faded, growing ever sweeter, more plaintive and melancholy, Glaughte redoubled his determination to land this monster. With a last harsh note, almost like the bark of a huge, vicious dog, Erma's song ended.

The fish led him on. The undergrowth slashed his canvas waders to shreds. All the little zippered pockets on his fisherman's vest worked themselves open, and spools of monofilament, bags of hooks and sinkers, jars of fish eggs, cans of insect spray and floatant, and all the rest of his tackle flew about, leaving a trail that shouted, "A fisherman passed this way!" Was this to be the proudest day of his life? It could be, he thought. It has to be!

Still hung on his belt by an elastic band, the traitorous landing net, instead of tripping him, banged his heels as he ran, would catch upon a bush, stretch its elastic to its extreme length, then spring free and smack his backside. But it never tripped him up.

As the fish rounded another of the myriad bends in the river, Glaughte's line went limp. Groaning and twisting, he waded into the river and clambered up onto a large flat boulder. Below him a great black pool, a backwater created by the boulder, swirled like Poe's maelström. Away from its center the water grew calmer. His line spiraled in and out of the vortex, where the fish must have sought sanctuary. "Damn you!" Glaughte yelled, "you better still be hooked, you bastard!"

He reeled in the slack line, frantically working the reel's little knob in furious circles. The tip of his fly-rod twirled, whipped and flipped, almost fouling the line. Finally, the line went taut again, aiming at the heart of the great charybdis.

Glaughte reared back mightily on the fly-rod. It doubled down, its tip rapping his white knuckles. The trout shot straight into the air. He could see its face, how, as though smiling and then laughing out loud, its jaw line stretched, and its mouth showed teeth. The fish threw the hook, which flew at his eyes. He ducked and it caught in his hat. Fishline coiled around him like baby snakes. Glaughte moaned and swore. Then something heavy and wet struck him in the face. He fell on his butt. As he watched, the fish panted its last pant, its eye a glazed glare.

"Well done!" someone said—a feminine voice, shimmering and lovely.

Ignoring the sound, he grabbed the fish, yanked open his vest, popping buttons, and tucked it under his left armpit.

"Don't worry. It's yours," came the voice again.

Glaughte gave the still fish a bear hug just to be sure. Yes, it's dead, he thought. He looked up where the voice repeated, "Well done!"

On a second flat boulder, across a narrow cataract, lay a naked woman. Sun-bathed, glistening with oil, every inch bronzed, her body stretched, stomach flat against the baking rock. Around her lay all of the paraphernalia of a fly-fisherwoman. Her large, round buttocks thrust up in shameless enticement.

"You deserve a reward," she said and turned over.

Glaughte stood up. The fish slipped from his vest and flopped on the stone.

"So it was you," he said, catching his breath, his voice like a bull-frog's.

"Couldn't let you drown, could I?"

He stepped to the edge of the boulder. He looked down at the roiling froth. The jump from his to hers was less than four feet.

"You can make it," she said.

"Maybe I should walk around," he said, staring at her peaked breasts, the pale delta between her massive, flat thighs, and the two rows of white teeth, closely set between her red lips.

"I might be gone before you could find a place to ford," she replied with feigned coquetry.

"I'm married," he said.

"I am, too," she answered and winked.

"Be right there."

He stepped back to get a running jump as she moved to the edge of her boulder to give him room to land. He took three quick, deep breaths, feeling strong, sure, and wonderful. Then he ran. His right foot landed on the trout. He slipped and executed the most exquisite pratfall of his life. As he disappeared into the whirlpool, never to be seen alive again, his last thought was of those three mad fish.

Approximately ten miles downriver from the place of Glaughte Blaugh's tragic mishap stood a little hamlet known as Yellow River, which straddled the watercourse, as much a part of the river as the water itself. It was ten years later that a young man of good family came upon a human skull wedged among some deadfall beneath the only bridge in the area. He quickly retrieved the skull and delivered it to the police, who theorized that it might be that of a drowned fisherman whose body had never been found.

Per protocol the skull was delivered to higher authorities. In time its DNA was tested and compared to that found in hairs in an old harlequin's mask still in the possession of the former Erma Blaugh, now remarried to an iron magnate named Horace.

The skull, clean of flesh and polished by the roiling sand and waters of the river that took him, was indeed that of Glaughte Blaugh. Due to her stature as an artist, Erma was allowed to keep the skull for one month to make sketches before a proper burial. Eventually, her drawings of the skull—which were, unlike all her previous work, fine and precise drawings on a par with Leonardo da Vinci and Albrecht Dürer—would be considered her crowning achievement.

THE
PIANIST

1

LIKE many of my fellow concert pianists, I hated my mother. It's a weird but entirely real occurrence that most of the successful pianists I know will forever resent their mothers for stealing their childhoods from them. There was always endless practice, plus the next competition, recital, or expensive lesson with some modestly famous pedagogue.

Maybe "hate" is too strong? In the end, each of us had to be thankful for great careers as soloists, pedagogues, principal pianists with major orchestras, or on the faculty at famous conservatories. Performing a Beethoven concerto with a major orchestra with your parents in the audience makes for a bit of redemption.

Ha! Not me. When I had my first solo gig with a regional orchestra not far from where she lived, I forbade my mother to attend. I said, "I won't be able to play a note, and all your work to get me here will have been wasted." All bullshit, of course. I simply refused any longer to share the credit. She died when I was on my second tour, of five cities that time. I couldn't cancel. I just couldn't. I missed her funeral.

You think that's cruel and ungrateful? But think! Us creative types—you have to cut us some slack, right?

She was a single parent and proud of it. Never did tell me who my dad was. What did she care? She was born rich to parents who moved to Tokyo when she left for college. I met them once backstage after my first recital in Tokyo. Though Mom had passed three years before, they looked ten years younger. At the end of a late dinner, after cordial questions on their part, and terse answers on mine, I asked them if they, since my Mom had written me out of her will, were planning to remedy her unfairness in their own last will and testament.

Grandfather handed me my Mom's last letter to them, explaining her decision on the will—my rejection of her—and asking them not, in her memorable phrase, "to give him a single yen." I handed back the letter and started to get up to leave.

"Wait a moment," Grandfather said, "I want you to sit down and tell us why we should not follow your mother's last request?"

"Because your daughter was a bitch."

Both of them flinched.

"Yes, I know she could be difficult. Even as a child."

Finally, Grandmother spoke up.

"Please apologize."

"I'm sorry," I said.

Of course, I could have taken the next hour to recite all the tyranny and selfishness of dear Mom in vivid detail, but it was exactly the last thing I felt like doing. Dredge up all that pain and drudgery again?

After a long pause, Grandfather said, "Well?"

I knew what he meant.

"The other reason is because I'm a genius and I'm not good with money."

Then I got up and left.

As I write this decades later, Grandmother's still alive, so I have no idea if I'll ever see a penny. However, I'm actually very good with money.

2

I'm also good with women, but before I get to that, let's get this "genius" business cleared up. I've never met a musician who's a "musical genius." Maybe some of them have IQs high enough to warrant the word "genius," but it has nothing to do with how well they play. My IQ number is 119; above average, but not by much. I am not a genius. But there is a reason why people call me that, and they call me that all the time, so I say it too. I play better than 99% of the pianists out there. I move, inspire, even thrill people with my playing. My recordings are as good as they come—everything from Mozart to Ravel. (Bach, not so great, so I just leave him be.) People tell me they've bought, say, my Beethoven "Hammerklavier" sonata, and have worn it out—I mean vinyl *and* compact disc!

To put it in practical terms, I've earned upwards of $50,000 per concert or recital for many years, and I have never been without a lucrative recording contract.

There's a simple explanation why. It has nothing to do with the endless hours of practice, or the fact that I studied with two of the greatest piano pedagogues of the last forty years. Sure, those are reasons for my technical facility and for some standard portion of my interpretive abilities. This is something altogether unrelated. I call it the "musical gene." I don't know if there's really such a thing or not, but it's as though I was made out of music. I've only met a small number of people I can say have the "gene," some of them even conductors (something, in all cases but one, I hate to say). What I'm getting at is that I have the ability, unerringly, to find the "line" in a piece of music. My "line" is unbroken from the first note to the last. It never varies (even if I make a mistake). I can make it do things so beautiful even the composer didn't envision them. The other 99% of pianists out there don't have such a line, wouldn't even understand what I'm talking about. Their line, such as it is, is not quite as bad as Morse code, but if you listen hard, you hear the bending, even breaking of the line—but what you'll miss most is the "purpose" in their line. Things speed up too fast, slow down too slowly, get too loud or too soft without any reason for the emphasis. There's no infinitely insistent intentionality. Or call my gift the "pulse" of my music—and I don't mean the beat. The heart's pulse can go up and down, but you can't break it. My playing has that pulse, and it's inexorable in everything I perform.

3

As for women, I didn't do so well at the conservatory. Frankly, I'm not that handsome, and like any good Pavlovian creature, I couldn't keep from studying and practicing more than anyone else. If I took a day off, Mom (who called every single fucking day) would say, "Tell me what you learned [or worked on or with whom]?"

I couldn't lie, so that barrage, part snippy, part hurt, and part demanding, would begin until I promised to do better tomorrow. And I always did.

Yes, I know it was worth it. I *understand.* All that hard work and all those lost pleasures made me what I am. Let's just say that when it comes to women, eventually I made up for lost time.

It was on that first European trip. I was no virgin, thanks to the pure charity of a rather plain but shapely cellist in my last year at the conservatory, but I was otherwise just naïve enough to be bold. In Paris, I gave a Chopin recital in an old church, long since desanctified. My hosts were members of a Chopin society, most of them elderly. My agent had arranged the performance for one of my days off between orchestra appearances. In the dressing room, after the recital, I was about to change to a suit. Then I looked at myself in the mirror. I had to give Mom this: she dressed me well, and I looked like a movie star in that tuxedo. I kept it on.

The reception turned out to be a sit-down dinner in a back room of one of Paris' fancier restaurants. I found myself seated next to the youngest woman in the room. Later I'd learn she was the daughter of one of the society's richest women. I drank two glasses of champagne right off and that loosened my tongue.

The young lady was in her early thirties—ten years older than me—cute, not beautiful, short blonde hair, but dark eyebrows, in a little black dress that hid nothing, her fine breasts in particular. We talked and talked. I was probably rude to my other hosts, but I couldn't help myself. During dessert, I put my hand on her thigh. She smiled at the person across the table. She grabbed my hand and drew it up under her dress, all the way to her damp panties. I withdrew my hand, put my hand on her forearm and whispered, "Let's go." We didn't even bother to hide it. We stood up and left together, after a perfunctory *"merci"* and a handshake with our hostess.

Later, she said something I lived by for almost a decade.

"You might think it's because of your playing, which is partly true. You moved me more than once, though Chopin always moves me."

"Well, it can't be my looks."

"Oh, that's not fair," she said without turning toward me. "You have the looks of a genius. Normal standards don't apply. Still, it wasn't your looks either."

"Tell me."

"The tuxedo."

4

You probably won't believe this, but a solid seven out of ten women, single or married (sometimes with the husband sitting right there) have responded to that hand on the thigh move just as the first one did. I always made a point to ask them later and the tux always fit into the equation.

It's no big secret that the best kept "secret" in the history of humankind is that women like it even more than men. It's such a joke that even today, more often than not, the man still has to make the first move, still has to ask. Sure, there's the come-hither look, even flirty words, but nothing happens if the guy doesn't make a move. Does that make sense to you?

And those three out of ten? Well, you take a risk, right? I've had them turn to their husbands and say, "This creep just groped me," with predictable results. I've been stabbed with a nail file and with a table fork. One woman tried to break my pinky, and damn near did. (I almost had to cancel a concert!) I've been punched, scratched, and bitten. Oddly, I've never been slapped, maybe because it's noisy.

Grant me this. Scientifically speaking, I'm on firm ground here. And I never once pressed the issue. I could take a hint. Boy, could I.

I also had a rule I never broke, which is I never once made my move when I was alone with the woman. I wasn't stupid. And the victory was all the sweeter when it happened in a room full of men and women who thought I was a genius, so it was okay if I behaved like one.

5

But when it comes to women, all that changed in 1989.

I fell in love.

I spoke slightingly of conductors a moment ago. I was being honest. I have always disliked them. I never showed it, because too often the conductor is the only reason an artist will be re-engaged. But I've always detested their every word. Rehearsals have been a torture to me. Once conductors shut up and follow my lead, I'm fine, but there's no species of musician more quixotic, petulant, inept, oblivious, and rude than a conductor.

And my general opinion about them didn't change, even when I fell in love with one.

Her name was Sofia Amber, the music director of one of the lower-end top-twenty orchestras in this country. At the time, she was the first and only female to rise to that level.

Because of a delayed flight, I didn't get to meet her before we walked on stage for our first rehearsal. I'd heard good things about her, and, unlike many of my colleagues, it never occurred to me that a woman could not conduct as well as any man, just as there's no gender disparity between pianists or violinists, or any other instrumentalists. Perhaps my flourishing sex life, you say, was the reason I felt that way, but no. I knew who had the "gene," the "line," and who didn't. That a stupid industry refused to recognize let alone embrace the fact that some major orchestra podiums were held by mediocrities, while truly gifted women were relegated to the minors, wasn't an idiocy confined to the business world.

Still, Sofia was a conductor, and I disliked conductors, even if they had the "gene," which she most certainly did. What made her different is that she proved in just the first twenty minutes to be one of the sweetest persons and most accomplished conductors I'd ever met. And, best of all, she hardly said a word! She didn't have to. The music just came pouring out. She was also one of the best accompanists I've ever worked with. She didn't lead, she didn't follow. She simply bonded with me musically like long lost twins.

She was tallish, and standing on the podium exaggerated the effect, all to her benefit. She wore blue jeans and a white blouse. No makeup. No jewelry. She reminded me of that French sweetheart, only prettier—blonde, but dark eyebrows, a smile shy when it didn't blaze in happiness, and like many female musicians (and athletes), demure in bra-size.

To get us from that rehearsal to her acceptance of my marriage proposal of one month later would be to roll out one cliché after another. I'll say only that I didn't wear a tuxedo after either of my two concerts with her.

It was only after she'd accepted my proposal that things got interesting. Early on, we agreed to wait on sex until our wedding night. It was my suggestion, and she was charmed (or so it seemed). We also agreed not to speak of our previous encounters with the opposite sex. That was her idea, which I, for obvious reasons, endorsed.

Kids were out of the question for the foreseeable future.

We were a couple of high-octane musicians, ambitious, supremely talented, with nothing but great success prepared for us by our mutual fates.

She had two orchestra jobs at opposite ends of the country, the second being a summer festival. She also was a frequent guest conductor in smaller cities around the country, and tapped now and then by the majors as a substitute on short notice.

I played 100 concerts and recitals a year all over the U.S., South America, Europe, Australia, and Japan. We both had apartments. Mine was in New York. We both made multiple six-figure salaries, but whose job was to take precedence when there were conflicts (such as the one that caused us to move our honeymoon in Hawaii back six months)? She had the relative security of a music directorship in a large city. I lived with the insecurity of not really knowing how much work the next season would bring—though I had yet to be disappointed.

With the wedding only a week away, we had our first and last verbal confrontation (not really an argument) about how we should arrange our lives together. We sat in a secluded booth in her favorite Italian restaurant, having escaped from another of the endless receptions inflicted on both of us, a professional hazard. With perhaps a few glasses of wine too many in her after the late dinner and a successful concert, she suggested she'd give up her festival if I cut back on my guest work and took a job at the city's prestigious conservatory as a pedagogue. I could get rid of the New York apartment, and we'd buy a house. As a base of operations, this airport was more convenient than New York's and, of course, we'd see much more of each other.

I couldn't quite take in what she was saying. Was she trying to get out of it? I decided to take an indirect approach.

"This is about loneliness?"

"Don't be silly," she said, a little miffed. "I did some calculations the other night and figured out that, with luck, with things as they are, we'd be in the same city no more than 120 days a year."

"This is about sex, isn't it?"

"Yes, partly," she said, seeming surprised at herself, and when I smiled, she hurried on. "And money, saving money, and a home to call our own, having friends, spending time with family, and, and security."

"Well, I'm glad you brought all that out into the open."

She took another gulp of wine.

"I'm an idiot."

"No, you're lovely," I said and took her hand. "Let's leave all this until after the wedding, okay? There's no reason to turn both of our careers upside-down before we know what we're *really* getting into."

"But won't it be too late?"

"Are you saying you're having second thoughts?"

"That's not what I mean, and you know it."

I took a drink and smiled. In spite of what she was saying, her manner was entirely charming.

"Do you know what a 'lead job' is?" I asked.

I sounded like a high school social studies teacher.

"Of course, in a marriage where both spouses are employed, one tends to have the 'lead job,' usually because, and it's usually the man, okay, usually because he makes more money."

"Exactly. You're suggesting that yours is the lead job."

"That's absurd."

I quickly realized my mistake. She was hurt.

"I'm sorry. All I was trying to say is that this is a marriage of equals."

She nodded.

"And we're going to have to figure it out."

I still don't know how this juncture of the discussion caused me to say, "As it is, I'm giving up quite a lot. You can't imagine."

"Me too," she said with a sigh, as if reading my mind. "I think we need to talk about something, and the sooner the better."

"Okay."

I don't know how I saw this coming, but I did. I resolved not to get in her way.

"I know it was my idea not to talk about our past, uh, lives."

"You mean sex," I said flatly.

She blushed, but it was without any charm at all, as if she'd been found out.

"Yes. It's one of those good things, bad things."

She bit her lip then took another sip of wine.

"You need to understand something. Let's just say," she paused and maybe swore under her breath. "I am a very passionate person."

"One kiss told me that, sweetheart."

" 'Sweetheart,' I love being called that. You can't *imagine*."

"Imagine?"

"The number of times I've been called that."

I laughed.

"Sweetheart, I'll bet every man you've ever met has thought 'sweetheart,' whether he said it or not."

"I am, you know."

"I know."

"There *have* been a lot."

"Look, I accept that. We're both over thirty. We travel a lot." I was about to go on, but I was already in dangerous terrain.

"And?"

"What does that mean? I mean, for you?" I asked.

"Well, it's not a matter of travel, though sometimes it has been."

"Okay, so you've had boyfriends."

"Not really. I mean not what you'd normally call boyfriends. I'm just too busy."

I was beginning to understand.

"What I think you're saying is that your life has been rich."

Some women would cry as they said what was to follow. She didn't blink an eye.

"I've slept with almost every visiting artist here in the last five years."

"Tell me."

She frowned, as though she couldn't believe I was taking it so calmly. But she could see I wasn't jealous.

"It's weird, really."

I sat there feeling like the kindly, attentive psychologist.

"We hardly ever say a word beforehand. At some point, usually after the concert or reception, I whisper in his ear. It's always me. They never, ever say no, even the married ones."

"And that's why you want me to move here. To save yourself from yourself, for me. You don't think you can be faithful if I'm gone too much."

"Yes," she said flatly. "But no. Not really. Not the way you just phrased that. 'Miserable' is more like it."

"That's sensible and quite understandable. Now, let me respond. As you'll recall, you didn't whisper a word to me at that first reception. Why is that?"

"Because you're different."

"And I didn't put any moves on you, like placing my hand on your thigh under the table, like I have with a great many adoring fans."

"No, you didn't."

"That hand/thigh thing? And my tuxedo? Almost as effective as your little whispers."

"You do look great in a tux."

"Thank you. But, let's do the math," I continued, very business-like, "By my calculations, between all the concerts you do here, and your guest conducting, which is a fraction of my guest work, you probably have the opportunity to sleep with twenty men a year. Is that close?"

"You're being awfully cold-blooded about this."

I laughed.

"Coming from a 'passionate' woman, I don't know how to take that comment. Not at all."

"This is not funny."

"No, certainly not. But let me continue. I sleep with roughly forty or fifty women a year."

She gasped. I hurried on.

"But let's get back to your question. Why didn't I come on to you? My first response is my question. Why didn't you come on to me? You answered that question. You said I was different. What did you mean by that?"

"I don't know."

"My response to the same question is the same. I don't know why I didn't come on to you. You're different. I can't remember the last time I hesitated making a pass at a woman I desired."

"We both desire each other?"

"Yes, sweetheart. I think that cuts right to it."

"More than all the others."

"More than all the others."

I suspect the reader will find all this rather unbelievable—two serial sensualists declaring fidelity to one another. I would have to side with any skeptics, except for one more thing that happened that night.

After an extended silence spent just looking at each other and smiling, she excused herself to go to the lady's room.

When she returned, she slid in next to me.

We smiled again as I put my hand on her thigh. I slid it all the way up to her panty-less sweetness.

"Time to fuck," she whispered in my ear.

I found her clit and pressed.

She rose up slightly on the bench, turned and shouted, "Check, please?"

In her bedroom, we made love three times before dawn. At the moments of her greatest passion she hummed, softly, then urgently.

During the first lull, I said, "You have the line, Sofia." Then I explained to her what I meant. In great detail, I described how the few truly great pianists we both knew were like me. And, like her.

She stuck her tongue in my ear and said, "My word for it is 'shaping,' " she said, "but I think we're talking about the same thing."

I put my hand on her perfect hip.

She reached down and grabbed me. I quickly responded.

"Isn't this your line?"

"One of them," I said.

THE NOSE
II

1

*T*HE operation was a complete success. Crito proved an astonishingly quick healer. When the nurse removed the bandages the next day to change them, the doctor gasped. The surgery had completely healed. Crito's nose was gone, of course, leaving nice smooth flat skin between his cheeks—all as planned—but so quickly! The doctor tweezed out a few stitches and passed Crito a hand mirror.

"It's perfect!" Crito cried and in fact began to cry in earnest. "Thank you, doctor, thank you! I don't know how I will ever repay your masterful workmanship!"

The doctor, a large young man whose name was Capriccio, turned to his cute (girlfriend) nurse and said, "Damnedest thing I've ever seen."

"Damnedest!" she replied, and squeezed his big left bicep.

Turning back to Crito, Capriccio enquired, "Can you smell anything?"

"Well, now that you mention it, I can smell a sort of nasty hospital smell."

"Don't worry. It's the last thing you smelled before we put you under. Think of it as the phantom feelings an amputee has, as though his arm is still there. It will fade very quickly, I assure you."

"I certainly hope so," Crito said, wiping away his tears. "Hey, it might be fading as we speak."

"I was going to keep you here one more night, but now I don't think it's necessary. You can go home. Just get a good night's sleep, okay?"

"Doctor, you're forgetting something," said Crito.

Capriccio turned to his cute girlfriend and raised his eyebrows, as if to ask, "What is he talking about?"

She stood on her tiptoes, whispered in his ear, "The nose," and gave his ear a kiss before stepping back.

Crito experienced a twinge of dark green jealousy. He chose to ignore it.

"Of course. I almost forgot!" The doctor dug in the pocket of his white coat and brought out a little burgundy velvet box such as you'd use to present an engagement ring to a young lady. He handed it to Crito.

"With my compliments. Everything is now up to you, as agreed."

Crito's eyes were as wide as hubcaps. He looked at the box, then at the doctor, then at the nurse. "Can I open it?" he asked, rather timidly.

"Why, it's yours, isn't it? At least for now."

Crito held the box close to his eyes and opened it just a bit, then let it shut with a snap.

"It's perfect!" he shouted at the top of his lungs. "Do you want to see it?"

The doctor and the nurse backed away, holding up their hands.

"Not necessary. Seen it. Yes. Perfect."

As they left the room hand-in-hand, Crito hugged the box to his chest and hummed a tune from a Strauss opera. Ten minutes later, as he was dressing, the phone rang. Crito listened and said, "Yes. That's fine. Four this afternoon at the diner will be just fine."

2

It's important now for the reader to become acquainted with our Crito. Crito was his only name. He might once have had a second name, maybe a first name, or a last name, but he had only the one name now. He couldn't tell you why, but it was a certainty that everyone, even the Department of Motor Vehicles, knew him only as Crito.

Crito was an orphan abandoned at a fire station who grew up in foster homes until he was sixteen when he ran away to the big city where he flipped burgers in order to rent a one-room apartment where he lived for five years. During that time, he was never without a girlfriend, though the rules prohibited his ever bringing them to his room. That was fine with him.

Crito was five foot five inches tall, deaf in his left ear since birth, with straight but grayish teeth, a tonsure surrounded by peppery hair, a strong chin, shapely, smallish ears, faded purple eyes, and hardly any eyebrows. He was neither handsome nor homely, though he was secretly vain about what he saw in the mirror—except for his nose. More on that in a moment.

Since turning twenty-one, Crito had been an assistant clerk at the largest drug store in the city. That was thirteen years ago. Not once during that time, even though he now lived in a nicer apartment, did he ever bring a single one of his unbroken string of girlfriends home. That's just the way things were. When he toasted the health (and the looks, when it made sense) of a lady with a glass of champagne at a nice restaurant, he thought himself the happiest man in the world. Invariably, the lady would say something like, "No one has ever treated me the way you do, Crito. This dinner must have cost you a fortune!"

But his life was not without its challenges. His salary just wasn't enough. After his rent, food, and the cost of entertaining his girlfriends, there was never a dime left over even days before his next paycheck. Each lady complained, "Why don't you get a better job?" whenever he had to beg off a date for lack of funds. His answer was always the same, "You're right. I'll start looking for a new job right away." But he never did, and if that meant he had to move on to a new girlfriend after cashing his next paycheck, well, so be it.

The fact was that Crito loved his job. He loved the people he worked with, even though they hardly ever spoke to him. He loved his manager, even though he never gave him a raise. But most of all he loved the smell of the place, a fact that he was not aware of in the least. No, it would be more accurate to say that he was actually addicted, without knowing it, to the smell of this particular drug store.

Which brings us back to Crito's nose. As noses go, his was as handsome, even as elegant as you would ever want to see. It was aquiline, yet retroussé at the tip, with perfectly shaped nostrils, almost teardrops of darkness, and of a nearly transparent luminescence that not once had been marred by a blackhead. Still, Crito would say in the mirror, "You horror! Why am I cursed with such a nose? A bullfrog has a finer snoot than you!"

He couldn't tell you why, couldn't even explain it to himself. He just hated his nose. If just one of his girlfriends had told him that his nose was his most attractive feature, everything might have turned out otherwise. But what woman singles out a man's nose for compliments when it's his only actually attractive feature?

3

This story begins for real some two weeks before Crito's operation. Three things happened almost the same day. The store manager was fired and jailed for stealing drugs and immediately replaced. For the first time ever, Crito found himself in debt. His three credit cards were maxed out. He owed thousands. He had absolutely no idea how this could have happened. And he found himself without a girlfriend, or even the prospect of a girlfriend (because of his debts). Lucia, whom he'd been seeing for almost two weeks, had been admitted to a sanatorium for alcoholics.

As if this wasn't bad enough, the new manager gathered the staff together after closing on his first day and announced, "This place has roaches. I could smell 'em when I walked in the door. I blame every last one of you for letting them get in and doing nothing about it. Tomorrow, I'm having the place closed and fumigated. The exterminators will be here until every last bug is dead. Do you hear me? Even if it takes a week. So consider this a nice vacation." He started to tromp away, then turned and added, "Without pay!"

If you've ever had roaches in your kitchen, you know how they scatter everywhere when the light's turned on. That's what the entire staff looked like getting out of the building. Crito just stood there, as if struck by brass knuckles, and didn't wander toward the door until he was entirely alone.

Fortunately, the extermination took only forty-eight hours, and they were all called back on the third day. The store wasn't opened until the following day as the manager had every employee sweeping dead bug carcasses until the floors were spotless. For this he was glad to pay them a half day's wages.

While it would take Crito his next twenty paychecks to get himself out of debt, at least they would keep coming. But no more nice apartment; he'd have to move to a small room as soon as possible, and he wouldn't be able to even think of getting a new girlfriend for months!

But dear Crito, while no stoic, who would gladly have escaped his impending penury, even at the cost of his good name, stepped bravely into the future.

That future was short-lived. On the day after the big sweep-up, Crito became unaccountably agitated, downright nervous, and his stomach hurt. As the day progressed, he began to feel an itch between his shoulder blades he couldn't scratch. He grew momentarily dizzy on several occasions, especially in more idle moments. An hour before closing time he began to get the sniffles, then to sneeze repeatedly. His sneezes were so loud and frequent, like Harpo Marx's horn blasts, that the manager ordered him to go home early.

As he walked home, within moments his sniffles and sneezing disappeared. He thought nothing more about it until the next morning, when, as he was restocking the liquor shelves, the sneezes returned, even more violently than before.

The manager cornered him in the back room and said, "You want to get the whole staff sick? Get the hell out of here, and don't come back until you're well again."

"But I'm not, ah ah ah, choooo! sick!" Crito explained.

"Get!" yelled the manager, pointing at the exit.

It wasn't one minute later as Crito was taking off his white coat that he understood what the problem was. The store stank. It didn't stink from the extermination. That smell had dissipated. No, the place had a whole new smell. Crito wasn't a particularly well-read individual, but he was a crossword puzzler of prodigious talent and experience, so the following words immediately flowed through his mind: noisome, malodorous, smelly, rank, mephitic, and iffy, not to mention foul- and evil-smelling, fetid, olid, reeking, and rancid.

He pinched his nose and ran, stumbling for the door.

For the next six hours Crito wandered as through a mist or fog, without any two thoughts following logically on each other, without seeing his hands or feet in front of him, though he seemed to be able to see the nose on his face—that culprit, that betrayer!—with no difficulty at all. At one point he stood on a bridge and wondered how cold the water was down below. He hated cold water. Later, he stood in front of a large sculpture shaped like he knew not what, only that it made his eyes hurt, in front of an art museum. As the afternoon drew on, he found himself in a seedier part of the city full of row on row of old shops selling who knew what. As he passed each store window, his brain was incapable of registering what was behind the glass. All he could see was his own reflection.

Exhausted, he sat down on a filthy bench and tried to think. Knowing he could never go back to the drug store—a tragedy in so many ways—his first concern was money, and lots of it. Every other misfortune flowed from that, just as his future couldn't be brighter if he only had money—enough money, he let himself dream, that I'll never have to be without a girlfriend for another day as long as I live.

"That's a nice nose you have there," said an elegant woman in a fox fur stole with the mouth clipped to the tail, sitting on the other end of the bench.

"Thank you," was all Crito could think to say.

"I heard you talking to yourself."

"Oh, I'm sorry. Very bad habit."

I've never talked to myself in my entire life, thought Crito.

"I know how you can get money. Enough for a lifetime!" the woman said with a little laugh at the back of her lovely throat. Crito saw that the fox had a bright black nose.

"What's that?"

"Yes, more money than you could even dream of."

"Tell me!"

"It's your nose, you see. It's really quite exceptional. I know someone who would buy such a nose for a million dollars, maybe more."

Crito stood up abruptly.

"I'm sorry, madam," he huffed, "It so happens, and I admit it willingly, that I'm not particularly fond of my nose, but parting with it for a million dollars is the silliest idea I've ever heard."

"Really? Is that really so? And if what I'm saying is absolutely true? Why, I've brokered the selling of noses a hundred times over. I specialize in noses. You can keep your ears. Too apt to lose their shape. Or your fingers. Anyone can sell fingers. They don't need my help. But, dear sir," she concluded, standing up and digging into her purse, "I have a very special clientele for noses, and for one as perfect as yours, well, we could both do nicely, if you know what I mean."

She handed him her card, which read only "NOSES" with a phone number underneath.

"Call me if you change your mind." As she stepped past him, she whispered, "You won't regret it."

Crito turned for home. Somehow, the experience of this odd, but rather attractive older woman had cleared his head and sharpened his senses. On the way, he stopped in a diner and ate a burger and fries, enjoying every bite. As he went to pay his bill, he was astonished to find two crisp $100 bills still in his wallet. At least I haven't paupered myself, he thought. Then he stopped at a bar and ordered a beer. As he nursed his drink, he came to a sudden revelation. Tomorrow, he thought, I take control of my life once again. Somehow, I've managed to lose my way. That's an end of it. I will move to a studio apartment immediately. I'll find a job, a good job, and pay off my debts in weeks instead of months. Then the money for the ladies will begin to flow like before, and all will return to normal.

He marched home full of renewed self-confidence. When he turned on the kitchen light, the roaches scattered frantically. As always, he drew in a deeply satisfying nose full of air.

4

The next morning, with no job he had to dress for, Crito lay in bed all morning long. You might think he was making plans per his resolutions of the night before. At first, he deceived himself that he was about precisely that. First the apartment; he'd start looking right away. Thank goodness his lease was month-to-month. Then he thought of running out to get a paper to check the want ads for both a room and a job. But he just couldn't bring himself to move. Instead, a parade began in his head. Crito had quite a memory for the ladies; in fact, he could remember the names and the faces and even the clothing of every single one—even the months and years in which he dated them. And all in the order in which they came and went. The only thing that tended to escape him was their bodies, but his head was crammed with so much else about them that this hardly mattered.

His reverie took him well into the afternoon when he began to feel hungry. Finding nothing in the kitchen that appealed to him, he dressed and went out to the same diner he'd been to the night before. As he was scanning the menu, a stranger sat down across from him. Crito found this quite objectionable, particularly as he was a rather large, imposing fellow, but before he could ask him to leave, the stranger said, "Yes, she was right. It's quite a masterpiece."

"What the hell?" said Crito angrily.

"My name is Capriccio," said the young doctor the reader has, of course, already met. "You're Crito, if I'm not mistaken."

"How did you know?"

"You know exactly how. Attractive older woman? A rather old-fashioned fox stole?"

Crito began to get up to leave.

"Please," said the big fellow, grabbing him firmly by the arm and seating him, "You have nothing to fear from me. I'm here to restore your future."

Crito was speechless.

"You're one for the ladies, aren't you?"

"I guess," Crito whispered.

"That's what she said. Well, ask yourself. What do women really want?"

Crito thought back over the last nineteen years and the answer was as clear as the handsome nose on the doctor's face.

I won't waste the reader's valuable time with a lot of details about what happened over the next two weeks. After a thorough examination, Capriccio determined Crito fit to undergo nose removal surgery. The mysterious woman whose name Crito would never learn took a dozen photos of his nose and the next day negotiated a $1.5 million fee for Crito's nose with a purchaser whose identity was never revealed. On delivery of his nose, the woman would present him with a check for $1 million. She and Capriccio would split the remaining half-million.

5

Which brings us back to the beginning. Crito left the hospital the next day, and the minute he got home, took out the little purple velvet box containing his nose. He wanted to take one last look before he turned it over to the fox-stole lady later that afternoon. The first thing he noticed was that his nose was encased in an extremely thin translucent soft plastic film. The incision—where his nose had been secured to his face—was hidden beneath an equally thin opaque film. It was incredibly light and dry and not as ugly as he remembered. Most interesting of all, where the two types of plastic came together there was a thin, barely visible slit on each side just above where the nostrils bulged out. He looked in the box again and took out two strips of flexible plastic with little ridges each on one end. He threaded the strips through the slits until the ridges kept the strips from pulling free. Taking up the two strips, Crito went into the bathroom and looked in the mirror.

He didn't even pause to reassess his noseless face but held the nose right in place above his philtrum. He pulled the strips behind his head and they clicked together almost like magnets.

"My goodness, what have I done!" he cried.

Imagine the conflicting thoughts and emotions he must have felt as he realized that his face was even handsome with his now irrefutably handsome nose. How had he never understood it before? It was exquisite! Why hadn't even one of his ladies told him how much they liked his nose? Why hadn't they noticed? Yes, I'm about to become a millionaire, and I'll never have to work another day in my life or smell anything so dreadful as that damned drug store again, but as he untied the nose and held it away for a moment, he wondered, what will the ladies think of me now? Will it even matter that I can buy them whatever they want? I might even be hideous. It's too soon to tell with certainty, but I might be looking at the ugliest face on this planet!

He realized that he was trembling, from his fingers to his knees.

He put the nose back on. There, he thought, that's better. He turned away from the mirror and walked around his apartment feeling calmer. The nose felt perfectly natural. The straps almost seemed designed to feel like they weren't there. He went back to the mirror, turned his head from side to side; the straps were perfectly invisible and fit snugly, neither too tight nor loose.

"Damn me if I'm not the handsomest man in the world!" he said aloud.

"To hell with the million dollars!" he shouted. "I'll go back to the drug store, smell-free, work hard and pay off my debts, and I'll bet I have a new girlfriend in less than a week. Maybe two or three!"

When the hour came for his appointment with the nose buyer, Crito was strolling along one of the busiest streets downtown as, he could swear, one after another, the ladies turned to stare or grin.

On the way home, he stopped at a bar and began a conversation with a redhead. Thinking that he still had $150 in his wallet, Crito invited her to dinner at eight at a very nice restaurant indeed. As they parted, she gave his cheek a pinch, which slid his nose slightly aside. Without giving it a second thought Crito moved the nose back into place and hurried home.

Crito opened the door to his apartment and turned to slide on the chain. Turning back, he found a tiny derringer pointed straight at his nose.

"You blew it," said the mysterious lady, as she tugged the nose and its strap up and off his head. Now the derringer was pointed straight at the flat space in the middle of his face. The gun was beautiful, the barrel spotless silver, the handle a brilliant mother of pearl. Crito thought, my goodness, what a beautiful nose it would make! Or would it?

CAT
MURDER

LLAN heard it as he reached the bottom of the back door steps, a crunching, almost a cracking noise. As he turned toward the patio, he found his wife cradling the cat. Something was wrong. She took her right hand off the cat's head. The cat hung limp in her arms. She'd just broken its neck.

He took the cat from her, encountering no resistance, and walked back toward the house.

He turned to her and said, "Come on."

She followed him to the place beneath the steps where they kept the garbage cans.

He pointed at one and said, "Take off the cover."

She did as she was told.

He dropped the cat in the garbage.

"If that's all you cared for the thing, then you're not allowed to give him any better burial than this."

He took the lid from her and put it back on himself. She wandered back to the house. He went for a long walk through a nearby park. When he returned, just before dark, she was asleep on the couch.

She always maintained she didn't remember any of it. Yes, she loved her dog, and, yes, the dog and cat didn't get along. And it was just a stray they'd taken in a few months before. She remembered that much. It didn't seem to register when he said that the dog had died a week before, and that he had liked that cat. It was clean and playful. It liked to sleep in his lap. When he asked her, a dozen times, "Why?" she'd say, "I don't remember."

But these conversations, nasty and accusatory on both sides, were days later.

Before she left that next morning, he said only, "You remember, right? That you killed the cat?" After she'd rushed out of the house without responding, he made same coffee, then gathered all the trash from around the house and took it outside. He tipped the trash can under the stairs until he could reach the cat. He topped off the trash can with everything he'd brought outside, then carried the cat into the rear of the back yard. He laid it beside a tall pine and retrieved a spade from the garage and dug a hole under the limbs. The cat was a long-haired black and white mix with a white "scar" of fur over his left black eyebrow. Before he poured down the first shovelful, he said, "Poor little thing."

It was Saturday and the one day he had all to himself, because his wife worked in an antique store Tuesday through Saturday. He spent the morning reading and making notes in anticipation of next week's lectures in the American novel and the afternoon watching baseball. Normally, Annie came home after five, but she woke him from a nap in front of the television at three, screaming, "I didn't kill any fucking cat!"

"What are you doing home?" he said blearily, turning the TV off with the remote.

"I quit, that's what, as if that should surprise you at all! Now what did you do, get me so blind drunk I'd believe anything you said?"

"You killed it."

"What?"

"The cat."

"What cat? I just dumped out the whole trash can and there's nothing in it but trash. Trash! What is this? Some kind of, of…" She calmed down a moment, then asked, "What was that old movie we just saw where the guy tries to deceive the woman?"

"Gaslight."

"That's it! You fucker! You're gaslighting!"

"You saw me put it in the trash can."

"So where is it? And don't lie to me. You're a terrible liar. You lie to me all the time!"

"I'm telling you what happened. What you did."

"How about what you did?"

"Go ahead. You've got a whole list. Pick something. Pick something really good," he said with venom.

"How about you and your little teenage twat?"

"Good, let's get to it."

She turned away and said something he couldn't hear.

"She was twenty-one, and that was fifteen years ago."

"It was exactly fourteen years ago next month when I found out, though you never did tell me how long it had been going on."

"Old news."

"Not to me."

"I buried it."

"Don't you wish," she said, turning back. "Some things will never be buried. I just choose not…"

He raised his hand to interrupt her.

"I buried the cat."

He watched her face and nothing registered. Finally, she shook her head slightly.

"Why?"

"Why?" He was used to keeping his voice at level calm.

"Why did you bury it?"

"Well, you were content to let the cat rot with the trash."

Then, what would have shocked another man, she dropped to her knees wailing. "But I was going to bury it! Why else do you think I looked in that goddamn can?"

"Not because you meant to bury it."

"Of course that was why."

"You're lying. Again. You just wanted, like most desperate drunks would, to prove to yourself what actually happened last night."

She stood up quickly.

"I think it just died or something and you threw it in the trash and made me look at it. That's what happened. And I've been thinking about it all day and decided to bury it the minute I got home."

"You really don't remember, do you?"

"Fuck you."

"You broke its neck. I saw you. I heard the sound."

"And threw it in the trash, you bastard. What a thing to do!"

"Annie, there's something that's going to upset you even more than that poor kitty."

"How many times do I have to say 'fuck you' to get you to fucking shut up?"

"I found them. While I was collecting trash to seem to hide the cat I'd already moved and buried because I knew you'd do exactly what you did, which was to look—while I was doing that, I looked everywhere until I found them. A tidy little stash it was too. I buried them all with the cat."

Now he was lying. He knew it was a mean trick. He'd found just the one empty scotch bottle under the stairs. In her state, she'd believe he'd found a lot more. More. More. More. And now it was gone.

"There's no stash," she scoffed. "There was one fifth of scotch. I drained that fucker while you were watching the news. I drank it so fast I puked up the first few swallows in the irises."

"It was a quart."

"There was no stash."

"There were five bottles. Some whisky. Some vodka."

"You're lying."

"Probably you yourself forgot they were still there. Leftovers from some bender maybe months ago."

"You buried five bottles?" She could hardly believe it.

"Much sadder than the cat, isn't that right?"

She stepped toward him, looking right down on him.

"I repeat, 'Fuck you.'"

"What do you care? You're in AA, right? You're just fine. Sober for how long? I thought it was four months, but maybe last night doesn't count. That was just a little slip, a toast to the pledge you made to Penny and me, and to everyone else you've hurt, that it won't happen again. Except you decided it would be nice to sanctify your toast with a sacrificial cat."

She turned away, whispering, "Motherfucker."

"Why did you quit the shop? If, as you said, it should be no surprise to me, it must mean that they caught you with a bottle again."

Turning on him angrily, "No, they didn't find another bottle. They smelled it on my breath. It must have been from last night."

"Oh, that's a good one, Annie. I don't think you've used that one before. It's not your fault your breath still stinks of booze fifteen hours later."

"It's true."

"No, Annie, it's not. Why are you still standing there over me like that? Please sit down."

She did as he suggested, turning her face toward the doorway.

"I had a nip while you were sleeping this morning."

"Where's the bottle, Annie?"

"It was yours."

"I don't drink, Annie."

Another lie. He had to be careful. His Irish whiskey was beside the point. The bottle she found was his only one, unless it was another one of her own.

"You do, and the bottle was almost empty."

"Then where is the bottle?"

"I threw it out of the car window."

"Of your myriad lies, that one might be the most inventive. That you could possibly destroy even one bottle is beyond conceiving."

"I said it was almost empty. I just finished it off."

Before he could ask her where she'd found the bottle, she wiped away a tear.

"Please don't use that word."

"What, 'conceiving'?"

"Yes," she whispered.

"Okay. I sure wouldn't want to bring up any more unpleasant history."

"Shut up, damnit!" she screamed. "You're the worst person in the universe. Here I am, so sick, so sick of my life, so sick of you."

"And cats, too, apparently."

She jumped up, grabbed her purse, and was gone.

She came back three hours later. He'd kept to the chair and the television, which he turned off when he heard her car in the driveway. He wanted her to see him exactly as if she'd been out of the room for less than a minute. She was drunk, in what was for her an early stage, though most people would have noticed.

She sat in the couch opposite his easy chair.

"Where's your purse, Annie?"

"It's in the car."

"I'll bet. How many times have you forgotten it? What bar did you leave it in?"

"I won't lie. I don't lie. It was Benny's. I'll call about it tomorrow."

"Yes, it won't be the first time for Benny's."

"You're just going to keep on me, aren't you?"

He waited to see if she had anything else to offer. Nothing.

"Yes, I will, until you tell me what I need to know, and that's 'why'? What set you off this time? You actually were doing pretty well for a while."

"I'm not going to tell you. You don't deserve to know."

"'Deserve.' Interesting word choice."

"Leave me alone."

"Annie, I don't mean the cat. We can leave that to later."

"Fine. I don't want you to mention that stupid cat ever again."

"Don't count on it."

"What do you want from me?"

"I want to know why you drank last night."

"I've given my answer."

"Okay, if we can't talk about that, let's talk about 'conceiving.'"

She screamed and fell face down on the couch.

"We can talk about that, or we can talk about last night. Annie, I want to know what set you off so badly you puked just to get it all down."

He had turned away for a second and she threw her keys at him, striking him on the jaw.

"Lovely," he said, picked them up from his lap and tossed them into the fireplace. "You can dig them out of the ashes later, dear."

With pure defiance, she said, "I apologize!" lifting her head just enough to get the words out.

"Excellent. Do you remember? Are you sober enough to remember how long ago that was?"

She whimpered, her face still in the pillows on the couch.

"What's that?"

He could barely make out "Fuck you, you cheating bastard."

"Look, Annie. I thought we agreed that the statute of limitations on that expired long ago."

She got up on her elbows, pleading and hope in her eyes.

"And the, the…?"

"Yes, I can agree to that, if you tell me what happened last night."

She turned on her back, sat up, then stood up.

"I bought that bottle yesterday when I saw you driving with a blonde on Fairmont."

"That was my secretary, Annie. She's not a blonde, she's gray, as you know. She's sixty-three years old."

"You're lying."

"No."

"Stop trying to confuse me. I don't care who it was. It was a woman and you were alone with her."

"So?"

"Nothing. I knew nothing was going on. But it made me remember."

"Well, I guess I can understand. I think. You have never forgiven me, even after what you just said."

"Statute of limitations, ha! That doesn't have anything to do with forgiving you."

"I could say the same thing, dear."

"You don't?"

"No, never."

"But you manage not to think about it too much?"

"I think about it every day. Every fucking day for the past ten years. Can I remind you of something?"

"No."

"You were a drunk long before either thing happened."

"Oh, so that's your excuse."

"No. I have no excuse. It was a stupid mistake I'll regret forever, but I've never reversed the proposition and rationalized my sleeping with a student as revenge for your getting bombed every night."

"Good for you, not that I believe it."

"And your excuse? What's your excuse for…?"

She started to cry again. He let it go.

"Yes, I did, darling. I slept with a twenty-one-year-old student. It was because I was a stupid, arrogant asshole back then and I felt, like my fellow professors, that I had the—almost the right to do it."

"Yeah, yeah. I've heard it a thousand times. And I'll bet you've had others since."

"You know that's not true," he said, raising his voice slightly.

"I don't know anything about you anymore."

"And the reverse is true."

"If you say so, though you act like you know my every thought or feeling, which allows you to judge…"

He cut her off.

"You saw me with 'another woman' and that's what set you off?"

"Yes."

"I don't believe it. I believe it's you who's been unfaithful."

"What?"

She threw her arms up and brought them down on her thighs with a smack of exasperation.

"You've been cheating on me."

"Right. That's obvious. I got drunk. Big news!"

"You know that's not what I mean."

"So I killed your cat too, *supposedly*, though that's a weird kind of being unfaithful."

"You know that's not what I meant either," he repeated with exaggerated patience.

"What's wrong with you? I know what's wrong with me! I slipped off the ole wagon last night and I'm still not sober. What do you think? I'm too stupid to understand I've broken my word, if that's what you mean by unfaithful?"

"For the third time, Annie, you know that's not what I meant."

He decided it was time.

"It took me a while to even begin to suspect. There was something about your sobriety that seemed too dutiful, too calculated, like you were hiding something."

"What the fuck are you yammering about?"

"Most of our married lives you've been almost defiant about drinking, and the two other times you've been in AA you complained until I couldn't stand to be in the same room with you. But this time was different. You actually volunteered. Remember? You sat me down and said you'd come to a decision and for my sake—Annie, you said for my sake, and Penny's—you were going back into the program. What surprised me is that before that you were actually doing pretty well, keeping things under control, though I could never count on you staying sober for more than a week at a time. But it seemed like progress anyway. All of a sudden you'd seen the light!"

"Now you're being snotty. First time I take control of things on my own and you make fun of me."

"Yeah, I'd be a real jerk if that was all. But I just wasn't buying it. I had no idea what was wrong, but I didn't believe you. Like I said, I began to wonder if you were hiding something. And it turns out you were."

It finally came to her, and she slumped onto the couch.

"I even know his name. I know where you met him and I know where you two go to fuck."

"Don't say that word to me."

"Fuck. Fuck. Fuck. Fuck. Fuck. And a million more fucks. But you know what?"

She cringed then put her head down to her knees.

"I've known now for three weeks. And here's the goddamn truth. I decided not to say a word. I couldn't believe you were doing it, but I had to act like all was well. You see, I figured you felt you had the right to do it."

"You're damn right."

"So you admit it?"

"I don't admit any more than you did."

"Well, that's enough. At least it's out there now. But, again, I wasn't going to say anything. I can't say it broke my heart. I don't have anything left for that. But I had to look in the mirror and talk to myself for fifteen minutes to convince myself to just let it go. 'It won't last,' I said to myself. 'Then we'll be even and who knows, maybe she'll stay sober as a result.' Boy, was I wrong about that!"

"You don't understand a damned thing. You have no idea what's been going on. You're a ruin, an ancient ruin, like fucking Stonehenge!"

"You're right on one point. I don't know what set you off. You blew your cover, Annie. So what happened that you had to puke in our irises and murder our cat?"

"I don't admit to that." She looked up, warning him.

He ignored her.

"What happened? Did his wife find out?"

"You don't know anything, do you?"

"They're separated?"

She looked out the window. Said nothing.

"So it was okay for him, but it sure as hell wasn't okay for you. And to be perfectly clear about it, my prior refusal to confront you, and to condemn your infidelity, is at an end. You see, I believe there has to be some balance in these things. You cheated on me in revenge, except I slept three times with that student, as I've said a million times, and you slept with this man by my count more than twenty times. Do I have to conclude that you are in love with him?"

"Maybe I was."

"Maybe. Well, let me repeat to you I wasn't in love with my student."

"It doesn't matter. You don't love me."

"Oh, if only that were true. And now you don't love me? Are you sure? Because that leaves you in limbo, Annie. You don't love me and you only maybe love your lover."

"He's not my lover!"

Then he got it.

"He left you, didn't he?"

She covered her face with her hands and started softly crying.

"He left you and you bought a bottle. Is that it?"

She nodded and cried more loudly. He knew what he was about to say was cruel, more than anything he'd said so far, but he couldn't help himself.

"You must be some lonely bitch, Annie. You give up your beloved bottle just to get out of the house and fuck a fucking realtor, who must be ten years older and certainly not the most handsome old dude I've ever seen, just to get back at me for fucking a twenty-one-year-old cutie fifteen years ago. And it must have been pretty good fucking for you to go back to his apartment for a quickie after your meetings and for your little nooners so many times. And now your little revenge is complete. And if I have to guess, you didn't love him at all. You could hardly even stand the fat prick. But what joy in sticking it to the old man by having it stuck in you."

He paused, chuckling in spite of himself.

"Sorry for the poetry. But to continue. What's left? No lover, no AA, and no cat. And here's the real kicker. I forgave you the moment I stood in front of that mirror. Because what's the point? If I'm going to live with it, I have no choice. I forgive you. You evened the score. Good for you. And he kicked your ass out. Good for him. Goddamn smart of him!"

He was letting it get too much of him, so he reined it in.

"But, remember this. While I've grown numb forgiving you for getting bombed in violation of every promise and trust and bond there ever was between us, I will never let you forget that cat."

He took a deep breath.

"And don't think I'm willing to see it as some final death-throe, so to speak, of your murdered revenge. That would be much too easy. No, I don't think the cat has anything to do with anything—me, Carl, the bottle, Penny, anything. In the very depths of your drunkenness something inside you got free and killed that poor creature. In short, there is something twisted, almost evil inside you, and you disgust me."

Then he stood up and said, "I'm going to bed. You stay down here and sober up. By tomorrow I'll have figured out what I'm going to do next. And make no mistake, it will be me who decides."

When she heard the bedroom door close, she got off the couch and went out to the porch stairs. She took a quart of scotch from behind a potted plant. She closed and locked the door and sat on the couch. She unscrewed the top of the full bottle and took a long swallow.

Then she lifted the bottle toward the ceiling and offered a toast.

"Here's to my next lover," she said, without lowering her voice.

THE
METAMETAMORPHOSIS

(With apologies to F.K.)

As Gregor Samsa awoke one morning from uneasy dreams, he found himself transformed into a small insect. Having also fallen out of bed, he wasn't sure at first what upset him the most. Spinning slowly on his back on the hardwood floor, Gregor gazed up at the edge of the bed, which looked exactly like the white cliffs of Dover, or at least like a bed the size of the white cliffs of Dover. Maybe my bed has grown to be as big as the white cliffs of Dover, thought Gregor. He lifted his head a little and saw his brown pot-shaped belly, which seemed only a bit darker than he remembered. He saw his numerous, barb-heeled, incessantly gesticulating legs, much thinner than his legs usually looked, and he thought, if I had to say, I suppose falling out of bed is less objectionable than waking up in a state of transmogrification.

What has happened to me? he thought. I've turned into a bug, that's what. But what kind of bug? A cockroach? A cockroach is flat in shape and I am anything but flat. I'm convex, belly and back. Really, I'm like a cockroach only in that I am brown. But let me pursue this. My belly is divided into segments, it would seem, though it's difficult to see. I have a hard rounded back, surely suggestive of wing cases. That's it! The cases conceal flimsy little wings that can be expanded to carry me for miles in a blundering flight. Further, I have strong mandibles. Who ever saw a cockroach with mandibles?

Indeed, I have assumed the shape of a beetle, a stag beetle, or a cockchafer perhaps.

His room, a normal bedroom, only rather too gigantic, lay quiet between the four familiar walls, behind two blind-drawn windows. Above the table, on which—beyond his vision—lay a collection of cloth samples, unpacked and spread out (Samsa was a fashion designer) hung the photograph, from a magazine, of his latest creation. It showed a lady in a fur coat and cap that covered her from head to toe, with the hem drawn tight around her ankles, and into which her entire body had vanished! Only two beady little eyes peeked out between the fur collar and the fur brim of her cap. He couldn't see it in the photo, but Gregor knew that behind the collar the woman wore a frown.

"Ah, Grete!" Gregor sighed, "You are lovely, I'll grant you that."

Gregor's eyes turned to the window, where raindrops falling made him quite sad and melancholy. Why don't I sleep a little longer and forget about all this nonsense? But he couldn't sleep; he could only sleep on his side. However violently he tried to roll over he always rolled onto his back again. The sight of his legs flailing about was a constant irritation. I'll bet real beetles don't have this problem, he thought. He gave it up only when it occurred to him that all the stress he was laying on his back might damage his little wings and he might never get a chance to fly.

"No," he said to himself aloud, "relax. Go with it."

Gregor stared up at the ceiling, which was like a white sky, with a globe fixture, even turned off, as luminous as the moon. He remembered that whenever he'd taken it down to change the bulb, it was always full of dead, dry insects.

This sleeping late, he thought, makes one stupid. Other people get up at a decent hour and come home to a pleasant evening in front of the fireplace. I didn't get in until four this morning, at least. My head! Grete pouring me all the Courvoisier! If I ever make it in this business, big enough to afford putting Mom in a home where she belongs, I'll just have to settle down. But with whom? he wondered. Not Grete! She only loves me for my connections.

He looked at the clock on the dresser. Would you believe it? he thought, it's only noon! I can't live on less than ten hours sleep. Without his blanket, which was nowhere to be seen, probably tied into knots on top of the bed as usual, Gregor would never get back to sleep on the cold, hard floor. In fact, he didn't feel the least bit drowsy.

This is silly, he thought. I may as well get up, put on that new pinstripe I've been dying to wear all week, and go down to the studio. Nobody but Chester will be there, but perhaps I can do a few more sketches for the gala this fall. If I can sell them on that bottomless leotard, I'll be as rich as everyone thinks I am.

Fully resolved to get to his feet, Gregor tried rocking back and forth, stretching his head back and to one side like a turtle. He rocked ferociously. I'm like a cradle! he thought. But it soon began to hurt. The top of his head ached so much, he wondered if he wouldn't pass out from the pain. At all costs, he must not lose consciousness, not when he'd made up his mind to put in an extra two hours of work that day.

With joy, Gregor discovered that he had made some progress after all. He was now much closer to one of the casters attached to a leg at the head of the bed. If he could move within reach of the wheel by continued rocking, he might grab hold of it and lever himself onto his legs.

He began to rock himself as furiously as before. He would have to nerve himself mightily to withstand the pain long enough to reach the wheel, which was, he noticed with some irritation, absolutely filthy with dust and other questionable matter. Then the doorbell rang. "Who in hell could that be?" Gregor groaned. His whole body twitched from the frightful pain in his head; his legs jigged wildly, like dancing exclamation marks. He was barely an inch away from the wheel. An inch, an eternity, Gregor thought with despair. He began to repeat over and over, "Why me? Why me?"

"Is he up?" asked Chester when Gregor's mother opened the door.

"Are you kidding?" came her feeble croaking whisper.

"Something terrible has happened!" cried Chester.

Hearing the words, Gregor didn't wait for his mother's response. He rocked as hard as he could. The pain set his thoughts spinning.

He's got troubles? What's it now? His girlfriend's moved out again? A drop of gravy's fallen on his blue suede shoes? It had *better* be terrible for him to disturb me in the middle of the day. Yet, I can't let him see me like this, and Mother would have a coronary! This would be her biggest shocker since Dad left her for that cosmetician, K. The way she sits in that chair knitting God knows what, day after day, year after year. She never knitted anything for me, that's all I know. Now it looks like the thumb, just the thumb of a glove is *all* I'd need. I must get to my feet. I must!

As Chester rapped the bedroom door, Gregor felt the edge of the wheel against his left side. I've done it! he thought.

"Gregor? You up?" Chester asked.

"Go away," Gregor responded. "Can't you let a man sleep? I was up with Grete until God knows when. The poor kid's driving me crazy with her ambitions. Even *I* can't help her. I mean I *won't* help her. And nothing you can say can make me, so leave me alone. I need my sleep. I'll see you at three, as always."

Saying all this in a tone of voice Gregor felt remarkable for its civility under the circumstances, he managed to grab hold of the dirty wheel that was, now that he was right under it, as big as a room. He was gratified to discover that his little legs each had a sticky substance on the soles. By pulling at the wheel from a gradually lower and lower position with his left legs and steadying himself with his right legs, Gregor finally managed to turn himself over and to stand on his feet.

"Gregor? You there?" said Chester, sounding more and more anxious.

Chester's apparent deafness vexed Gregor. Hadn't he provided more than sufficient dismissal of the fellow? What a pest he was! Gregor shouted, "Damn you, Chester! Get the hell out of here. I'll see you at three and not a minute sooner."

"Did he come home last night, Mrs. Samsa?"

"I didn't hear him, Chester. Not that I ever listen," said Gregor's mother, "I go to bed at ten o'clock like all good God-fearing people."

"The door's locked, but I don't think he's in there. It doesn't feel like anyone's there," Chester said in a voice tearful and quavering.

Gregor's mother said, "That would be about the size of it in any case."

That's it! Gregor thought. She's starting in again, and he's in one of his states! If he weren't so clever with needle and thread, I'd have sacked him years ago.

Then a thought struck Gregor, clearing his mind of everything else.

"Wait a minute!" he said aloud, "I'd nearly forgotten."

Gregor had remembered his wings.

"Gregor! Wake up. Unlock the door. I must talk to you," shouted Chester.

"Something horrible has happened!"

"Call me if you raise him, Chester," Gregor's mother said, "I've got work to do, but I would like to give him a piece of my mind. He hasn't paid the rent this month!"

Hearing his mother trudge off, Gregor scurried under the bed, feeling more and more sure of his legs every second. He flexed this muscle and that, searching for the right ones. He could feel the hard shell of his back split apart. He could hear the crackle, like wax paper, of his wings unfolding. He tried other muscles. All of a sudden, he jumped. Astounding! His first airborne experience! He jumped again. Ouch! His head hit one of the enormous metal spirals under the bed. Wait a minute, he thought, let me get out of here before I brain myself. Away from the massive roof of the bed, Gregor tensed the now-familiar muscles and up he went. "Yikes!" screeched Gregor, veering to his right just as he was about to collide with a brass floor lamp. "Wheeee!" Gregor flew, rather blunderingly, about the room. He'd never felt so wonderful in his entire life.

"Gregor? Unlock the door!" Chester yelled.

Damn him, thought Gregor. He'll never leave. Well, if he wants to see me, then he'll just have to see me. Mother, too. And the Devil take them both. I can fly! There's nothing to be ashamed of in that.

Veering unsteadily, he made several practice runs at the doorknob. Now, he thought, I've got to be going slowly when I land so that the sticky stuff on my feet grabs on and my momentum doesn't pull me loose. His next two passes were just slightly too fast. I've got to hone my timing, he thought. Concentrate. Careful. Then, there he was, standing on the doorknob, sawing precariously. He steadied himself and sheathed his wings.

"I did it!" Gregor shrieked.

The key, Gregor thought. Trusting his ability to cling to even the smoothest surface, he crawled under the great brass ball of the doorknob, onto the wall, and down to the key. Now for the hard part, he thought. Tensing the muscles in his face—there seemed to be dozens of them—he soon found what he was searching for. The mandibles opened effortlessly. He snapped them shut; they made a great, scraping noise. "Ooooo, how terrifying!" he screamed with delight. As he bit the disc of the key, he heard Chester's voice booming through the door.

"Gregor, if you're there, please come out. She's thrown herself from Brooklyn Bridge! Oh, Grete! What could you have done to her, Gregor?"

His great jaws gripped the hard key and his body swiveled across the round brass plate of the lock. An indescribable pain shot through

Gregor. Brown fluid dropped from his mouth and the meaning of Chester's words seared his brain. He dropped to the floor.

Chester could have sworn he'd heard a noise, ever so soft, from Gregor's bedroom. He began to fear that Grete's death—"Gregor, I'll see you in hell!" her note had read—was not the only one. A suicide pact? he wondered. Quite beside himself, he ran to Mrs. Samsa's bedroom.

"Mrs. Samsa!" Chester cried, "He still doesn't answer. But I heard a noise. I'm afraid something's happened."

"Something terrible?" asked Mrs. Samsa, cocking her head to one side.

"Yes!"

She looked up at him, rocking comfortably, a twinkle in her tiny old eyes.

"He doesn't know it, but I have a key."

"Get it!" Chester shouted. "For God's sake, Mrs. Samsa, get it!"

The tinny, rasping sound of his mother's key in the lock brought Gregor back to consciousness. He was on his back once again. His wings, having spread during the fall—perhaps, instinctively, to break it—felt crumpled and torn beneath him.

"Grete!" he moaned, remembering, "you *loved* me?!" He saw her young body stretching, her long, wingless flight down.

The door opened, swinging over him with a great blast of wind, blowing him halfway across the room and flipping him onto his feet again.

"There's nobody here!" shouted Chester hysterically.

"Greetings!" said Gregor, gritting his mandibles against the pain, determined to put the best face on his predicament.

"Ugh! A cockroach," Mrs. Samsa cried out.

The last thing Gregor knew was his mother's shiny black shoe descending upon him like that of some colossal goddess.

ORCHESTRAL

1

L IKE many of my colleagues who run symphony orchestras, I am single. I'm almost forty, executive director of an orchestra in a mid-sized city in the Midwest for the past ten years.

I'm a bachelor because I entered this field when I was only twenty-five, and from the first month on the job I realized that a career in the orchestra field would be all-consuming: fifty-, sixty-, seventy-hour weeks, were not unusual. I loved every minute of it, and the last thing I wanted was to send my children off to college total strangers. So I hadn't married. At least, that's how I felt about it for a long time.

Two questions might occur to the reader. Have you had no love life at all? Why, after fifteen years in the business, aren't you with a bigger orchestra?

The short answers are "I have," and, "I've tried." Yes, there was someone in college that took me a long time to get over; and I have dated a number of women, and every relationship of substance ended when the question of marriage emerged. But, more recently, I met the manager of another orchestra, and I'm in love with her.

I only learned the following about Eliza Ohtera after the events I'm about to relate. She was a third-generation Japanese-American. Her grandparents were interned during World War II for almost two years. She went to Juilliard in the '90s and graduate with a per-formance degree in piano in 2000. Like many talented musicians in the past four decades, she discovered how difficult making a living as a classically-trained musician actually is. In 2006, she applied for a management fellowship with the American Orchestra League, the umbrella organization of the symphony orchestra field. Her first full-time job was as the Artistic Administrator for the Cincinnati orchestra. In 2012, she became the Executive Director of the West Florida Philharmonic. By then, I too had become an executive director, for the Evansville Symphony in Indiana.

This story is as much Eliza's as mine.

We met three years ago in 2017, as far away as possible from anything connected with an orchestra—on a flight to Paris.

It was the first time I'd taken a vacation in five years. I went alone because I needed to utterly expunge music and musicians from my thoughts. I would spend all my time in the Louvre and the Musée d'Orsay, and on the beaches of the French Riviera.

Eliza and I were seated together, with an empty seat between us. She was slightly pale, with a swept-back cap of lustrous black hair, high cheekbones, a medium, slightly pinched nose, full lips and beautiful teeth. For lack of a more poetic description—she was uniquely attractive. Once she seemed comfortable with me, I couldn't take my eyes off of her. She was relatively short but trim, almost athletic. She wore a light summer dress, white flowers against blue sky.

We started talking as soon as the drinks were served. I led things off and told her my name and where I worked. At that moment, she must have decided not to tell me anything about her similar connection to music. She called herself Ginger. She didn't lie outright about her career, but it was clear she didn't want to talk about her job as a manager of "a company I'd rather not even mention," she said.

Early on, I asked her, "Do you know who Mitsuko Uchida is?"

"The concert pianist?"

I was impressed. "Yes. You look a lot like her, only lovelier."

She blushed, flattered, and also smiled, as though I had said more than I thought I had. We went on to talk about everything except our careers. We were both well-read with proudly snobbish tastes, loved music of all kinds, loved theater, movies, art museums, and dance. We both loved skiing, running, and biking. She was also an avid fly fisherman, as I was.

When we began to talk about our personal lives, things began to warm up. She asked me if I'd ever found the love of my life, and we agreed to tell the stories of our respective experiences. Both, going back to our twenties, were sad, but the telling (she went first) revealed to me—and I think to her as well—that we were two people of decency and deep feeling, even if we were still single. She was two years my junior.

At one point, in the middle of my story, she got up and moved into the middle seat. At the end she took my hand and kissed it. Then our lips met.

I asked her if we could meet in Paris.

"No, I'm sorry," she said, "I will be very busy with work."

"Even in the evenings?" I pressed.

"Especially in the evenings," she said and kissed me again.

Then she said, "Can I ask you a favor?"

"Of course."

"Will you hold me and really kiss me for as long as you can?"

I didn't answer. She unbuckled her seat and we turned off the overhead lights and flipped up the arm rest. We were maybe two-thirds through our eight-hour flight and the lights were dim in the cabin. She turned and crawled onto my lap; I held her in my arms and we kissed and kissed as passionately as any two lovers can. Once or twice she squirmed to accommodate my unavoidable erection.

At one point, she whispered in my ear, ever so softly, "If I was ever to want someone to be with me, it would be you."

After much more kissing and talking, she sat up, looked around, then lifted her skirt and wriggled her white panties down below her knees. She reached for my zipper.

"My fingers know what to do," she whispered, "And I can show you what to do if yours don't." she giggled. Her tongue probed my ear, sending an electric shock down my spine to my penis.

"I think I can manage," I said, already trembling.

She came first, her pelvis shivering like a minor earthquake—and as I was close to it, she leaned over and took me between her lips and casually swallowed my seemingly endless ejaculation.

"I'm sorry," I whispered as she sat up and touched her forefinger to her lips.

"Sorry? That was lovely. I came again when you came."

Then she snuggled into my shoulder and fell asleep, not waking until we'd landed.

We hardly spoke again, except to say goodbye at the end of the jetway.

"Can I walk with you?" I asked.

"Please don't," she said and kissed me deeply one last time. "I love you, sweetheart."

"I love you too," I replied.

Then she walked away, but hardly out of my life.

2

Almost a year later I was approached for the job of Executive Director of the Salt Lake City Philharmonic. I was flown out and spent two days interviewing with the music director, musicians, and members of the board.

This was not the first time I'd been a candidate to manage a larger orchestra and had turned down one offer already. Here there were two things that made me cautious. The orchestra was in deep financial trouble. It had squandered its endowment and had millions in debt it was floating with a line of credit. The other issue was the Mormons.

The financial problem was not unlike that of most orchestras in this country. Evansville had similar problems when I was hired, and

I'd managed our way out of the mess. Perhaps I could do the same in Salt Lake, though it might take years.

During a pause in the search committee interview, one of its members took me aside and asked, "How do you think you'll get along with us Mormons?"

"I'm sorry?"

"I know," she said. A large blonde woman with a brown mole on her chin, she gently grabbed my arm. "I know it's not proper to ask, but this is the Mormons we're talking about."

I wasn't about to blow the interview this early, so I replied, "I don't think it's a question. I can get along with anyone."

"Can you tell me your religious beliefs?"

"I don't think I can."

"You mean you don't have any?" She seemed shocked.

"I mean my beliefs are a private affair."

She relaxed, smiled, squeezed my arm and said, "You know, of course, that we have other candidates?"

At first I thought she was threatening me, however subtly. "Yes?"

"And one of them, a woman I rather like, said the same thing."

"Thank you for understanding," I said as we walked back to the board room.

Early the next morning, before the interview process continued, I had coffee with a musician who had once been in my orchestra and in Salt Lake was the Principal Clarinetist. We were good friends, and we spent most of the time catching up. Finally, I asked him about the board and mentioned my "private interview" with the blonde woman.

"Well, I'm sure you've figured them out by now," he said, with an "oh, what I know!" grin. "It's an issue, the Mormon thing, but, hell, I'm Jewish and I get along fine with them. I just act like the whole thing doesn't exist. I keep my mouth shut."

I pressed him a little harder, but he clearly didn't want to share his personal experiences. He had already said he really hoped I would become the executive director and probably didn't want to say anything to discourage me.

I told him I'd been doing my research and was curious about something I'd come across.

"The Utah Olympics were in 2002, right?" I asked.

"Yup."

"And before the year 2000 it was Mormon doctrine that the world would come to an end in 2000, right?"

He knew where I was going, and said, "Yes, and yes, they had to lobby to be selected by the Olympic Committee years before that."

"Yes."

He laughed. "You want to know why they bothered?"

"Do you know?"

"Well, in a way. When I first got here four years ago, I was invited to lunch by the board chairman. I think he wanted to prove he wasn't an anti-Semite," he added, laughing. "I'm the first one they ever hired, you know. He was very nice, so I asked him the same question you just asked. He admitted that he'd been involved in the campaign that brought the Olympics here. In answer to my question, he said, 'Son, one thing about the Mormons; we cover *all* our bets.'"

We both laughed, but the more I thought about it, the more I felt that these were people used to having it all their way. Would I succeed with them? I had led Evansville to solvency; would these folks follow me too?

Something else disturbed me. The orchestra's terrible financial position was mostly due to poor ticket sales. The fault was certainly not the players' or the conductor's—their playing was highly professional, at moments exquisite. On my last day there, I walked out the front door of the concert hall and there, not a few hundred yards away, was the Mormon Tabernacle. I had the sense to ask if the choir had an orchestra. A board member said, "Oh, yes, and they give free concerts almost every week."

I thought about that on the way home. On the one hand, Mormons represented a majority of the board and seemed genuinely concerned about its financial health. Yet, their church was running the orchestra's toughest competition. Nothing added up.

Though ambivalent, I was still open to pursuing my candidacy, but it was not to be. A week after returning home I received a phone call from the headhunter informing me that I had been much liked, that it was a very close decision, but the job was being offered to another candidate. I asked who it was, and she said she couldn't divulge that until negotiations were concluded and the hiring was made public.

I forgot all about it until two weeks later, when the headhunter called and asked if I'd be willing to meet her at the Evansville airport in two days. I said sure.

Before I relate what happened at that meeting, I should explain why my job is difficult, and why moving up is such an important decision. Being the executive director of an orchestra doesn't just mean long hours from constant rehearsals, cocktail parties, fundraising events, meetings, and concerts. It means, in truth, being regularly victimized, and often demonized.

Here are some examples: 1. the subscriber who calls after every concert to complain about the fat and malodorous man now sitting next to him, and wants him moved; 2. the musician who files a grievance because the French horns, which are right behind him, are deafening; 3. the board member, who is also a major donor, who starts a whisper campaign among other board members criticizing the executive director because he or she is not a "good listener;" 4. the volunteer who trumpets her resentment at not having been sent flowers or some other gift of thanks for chairing a successful gala; 5. the corporate sponsor who wants you to thank his company's involvement by speaking to the audience before the beginning of the concert, or, worse, the donor of whatever kind who can't stand new music and likes to walk out in the middle of its being performed, who then calls the following Monday to demand a committee be formed to tell the conductors what to program; 6. foundations who make you spend sixteen hours of staff time preparing a grant application only to refuse to consider it because it didn't contain a copy of the government's non-profit tax letter, a copy of which they already have on file; 7. the staff member who doesn't like his or her manager and snoops through the manager's desk looking for dirt, and who, when fired for cause, gets a lawyer; 8. and, finally, the music director who can't stand to be alone in his dressing room after a concert because he's so keyed up, and will guarantee you don't get home before midnight because he needs to talk, talk, talk and hear you say many times that it was one of the finest performances you've ever heard.

I've melded my experiences with those of other executive directors, but every word is true, and all of it together represents a small fragment of what goes on all the time. As a senior vice president of a Fortune 500 company once said to me, "I think you've got the hardest job of anyone I know."

I love my job, and I'm not complaining. I offer the litany to provide some context for the decision to move to a larger orchestra. In short, all the problems grow exponentially with the size of the organization and the number of its constituents.

Among these and other concerns, my reflections on Salt Lake had led me to believe it might not be the job for me after all.

I met the headhunter, Heather Kozlowski, at the gate. We hugged. We'd become friends, and I certainly didn't want to alienate her in case she was involved in another search down the road. She was dressed in denim blouse and skirt, and excused herself for dressing so casually because she was headed to Florida for a week's vacation.

We sat at a small table in the concourse after getting coffee.

Once she'd taken a sip, she said, a bit nervously, "I'm here to offer you the job."

She wouldn't let me respond, though I'm sure my face registered no surprise.

"Look, I know it sucks being number two. We didn't choose you and that was a disappointment. Maybe you're pissed. Now I've come here to offer you the booby prize. But it's not like that."

I didn't know what to say.

"If it helps at all, the first decision was very close—a matter of a couple of votes. Now they're unanimous."

"That's helpful."

"And they gave me full authority to negotiate your compensation package."

"Can you tell me who it was that turned it down, and why?"

"That's the right term, I suppose. Turned us down, even after we'd agreed on all the terms. I honestly don't know why. Please keep this to yourself, but it was Eliza Ohtera; she runs the West Florida Philharmonic. Do you know her?"

"No, I'm afraid not."

I didn't know at the time exactly why I said what I said next, except that it seemed now like a job promising nothing but money troubles and certain failure. I felt it likely that that was the reason the first candidate bailed out. And, though it sounds petty now, I didn't at all like the fact that I was their second choice—which could mean I wouldn't have the board's full support—and, frankly, I was offended.

"I'm sorry, but I can't take it."

"Please, hear me out."

"Heather," I said, putting down my coffee and touching her hand for a moment. "I couldn't help but guess why you're here, so I've thought it through already."

"Look, this is a great job!"

"Maybe, but enormous problems."

"The Mormons?"

"Funny that's the first thing you say, but it's not a major concern."

"What, then?"

"When I came home, I really wanted this job. I thought I'd won it. Maybe I got too excited, so when you called, I felt let down lower than I should have. Maybe. But then I began to feel relieved and almost immediately I felt exuberant, as if I'd just escaped something I would regret."

"But why?"

"I can't really explain it, Heather, except that I've always followed my instincts. And my instincts in this are perfectly clear."

Some of this I was making up on the spot just to make Heather feel better.

"I understand, I guess."

"I'll admit that sense of relief weakened slightly when you called wanting to meet me here. It was probably unfair of me to even have you come, and I apologize about that. I guess I just wanted to hear what you had to say and find out if it would change anything."

"And it hasn't."

"No. I'm sorry. I'm out."

She laughed. " 'I'm out,' that's what they say in gangster movies. Okay. I understand. No hard feelings, either way?"

"None. I think you're awesome," I said, and meant it.

"Good. Who knows what might come along in the future."

"Exactly," I said.

She looked at her watch and said, "My flight leaves in forty-five minutes. I think I should go to my gate and call the folks in Utah."

At the security gate we hugged and I said, "One word of advice you might pass on? Tell them not to ask their next candidate what they think of Mormons."

"Yeah, I knew about that. Good advice," she said, and walked away.

3

Six months later, I was a candidate for the presidency of the American Orchestra League. I had supporters from the ranks of the major orchestras, and though it was a long shot, I was encouraged to remain a candidate and went through several interviews.

During that process, I got a call from a Thomas Silvian, the chair of the search committee for a new executive director of the West Florida Philharmonic, which served Sarasota, St. Petersburg, and Clearwater.

He began with these memorable words: "On behalf of the organization, I'm inviting you to visit to explore becoming our executive leader. And to be clear, you are the only candidate we are interested in at this time."

"The only candidate?"

"Yes, we've done our homework and there's no one out there right now we feel has the track record of success and is as highly regarded, particularly by musicians."

I explained that I was a candidate for the League job. He was impressed. He asked when that would be resolved, and I told him in two months or so.

"If it's okay with you, we'll wait."

I was stunned and felt if I said anything he might correct himself. Finally, I said, "That's fine. I appreciate it."

"Good, then. Please call me when you know what happens with the other opportunity."

"That's very generous of you," I said, then, rather clumsily, "I'm honored at your approach."

"Good luck, and let me know what happens. Goodbye."

It didn't take two months. My supporters for the League job backed out on me a month later, preferring a candidate from outside the field who was favored by the most aggressive of the major orchestra managers.

I called a friend of mine on the League board, who said, "Don't feel bad. You've handled yourself very well. They just want to take a different direction." I thought he was just being nice. Of course I wasn't qualified for a national position. At least not yet. Nonetheless, I was crushed.

I called Thomas Silvian the next day, and we arranged for me to visit St. Petersburg in two weeks.

There was one hiccup. Thomas said that they planned to schedule a battery of personality and intelligence tests as a first step and had engaged a firm to conduct them.

"I'm sure you're familiar with them—Wonderlic, Myers-Briggs. They'll take up most of the morning of your first full day."

I shook my head and said, "No, I'm sorry. I've done them once before and absolutely hated it. In fact, I find them slightly offensive."

Nothing but silence on the phone.

"Look, Thomas, if you decide to hire me, I'll take the tests then, if you still want me to."

"You're sure about this?"

"Yes."

"Okay," he conceded, "Let's let it go. If there's pushback, I'll get back to you right away."

He met me at the airport and took me to a restaurant where we had dinner and wine. When he suggested a second bottle, I begged off, thinking it unwise to get tipsy during my first interview. He ordered a second bottle anyway, so I had one more glass. Having poured his fourth glass, and pushed his dinner aside half-finished, he proceeded to tell me the following. The board and the search committee, as well as the musicians he'd talked to, wanted me to know that they were all looking forward to meeting me. His musicians had talked to my musicians and had received very favorable reports, and that (along with my success with finances) was the main reasons I was called. It seems there'd been strife with the musicians in the past and everyone wanted a "peacemaker," which is how I'd been described.

"Now I should tell you some things that you need to know, but you must act as though you know nothing of the matter."

His discretion was certainly evaporating before my eyes, but I decided to let this rather commanding middle-aged lawyer continue.

"I guess you could call it the skeleton in our closet. It's a secret only three of us know, but I can't let you consider coming here without knowing. It's about the chairman of the board. He has two more years in a four-year term, and he's doing a fine job. He had a terrific relationship with our former executive director, Eliza Ohtera. Do you know her?"

"I've heard the name," I said. "She turned down a job I later turned down myself."

"Well, a terrific relationship, as I said. In fact, a little too terrific, if you know what I mean. It wouldn't have mattered, since they were both extremely discrete. As I said, only three of us knew. However, what makes it so difficult is that his wife was dying of breast cancer at the time. There's some suggestion that a moment of vulnerability consoled by Eliza was repeated, and eventually became a matter of pleading on his part. I won't use the word 'pressure,' but it's clear Eliza was in a situation that made her very uncomfortable. Even more so when the wife passed away. She started looking and was considered elsewhere and eventually took a position with the Denver Symphony, where she is today."

"It sounds like the situation resolved itself," I offered.

"For now, it has."

I didn't quite understand what he meant, but I let it go.

"I have no problem keeping this just between us, and I appreciate your telling me, just in case...."

"Really, it won't come up. I don't know why it would."

He looked away for a moment and seemed to have more to say and had to decide whether or not he should say it.

He turned back and said, "Look, there's one thing that's changed since we first talked. I said you were the only candidate. And for the vast majority of us, you still are. The board chair—his name is Simon Uzzutti—has told the search committee he wants to consider the interim manager for the job as well. This just happened this week. The interim's name is Daniel Wallace. He's been the number two here for three years, with the title of General Manager. He's a nice guy, everybody likes him, but no one thinks he has the experience we need, what we think you will demonstrate in the next two days. Still, we're forced to at least consider him as a candidate, though I think we'll let him down easy before too long."

This bothered me more than the adultery, but I didn't see it as a reason to walk away.

"Thanks for telling me," I said again.

"When you meet him, please treat him as if you didn't know he was being considered."

"I can do that, but I have one question."

He sipped his wine and looked at me slightly apprehensively.

"If Daniel is not a serious candidate, why is Mr. Uzzutti so…"

He put up his hand.

"I was afraid you'd ask that."

"Yes?"

"Uzzutti is *grateful* to Daniel."

He paused to formulate the next words carefully.

"He's grateful to Daniel for the same reason he's grateful to me."

"Because you have both been protecting his secret."

He smiled. "You're as smart as I thought."

He tipped his glass toward me in a half-toast.

"Well, enough of all that. It really doesn't matter anymore. Eliza's been gone for half a year. Let's talk about the orchestra. What can I tell you?"

The next two days were like a parade; no, more like a fraternity rush. Meetings with half a dozen constituencies all began more or less the same way: We've heard so much about you, and we're thrilled you're here. They did more than their share of selling me, and I was listened to with smiles and nods the entire time.

My dinner with Simon Uzzutti could have gone better. He took me to a Ruth's Chris Steakhouse. The meal was fabulous, and we each had a single glass of wine. Uzzutti was considered one of the richest men in Florida—the owner of likely the state's largest commercial development firm. There was hardly a city in the state that didn't have a major Uzzutti project downtown. He had dark hair and olive skin. He was dapper without being fussy in a herringbone suit and a yellow tie. Almost handsome with acne scars on a slightly bent nose, and perfect teeth; he rarely smiled, but when he did it said he lived to be the boss.

After dinner, he said, "That was pretty ballsy refusing to take our tests."

"I'm sorry," I said. "If you really need them, I can get you the contact information from the firm that did it for the orchestra I turned down two years ago. I don't know how much they'd charge, though."

"No, that won't be necessary. I just wanted you to know there was no ill-feeling over it. Like I said, it was ballsy. Some people like that."

I couldn't tell if he was trying to reassure me or not, but otherwise he was complimentary and deferential, but he didn't ask many questions, which bothered me. He rarely made eye contact. He seemed almost shy, but he could have been simply distracted by other matters. Nonetheless, I left the restaurant wondering at his lack of curiosity.

The orchestra wasn't the Chicago Symphony, nor would you expect it to be, but they played better than I would ever have expected. I even liked the music director, a fiery Spaniard with very little English. After the concert, we had a bottle of Rioja (I had a glass and he drank the rest). One thing seemed to bother him. I had ordered a side of blood oranges with my wine.

When they came, he actually pushed back from the table in mock fear of them. We both laughed and continued our conversation. We parted as if we were already working together, but I knew that he would prove a handful.

The only time I heard about Mr. Uzzutti's secret was during a tour of the city by their assistant conductor. At one point, he said, "I understand Thomas has told you about our little problem from a year ago. I wanted you to know that other than Daniel and Thomas, I'm the only other person who knows."

"How could such a thing remain secret when there are so many people involved with the orchestra?" was the only thing I could think to say.

"I wish I knew. It's amazing. And a blessing that it's now ancient history. And who knows? There may be others who know and just choose not to talk."

"That seems more likely."

"No matter. It's nothing you have to worry about. You've been blowing people away, man. As they say in golf, it's your job to lose."

Later that afternoon, Thomas drove me to the airport. At the curb he said, "You should know that the search committee met this afternoon and voted to hire you."

"Wow! That was quick!"

"After the executive committee meets on Tuesday to confirm the decision and discuss compensation, I'll call you. No later than Wednesday."

Finally! I exulted as I headed into the airport.

Tuesday night I received a call; both Thomas and Uzzutti were on the other end. Thomas did most of the talking. He said they were calling to extend a formal offer of employment and they hoped very much I would accept. He said that I would receive their compensation offer by email no later than the next afternoon. I should feel free to call Thomas with any questions. They both said "congratulations."

Without going into the details of the compensation offer, which arrived as promised, I can't describe the disappointment I felt reading that email from Thomas. The West Florida Philharmonic may have been in financial straits, but their budget was three times that of Evansville. I had expected a salary increase of at least fifty percent.

I called Thomas immediately.

"That was quick," he said chuckling. "Do we have a deal?"

"Not yet," I said.

"I was afraid of this," he said, softly, as though holding the phone away from his mouth.

"This wouldn't even be a lateral move for me, Thomas," I said. "I've done my homework and your taxes alone would eat up my increase from the outset, not to mention your higher cost of living."

"I'm sorry. It's what they authorized. I argued for more, but this is what they came up with. Of course, you can make a counter offer."

I told him a figure that was forty percent more than what I was making and said even that would hardly compensate me for the significantly greater rigors of the job.

"I'll see what I can do."

He rang back an hour later and said they didn't want to negotiate against themselves, but I should feel free to make another proposal.

I called him back an hour later with a three-year contract proposal that started at a figure five percent less than the first number I'd thrown out, but with a five percent annual increase.

"I don't think Uzzutti is going to like this," he said.

I kept silent.

"I'll call you back."

It took ten minutes.

"Now he's just pissed off," he said. "I can't tell you how frustrated I am. What you're asking for is completely fair and only a bit more than your predecessor made."

"Thomas, please be honest with me."

"Yes?"

"Uzzutti doesn't want me and this is the only leverage he has. Tell me he hasn't said you can't afford more than the original offer."

"Almost his exact words."

"And that to give me what I ask would be fiscally irresponsible."

"Something like that."

"But if he, as board chair, *recommended* they accept my proposal they'd agree to it in a moment, right?"

Now he just sounded guilty.

"Yes, that's right."

We ended the conversation with Thomas telling me he'd try to turn things around. There were so many people pulling for me. I just needed to be patient, and he'd get back to me.

He never called me again. Instead, a week later, I got a call from the assistant conductor.

"I'm really sorry, man," he said. "Thomas asked me to call. He was too pissed off and disappointed and was afraid you might think he hadn't dealt fairly with you."

"No deal, then. No counter offer either."

"I'm afraid not."

"And the job's going to Daniel."

"Yes. Yes, it is."

"Because of…"

"Yes, because of that. Uzzutti's a powerful man and he runs things his way. But none of us saw it coming."

"I did," I said and rudely, which the guy didn't deserve, hung up.

4

Before what I'm recounting begins to seem overly self-congratulatory, as if everyone wanted me, I should explain something else about the orchestra business. It is a very upwardly mobile industry, at least for staff members, because of burnout. Orchestras with $75 million budgets poach staff from $40 million orchestras, who poach from $20 million orchestras, who poach from $10 million orchestras, etc. Any competent manager can move up every four or five years. I was on that path, and for the past four years I had regularly been a candidate for either the manager of a larger orchestra like Salt Lake, or for the number-two position at a much larger orchestra, like Seattle or San Francisco, which I turned down once I learned that they were run by people who behaved like monsters because they thought they had to in order to survive.

As for Florida's exclusive interest in me, it was probably not just from musicians talking to musicians, but board members calling my board members, and the search committee talking to the American Orchestra League. It was likely also a matter of timing—fewer smaller orchestra managers were ready to move up at the moment. Certainly, if Florida had hired a headhunter, they would have had more candidates. But then, I concluded, that was part of Uzzutti's scheme as well.

It was not surprising, then, that within a few weeks of the Tampa debacle, I got a call from Heather. She had recommended me for the Denver Philharmonic, which was larger than the Florida and Salt Lake orchestras. Would I be interested?

"Isn't that where Eliza Ohtera went? She's left already?"

"Yes, she quit rather abruptly and left town. Frankly, I was a little miffed with her after what she did in Salt Lake."

I didn't think anything of it. Managers often had short incumbencies with orchestras, for any number of reasons—personal chemistry with the board, impossible music directors, financial or union issues—it was the nature of the business.

I said of course I was interested, and we left it that once she'd talked with the search committee, she'd get back to me.

Two days later I got a phone call.

"Hello, this is Eliza Ohtera," she said, "You know who I am, right?"

"Yes. I do."

"Good. I know this is going to sound very weird, but you need to listen to what I have to say. When I'm done, I'm going to hang up. Is that okay? Because if not I'll have to hang up now, though I'll call later after you've thought about it."

"No, that's okay. Go ahead."

"It's like we've been invisibly attached for a while. Or a better way to put it is I've been pulling your strings a bit. But in a good way, or so I thought.

"Now be patient with me and let me get this all out. It's difficult. You'll understand why when I'm done.

"First, the job in Salt Lake. I did win that job, and then I didn't take it. I found out you were the other candidate, quite by accident after the job offer came. I turned it down because I wanted you to have it. You deserve it. That you decided not to take it isn't my business, but I can guess why it might not have been totally appealing.

"Second, the Western Florida Philharmonic. I'm sure people told you I was the previous executive director. Right?"

"Yes."

"You can't imagine how strongly I recommended you for that job. You might have solved so many problems. I know you would have. Only I underestimated the board chair."

"Uzzutti?"

"He's a total bastard."

"But I thought…," I began, then realized what I was about to say was her secret too. But it was too late.

There was a long pause, then she said, "I don't know who told you, but I suppose it was inevitable."

"I think Thomas was just trying to be honest with me. And, perhaps testing my discretion."

"Let's drop that for a moment. The main reason I called is to tell you do not, under any circumstances, no matter how much money they offer, do *not* take the job in Denver. You'd have found out I was the executive director there, having come from Florida."

"Amazing."

"I can't talk about it, but if you think what happened in Florida was bad, there's something wrong in Denver that's immeasurably worse. It may take a while to come out, but when it does, it will tarnish everything. And the worst thing about it is you would find out very quickly and have to keep quiet or expose it all. Either way, it would make your life miserable, and possibly hurt your career."

"I have no reason to doubt you."

"But even that is not the main reason why I left Denver."

Another pause.

"Go on."

Now she was talking very quickly.

"Keep quiet now, I'm almost finished. And since you know about Uzzutti I might as well tell you. I'm pregnant. He raped me in a rage just before I left St. Pete. He knows, and now you're the only other person who does. I left Denver before it showed. In return for my silence, he's given me enough money to raise the child and to live on for the rest of my life. But I will never go back to him. Never. Even if he should be lucky enough to find me.

"I have only one more thing to say. We've met before. You know me as Ginger." She could hear me inhale. "Not a word, please. That night on the plane meant to me what I said it did when I left you. But even then I was entangled emotionally with Uzzutti because of his wife. I had yet to fall into his grasp, but it was soon after that. By the time of Salt Lake, which I kept secret from everyone, it was over for me. But I did try to look out for you. That's why I called. Don't go near Denver."

"But I want you. I don't care."

"I'm sorry. I have to raise this child and forget everything that came before. And you have to promise not to try to find me."

"I love you, Ginger. Don't go!"

"I love you too, sweetheart. Goodbye."

And she hung up.

If you've seen what has been coming out in the past year about the sexual behavior of conductors, you'll know what was eventually exposed in Denver. It had been going on for years, thus members of the orchestra and the board were complicit.

Ginger saved me that. I kept the promise she asked of me not to try to find her. But I never *actually* promised, did I?

I stopped taking calls from other orchestras and seriously considered getting out of the business. A small college thirty miles from Evansville was looking for someone to teach arts management; I had applied and so far had been encouraged.

That spring, I received a call from Magnolia Hospital in Evansville. It was a mid-sized facility known for expensive but top-notch treatment.

The caller was a nurse, and she said that a patient named Ginger was there and was asking for me.

The hospital was only a mile from my house. Ten minutes later, I asked for Ginger at the front desk, but had to explain I didn't know her last name.

"That's okay. She asked me to ask you a question. If you know the answer, I'm to send you right up to her."

"Yes?"

"Where did you meet Ginger?"

"On an airplane."

"Room 432," she said, thumb pointing up.

When I reached the door to her single room, I found her on her side, back to me. I thought she was asleep. I tiptoed in and then heard a cooing sound and realized that she was holding a baby.

"Ginger?"

She turned and smiled. "Yes, please call me that. That's my real name now. Ginger Kimura."

She waved me forward. I leaned and kissed her. She stroked my cheek. She looked impossibly beautiful, her face flushed with joy.

"Come around here and meet my daughter."

I did, but was too shy to touch her.

"What's her name?"

"I don't know. It depends on you."

Then she explained that after changing her name and putting her financial affairs in order, she'd moved to Evansville, where she'd been staying in a rented house with a live-in nurse and a maid until the baby came.

"Why didn't you call me before?"

"Because of her," she said, holding the baby's head up. "I couldn't ask you to see me pregnant. I couldn't know how you would be with the thought of where my pregnancy came from. I thought only see-ing the reality would make a difference…" She paused. "For both of us."

"Can I hold her?"

She reached up and I cradled the pink-swathed infant in my arms.

"How about Cinnamon—another spice?"

"Cinnamon," she whispered, then, without looking at me, she turned away and started to cry, to cry unconsolably.

PHILOSOPHY
000

"Sartre! Heidegger! A commie and a Nazi and the only thing they have in common is they both wrote ludicrously fat and unreadable books beginning with the word 'Being,' which I fervently wish they could not."

"Couldn't what?" she asked, propping her head on her right elbow and throwing her blonde hair across his face.

He brushed the hair away and pinched the satin flesh he liked so much just beneath her left breast.

"Be."

"Isn't that a bit unphilosophical for a philosophy major?"

"Look, imagine this," he said, facing her in the same pose. "Let's imagine that I, John Young, smuggled a corned beef sandwich into space."

"You mean outer space?"

"Maybe. Or maybe just the space in the teaching assistants' lounge behind the white board."

"I prefer outer space."

"Okay. I've become an astronaut and I can't stand the mush they feed us, so I smuggle the sandwich on board in my spacesuit."

"Good, I like that better."

"Happy to please. Now, what if I forgot the mustard?"

"What a tragedy!" she said and laughed.

"Ha. Ha. He responded with withering sarcasm."

"The point?"

"So imagine that the corned beef sandwich actually is. It exists. It has Being with a capital 'B.' It might have mustard or it might not, but it doesn't matter as long as I appreciate it, that I even study the sandwich for what it is, and disregarding what it isn't and everything else around it that isn't it. That's Heidegger."

"The man's a genius."

"On the other hand, the thought of eating such a sandwich without mustard is absolutely nauseating. My will to have the sandwich as I want it is thwarted, and I have only two choices, equally valid. Either I eat the sandwich without the mustard or I get off the damned spaceship and get the mustard, even though the effort will probably get me thrown off the mission. That's Sartre."

"I sense there's a catch."

"Yes, you smart golden hussy. The catch is that I have to choose. I can't just avoid the issue and let the sandwich rot in my spacesuit."

"What a relief! I like the character, but the plot not so much."

"English majors!"

"Live with it," she replied, pinching him back. "You still haven't told me what's the matter."

"I learned today, our first day of the fall semester, that I have to read both books and write multiple papers on each between now and December."

The golden hussy threw her leg over his stomach and said, "Well, you already have a firm grasp of their work, so what's the issue?"

"What I just made up is all I could glean from twenty pages in a book called *A Short Intro to Modern Philosophy*."

She giggled.

What happened next has been lost to time and nothingness.

✳

The reader is to know that the scene remains unchanged, though it is a week later, late summer, same time of day—mid-afternoon, mid-August, 1973. A brilliant slanting sunlight has set afire the shoulder-length hair of the young lady, whose name is Phoebe Stone. Even the disposition of their limbs is roughly the same as at the beginning of the previous scene.

"You think you have it bad?"

"Yes, I do," he countered, "Today I was sitting in our phenomenology seminar saying to myself, 'Not only do I NOT understand a single word my professor is saying, I couldn't even formulate a question that would allow him to clarify things for me.'"

"Agree. Not good."

"So what's bothering you?"

"A question first. I'll bet no one has ever written a book called *The Phenomenology of Sex.*"

"Funny you should ask," said John, pinching her in the usual spot. "I was sitting in the library yesterday, totally bored, thinking of anything to keep from reading, so I looked it up. There's actually a book with that title by a Suzanne somebody, I forget."

"Well, how was it?"

"Even worse than Sartre, if you can believe that. But she does mention that there's a very famous book on the same topic. It's called the *Kama Sutra.*"

General laughter.

"So what's *your* trouble?"

"I made the mistake of signing up for a class in the English Novel of the Twentieth Century. The teacher didn't write a syllabus in advance, but said that he'd make things up as we went along. That sounded amusing. What a sucker I was. The first day of class he assigned John Fowles' 600-page *Daniel Martin.* I call it the Green Monster because the cover is green. The second day he added James Joyce's *Ulysses,* and the third day the entire *Alexandria Quartet* by Lawrence Durrell. And he isn't done yet!"

"Quantity over quality. Sounds like a speed reading course."

"Ha. Well, we all know about *Ulysses* and I've actually read the first book of the Durrell, *Justine,* which is wonderful. But if he continues like this I'll have to read 200 pages a day just to keep up."

"My poor hussy."

"Golden hussy to you, mister," she said, pinching him back. "By the way, *Daniel Martin* is a glorious mess. It's basically a love story, but it has three, count 'em, three *ménage à trois.*"

"Ménage à trois à trois?"

She ignored this.

"One is only situational, another probably imagined, and the third coyly under-described."

"Sounds like my kind of book."

"More than you guess. It's full of philosophical musing, existentialism in particular. Tons of socialism and Freud, of course. And the damned narrator, who is Dan Martin, can't say something without adding the same thing backwards."

"Like?"

"I'm making this up, but you'll get the idea. 'If only I could legitimize the flagrancy of my transgressions, or transgress my flagrant legitimacy.'"

"Hey, that's pretty good! Tell me more about the threesomes."

"Read the book, you perv."

"That's golden perv, miss."

"Your hair is black."

"So what do I do?

"About what?"

"Philosophy. I don't think I can make it. I can barely bluff my way through class, and my papers will be laughable unless I cheat. Plato and Nietzsche write like human beings, at least. These guys are haywire computers, or that fabled room full of typing monkeys."

"Cheating sounds plausible. What would your Being guys say?"

"Let's see. I think Sartre would say I have three choices. I can study harder than I ever have in my life and get a D-minus. I can cheat, of course, as you suggest, just enough to get a C-plus and avoid suspicion. Or I can change my major to English Literature."

"Don't you dare!"

"Why not. *Daniel Martin* sounds like Philosophy 101."

"The last thing I want is to talk shop with you in bed."

"Isn't that what we're doing right now?"

"No, it's not. Imagine spending an hour discussing some scintillating topic, like, say, the metaphor of the snake throughout literary history."

"It has possibilities."

A knock came at the door.

"Phoebe, are you in there?"

"Yes, Jeanine. Give me a couple, please," she said, throwing off the covers.

"Now Mr. Being and Nothingness would suggest three possible options here. First, we could invite Jeanine in."

"Forget it."

"Are you criticizing Mr. Fowles?"

"Get dressssed," she hissed, an excellent snake imitation.

"Two," he said, getting out of bed and approaching the door, "I could let her in myself."

"Jeanine! Can you go away for thirty minutes. Please?"

"Phoebe?!" Full-tilt exasperation. "I have a ton of homework!"

"Pleeeese!"

"Alright, but not one second more, I mean it," Jeanine said, her voice trailing away.

What happened next has been lost to nothing but time.

✳

The scene is as before, the last day of the semester. It's snowing lightly, the sun beaming through the flakes.

"I did it. I'm ashamed to say it, but I did it."

"You sure did. Thanks. Why ashamed? Why now?"

"You have no idea what I'm talking about, do you?"

"Of course not. I'm too tired. I can't believe what just happened was even possible, I'm so tired."

"How do you think you did?"

She laughed.

"You tell me!"

"I'm talking about your grades. You got through the reading and the papers. I suppose you aced everything."

"Oh," she hesitated, "Yes. Sorry."

"For what, for being stupid about being smart?"

"I don't like that, as one of John Fowles' women would say."

"Sorry."

"So what did you do?"

"I cheated."

"You did not!" she said and punched his shoulder with her left hand.

"I did. It wasn't my fault though. At least not all of it."

"Explain yourself."

"You know I was sick last week."

"Yes. The reason it's been two…" she hesitated. "Go on."

"I missed the exam and I had to take it today in the professor's office."

"I can't wait to hear this."

"Here's the funny part. After writing four papers, all of them given D's out of sheer pity. No. One was a C-minus."

"Get to it."

"The test was multiple choice! When I first saw that I had a glimmer of hope." He held up three fingers. "Three possible answers. A one in three chance! Just the odds meant I might get a passing grade, but the questions were if anything more opaque and convoluted than the original texts! I sat there literally moaning in terror and frustration."

"With the professor there?"

"Nope."

"She wouldn't leave someone taking her test all alone. They might cheat!"

"Precisely. Instead, sitting at her desk was one of her PhD candidates, a rather lovely young woman as a matter of fact."

"Of course."

"Not a hussy, actually."

"Golden...."

"But attractive nonetheless. About ten minutes in, she stood up, sighed, rather loudly, and opened a filing cabinet. She took out a few pages and laid them in front of me."

"Don't tell me she gave you the answers."

"The only thing she said was, 'Don't get too many right. No more than fifteen. That will get you a C.'"

"I don't believe it."

"True as you," he said and kissed her lightly on the lips. "I took my time, making sure I got the hardest questions wrong. As much as I knew the difference. Then I handed her both my test and the answers, which she promptly returned to the filing cabinet as I stood there stunned at her composure."

"Did you thank her?"

"I was too ashamed."

"I know that look. You did something."

"I kissed her hand. I leaned over slightly, took her hand and kissed it, just like the courtly knight of olde."

"You're kidding," she asked, a bit too seriously for John. "What did she say?"

"Nothing. She didn't even look at me. And there was nothing in her expression, just as Sartre would have described it. An absence of expression. A nothing."

"I get it. She liked you."

"Don't be silly."

"Wrong!"

Then it was as if the covers exploded. Phoebe kicked and threw the covers off, stood up and shouted, "Get out!" Then she grabbed a white cloth robe from her closet and draped herself.

John scrambled out of bed and pulled the blanket around his waist. He started around the bed toward Phoebe.

"Stop right there."

"What the hell?"

"Get dressed and get out. We're done," she said, hiding every inch of skin she possibly could, even turning the collar up.

"Phoebe, please!"

"You expect me to believe a story like that? You really do think I'm stupid."

"Of course I do. I mean, yes, I do expect you to believe me. It's true. She gave me the answers and I passed the test."

"I said get dressed."

He dropped the blanket and she turned away. He grabbed his pants.

"I don't get it. I just don't GET IT!"

"No PhD candidate would do that and you know it. If they ever found out they'd destroy her career before it was started. And yours! I'll bet you stole the answers somehow."

"But she did!"

"Then why?"

"She took pity on me, I guess."

"You bribed her."

"That's ridiculous."

"Then you flirted with her. That's it. You made eyes and called her a, a, what color was her hair?"

"Black."

"A raven-haired hussy. You called her that, didn't you? You made a pass, didn't you? Hell, you probably had her right there on the professor's desk!"

"Now you're acting insane!"

"And that's not even what truly upsets me."

"What else is there?"

"You cheated, you asshole. You cheated!"

"Now wait a minute. I told you it might be necessary."

"Necessary? You were joking about Sartre. I never thought you were serious. How often do you cheat? This can't be the first time."

"I swear. Never once. What was I supposed to do? I was desperate and she just handed me the answers. I didn't ask for them, honest!"

"It doesn't matter. You cheated. You cheated that girl. You cheated your professor. And you cheated me."

"You?"

"Me."

"I don't understand."

"That's your problem, isn't it?" she said, with unadulterated spite.

By now, John was fully dressed and in seconds found himself on the other side of Phoebe's dorm room door.

＊

The scene is a different bed, different bedroom, more spacious, part of an apartment or house, rather than a dorm room. We've no idea how long it's been since Phoebe threw her tantrum. There's a large reproduction of the famous Karl Marx photograph above the head-board, which is made of a richly carved mahogany. The room is lined with bookshelves full of philosophical texts arranged alphabetically by author.

"You are a naughty boy," said a slender, attractive woman in her thirties with black hair. She is lying with her head on John Young's stomach, her feet dangling off the bed. She kicks her legs as though slowly riding a bicycle.

"It had to happen."

"You might have been a little more honest with her. The hand-kissing was a bit much."

"Revenge."

"What for?

"Acing everything in sight, for starters. Subtly rubbing it in all semester."

"Childish."

"I couldn't tell her it wasn't a PhD candidate."

"No. That wouldn't do."

"I had to tell her something."

"Yes, you did. She did expect you to fail, after all."

He reached around her front and dragged her up with him on the bed. He didn't pinch her. It didn't please her. Instead, he buried his head between her breasts, which did.

"I didn't mention this before," she said, stroking his hair, "but the only thing you wrote all semester of any merit at all was your corn beef sandwich analogy."

"Good enough for a C-minus?"

"Just barely."

"You don't feel compromised?" he asked, looking up into her dark blue eyes.

"For taking pity on you?"

"For helping me cheat."

"Have you read Camus, yet?"

"Yes, actually I have. *The Rebel.* I could actually write a decent paper on him."

"Ha!"

The light in the room was slowly dimming with the sunset.

"I don't like that."

She ignored this.

"You need to switch majors. Your next professor might not be so sweet on you."

"Any suggestions?"

"How about English Lit?"

"There's an idea."

General laughter.

What happened next should never happen, but it did.

GOGOL
IN PARIS

*N*OTE *to the Reader:* The following manuscript (I have taken the liberty of providing it a title) was found among the personal effects of one Alexander Post, who disappeared while walking home from work in January of 1940. His wife and her relatives all told the newspapers the same story. Post had been distant, nervous, and "unnecessarily sullen." The night before, he had quarreled with them (which was usual), then had laughed at them (which was not). They had feared a suicide, but he left no note. The effects in question were found in 1999, upon the death of one of Post's former business associates. In the man's attic was discovered a large wooden box that contained, along with the manuscript (dated August 22, 1939), a pair of filthy leather boots that Post's granddaughter maintains he had been very fond of; a large, cloth briefcase holding the manuscripts (unpublished) of some two hundred stories written by Post's great-grandfather, Wilfred Post; several articles of clothing of a flamboyant nature (a tuxedo, scarves, a top hat, three silk shirts, also a red brassiere); and, finally, a confession to the embezzlement, never of course discovered, of "approximately one quarter of one million dollars" from the investment firm of Paige, Paige and Page of New York (now defunct), where Alexander Post was employed for seventeen years before his absquatulation.

✳

My great-grandfather knew Gogol. His son, my grandfather, told me the story of their fateful encounter when I was fourteen; when I had just failed to reach even the semi-finals in a writing contest; when my ambition, already burning like "a flame-like gem" (if I may go Pater one better), was to become a writer of stories like my great-grandfather. It is true that Grandfather often bitterly censured the memory of his father's "aimless career" because of the hardships he and his family had suffered as a consequence, but I have never questioned the truth of his story of my great-grandfather and Gogol in Paris.

"Did I ever tell you, Sasha, that my father once met a very famous writer while traipsing through Europe?" my grandfather began, pulling a small rocker up close to my bed, where I, employing my pillow as consolation, lay prone and desolate.

"I never told you? The writer's name was Nikolai Gogol and he wrote a couple of outlandish stories about people who lose things. It seems to me he was a trifle obsessed on the subject."

Grandfather squeezed himself into the rocker and ruminatively began to rock.

"It was in the winter of 1848. Father was in Paris, staying in a very expensive English hotel, the Westminster. He was there, so he told anyone who would listen, to find inspiration for his work and to hawk his stories, dozens of which were secreted under false bottoms in his portmanteau.

"Enjoying one of his daily strolls, no doubt peering into gardens and peeking under bowers for something lovely to write about, Father was startled by a cough, like a mastiff's bark. Turning around, he saw a little man with a round, worn face, a large, pointed nose, and wispy, shoulder-length hair that gigged on the breeze. Dressed in breeches worn smooth at the knee and coattails too short by a foot, he was by all appearances a penniless, starving, exhausted clerk. The little man drew in his head and grinned sheepishly, then he laid his hand flat against his face, palm on chin, fingers—long, bony fingers —touching his forehead, like this."

Grandfather demonstrated, peeping at me between his first and second, and third and fourth digits, also long, but fleshy, thick.

"Thinking nothing of this, Father continued on his way. The cough sounded repeatedly, changing timbre, now more like a goose's honk, again like a bark, but always, clearly, a nasty human cough. Father stopped and looked around. Still with him, the little man stood quite nonchalantly gazing into space. Father preceded another hundred steps, then spun around without warning. He had hoped to catch the little man in the very act of spying in which it was now obvious that he was engaged, but his quarry, back turned squarely to him, was yelling something Father couldn't understand up at a tree. Determined not to take his eyes from the fellow, determined to confront him eye-to-eye, Father started off again, walking side-ways like a crab. The little man walked crab-like. Father walked back-wards only to be mimicked again.

"Father had had enough. He turned and walked toward his pur-suer, who of course turned and walked in the opposite direction. Father started to run. With a screech, the little man bolted. You never saw your great-grandfather; as odd as it may sound, he was tall, fast, very athletic, and didn't look the least bit like a writer. He had the little man by the collar in a trice.

"The little man shrieked something in Russian as Father spun him around. His face was a red mask of terror. A big pimple blushed on the tip of his nose. Not knowing a word of that garbled tongue, Father demanded in French to know why he was being followed. (He knew the language well enough to employ it gratuitously, you will notice, in those stories of his.) The little man squealed—what sounded like 'Nyet!'—and sawed the air with his arms.

"As Father lifted the unhappy fellow so that his toes barely danced on the ground, he continued the interrogation, shaking him earnest-ly until another hand, thin but powerful, came down on Father's arm so hard that he had to let go. His prisoner fell to the ground like an empty coat and pants. Father's arms were roughly yanked and pinned behind his back. He watched in dismay as the little man jumped up and ran off, the satin lining of his coattails flashing like the white tail of a rabbit.

"Father was surprised to see the little man disappear through the lobby doors of the Westminster. The painful grip on his arms was released. He turned to confront his assailant: a tall, elegant stranger dressed in immaculate black satin—a frock coat with a crimson collar—and top hat. On a red ribbon around his neck dangled a silver medallion, imprinted with foreign lettering. In the crook of his elbow he held what appeared to be the Bible.

"Father swore at him, demanding—again in French—to know why he should be treated in such mysterious and violent fashion.

"'But you were hurting Monsieur Gogol,' said the stranger, in thick, Russian accents, chuckling as though it were all a joke.

"Father explained that he had been followed, that he, as an American citizen, had every right to know why.

"'Monsieur Gogol is a famous man,' the stranger explained. 'He is a very great writer. You should feel honored.'

"Of course, in those days, the Russians were little known for their writings in this country. People like my father thought of them either as anarchists, monarchists, or slave-keepers. Again, Father demanded to know why the name of Gogol—he added, 'the *ludicrous* name of Gogol'—should grant anyone the right to follow him around like a suspect in a robbery.

"His interlocutor said, with continued chuckling, that Gogol did it all the time.

"'Actually, it is a very great honor. You are certainly being studied for inclusion as a character in one of Nikolai's famous stories.'

"Father thought about that for a moment.

"'Well, that's different,' he admitted. 'Why didn't he say so?'

"Father grinned. Here, after all, was a colleague! He decided to introduce himself—slipping into English in the process—but the tall one, still chuckling softly, cocked his chin and strode majestically off toward the Westminster Hotel.

"The rudeness of all this odd behavior left Father in something of a daze. He recovered his senses in time to dash after the tall stranger just as he stepped through the doors of the hotel. Bursting into the lobby himself, Father found neither Gogol nor his guardian angel. There was no one in sight except a bellboy, wrapped in a faded blue uniform three sizes too big, splayed and snoring raucously in an overstuffed armchair.

"The next morning, having quite forgotten the intrigues of the preceding afternoon, Father ate breakfast in his room. As he sliced into some fresh-baked bread, he noticed a small package next to his jelly jar. 'Where did this come from?' he asked the waiter, who was just about to leave. 'No idea, Guvnah,' he replied, 'I 'oist the trays. That's all I does.' A sly, crouching fellow, resplendent in a constellation of brass buttons. Father had never trusted Englishmen, and he didn't believe this one for a second. There was nothing, however, to be done. He dismissed the young lout by staring him down.

"The package was wrapped in crumpled newsprint, tied with three pieces of tired shoestring. Inside, he found his wallet, contents intact. A plain, white card read, *'Mes compliments.* G.' Father hadn't even noticed that the wallet was missing!

"I *must* meet this fellow, Father thought to himself. I've never known anymore more curious. *He* should be a character in one of *my* stories!

"The question was how to approach him? He might enquire at the front desk as to Gogol's room number, but Father's sense of good form, and the fear that such direct measures—bearding the lion, etc.—might further terrorize and alienate the little man, ruled this inadvisable. There was another way.

"Minutes later, he was walking through the streets of Paris, glancing repeatedly—like some mild paranoiac—over his shoulder. He hardly even noticed that it was raining in buckets. It wasn't until he had accomplished the circuit to the Tuileries and back three times, with no sign of anyone following him—except for a gendarme in front of the hotel, who, watching him pass for the fourth time, stepped out from a kiosk, only to look up at the drenched and somber sky, shake his head as though to say, 'To hell with it!' and return to his cozy shelter—that Father began to wonder if this weren't a futile manner in which to make contact with Gogol after all.

"Entering the hotel lobby, Father was surprised and gratified to find the tall, elegant stranger, having appeared out of nowhere, preceding him by less than a dozen paces, his long coat soaked and dripping. Father hadn't noticed him before, but perhaps, if he'd just then been deposited by some coach or similar means of transportation, which he had to admit, was a distinct possibility, then his little gambit had not been a complete disappointment. The tall man's shoulders shook violently, perhaps to shake off the rain, although Father couldn't be sure he wasn't having another fit of laughter.

"Father decided to confront the man. He concluded that if he handled himself with his customary gentlemanly mien, the fellow would certainly agree to introduce him to Gogol. Who better than Gogol's rescuer to enlist on his own behalf? Who better to clear up any misunderstandings between them, to put them on comfortable speaking terms, without which neither could ever profitably study the other? But then, without really knowing why, Father let the opportunity pass. He told himself that it wouldn't be polite to detain the man, who might possibly need a change of dress or a good stiff drink to warm his blood. He watched as the tall one disappeared through the doors to the clubroom, then he went to remove his own drenched clothing and to wait for it to dry."

Here Grandfather paused and took several deep breaths. Exhaling, he distended his pale and parchment-like cheeks. He shook his head as though two thoughts were at war within. He sighed as though the unpleasant had triumphed, then he proceeded with the account.

"Later that afternoon, Father ensconced himself in a thickly up-holstered armchair in the hotel lobby with the states news in his lap. Holding the papers at arm's length, he perused intermittently the latest word from home, and, around the paper's edge, each and every person who passed.

"Engrossed for a moment in a story about an acquaintance who was in a fix at the bank where he was employed, Father looked up to see Gogol's flashing coattails disappear through the lobby doors. Quid pro quo! he thought as he jumped out of his chair, tossing the papers in a heap on the floor. He didn't stop as the desk clerk yelled something and pointed at the mess.

"Sometimes, in this tantalizingly elusive and bafflingly enigmatic world, it is advisable to become a Hunter. Sinews stretched, eyes on fire, teeth bared in block-thick concentration, the Hunter plays the game of life and death. He crouches, he slithers, he levels his weapon, perhaps he doesn't even have one! The pursuit itself is sufficient reward for all the effort put to the test. The thrill of the chase! A man such as my father had never, up to this moment, enjoyed this particular exercise of power and cunning in the pursuit of that fleet-ing and intangible prey—Inspiration! Perhaps he wasn't even aware of it. Who can say?

"Keeping an even twenty paces between them, and chuckling into his fist, your great-grandfather followed Nikolai Gogol. The writer, coughing all the way, led him a merry chase indeed.

"Father had read about the more noisome streets of Paris, but never had he envisioned anything like those through which his quarry led him. The rain had stopped, but gloom and futility hung in the air like a noose. Everywhere the smell of some hot, thin gruel and old women in ragged clothes making their raids on limp-necked pass-ersby just as ragged and desperate. Beggars gathered near the doors of cafés where the drowsy Ganymedes, brooms held out in warn-ing, threw them stale pies and bits of fat. Nowhere in sight a proper lady, though now and then a gentleman of dubious breeding slunk through the garbage holding his trousers up like skirts. The women Father did see, he wished that he had not: pocky noses, hair coarse and dry, brown as spent dandelions, skirts faded and stained, and make-up so thick it would require a trowel to remove it from their cheeks. The children saddened him most of all. Rachitic orphans and limping tatterdemalions danced around him as he passed. They seemed actually happy in their ignorance, almost philosophical, as if to say, 'If we are lucky enough to have sufficient food and cloth-ing for today, why shouldn't we laugh and frolic and tease the visitor in our midst?' They laughed at Father as though *he* were the know-nothing. He gave them money and hurried on so as not to lose sight of his prize.

"And what of our famous writer? Father could not help but notice that he changed, that he looked more stooped and tired with each and every step, as though as he walked he took upon his own thin, cough-racked shoulders the weight of all the suffering and boredom that he met, not, like a Christ, with compassion and understand-ing, because he was stronger than all of it, but like a sinner, cringing under the weight of his own transgressions, seeing them mirrored in the lives of others, destined to take up and labor under their com-mon load without the knowledge that his own mortification would relieve even one soul's agony in this incomprehensible world—or in the next one.

"Now and then, Father heard Gogol's cough above the din of the street. Sometimes it sounded like a stifled yelp of laughter.

"Thus through the dingy, hopeless, ugly, most degraded byways of Paris—the little man not once turning around or stopping, walk-ing on at a slower and ever slower pace, almost to a crawl—Father pursued his former pursuer.

"Then Father lost him. Turning a corner, he was alone.

"He looked up the street, which seemed by far the most necessi-tous yet, a very avenue of destitution. Gogol was nowhere in sight. Nor was anyone else, for that matter. Being a proper man, Father could not bring himself to glance through a window, let alone knock on a stranger's door. All he could do was listen. For the longest time he walked softly up and down the bleak and deserted street, straining to hear a single muffled hack.

"Now, Sasha, I would like for you to imagine; imagine that you are a reasonably uninteresting person, that life is good to you when it offers three square meals a day, an occasional, vapid entertainment, and the friendship of similar folks; imagine the indifferent days and nights, the dog-eat-dog world in which you are trapped, a willing and unwilling prisoner; imagine, above all, the boredom. Then, out of nowhere, someone appears with an offer. With a wry smile and shifty eyes, she says to you, 'Take the mud from the street into your hands and make something of it. Make me sculptures from the mud. Make hundreds, thousands of them, until you've mastered the principles and techniques of making beautiful mud sculptures. Then make thousands more. Finally, when you've made the very best little mud sculpture that you can possibly make, then, only then, and then only perhaps, I will make you happy and never bored, to the very end of your life.' Imagine, my boy, that that is precisely what you do. You make the thousand sculptures, and then the thousands more, until you can make none better than the last. Imagine that you imagine it to be an excellent, a perfectly realized mud sculpture indeed. Only, what if it is snatched from your very hands, stolen the moment you have a chance to show it proudly, with great expectations, to your challenger. Can you imagine, imagine how you'd feel?"

At first I thought that Grandfather was being merely rhetorical, but the baleful intensity of his stare informed me that he expected an answer. I remember that the corners of his mouth curled up like the twisted tips of a dainty handle-bar mustache.

"I think I can imagine, Grandfather," I said meekly.

"Well?"

"I mean, I can *certainly* imagine what it would be like, Grandfather," I said earnestly.

"Yes?"

"Um, well, I'm not sure what you want me to say?" I said.

"Tell me what you think it'd be like, boy!" Grandfather shouted.

"Very, very unpleasant, I should think," I replied with utmost gravity.

Grandfather squinted at me.

"Yes, well, that's exactly right. Nicely put," he added gruffly, leaning back in his rocker. He patted the pockets of his worsted wool vest bemusedly, with satisfaction. His smile slowly broadened, then he went on.

"As you know, my boy, I have no sympathy whatsoever for the life your great-grandfather led. He was a brilliant man, a genius, perhaps, in his own silly way, but when I think of the things he might have accomplished…" Grandfather paused for a deep, apparently self-pitying sigh. "Well, *c'est la vie!* Enough of this maundering. What it all leads up to is that when Father returned to his room it looked as though a bomb had exploded in his suitcase. Pants draped the coat rack. His shirts, some torn in two right down the back, lay heaped in separate corners of the room. Underwear bedecked his dressing table mirror, and his collars encircled the base of a gilded lamp stand as though the thieves had whiled the time playing ring toss. Father looked under his pillow and found intact his precious, tiny cache of American dollars. Little did he care, however, because the product, the total output of his life and soul—two-dozen-odd manuscripts, short stories and a short novel—was gone! Someone had plundered the fake bottoms of his portmanteau!

"With that one moment in my father's life, I can sympathize," sighed my grandfather.

"He stood in the center of the room, his mind a glazed and fissured pot. The smell of rat grew strong in the room. Mr. Gogol, Father concluded, was nothing more than a clever, common thief.

"It came as no surprise when Father learned from the desk clerk that Gogol had checked out of the hotel just twenty minutes earlier.

Slowly, Father backed into the very center of the crowded hotel lobby, stunned like a steer at the slaughter. He tried to calculate the extent of his loss in terms that might register on some scale, any scale. He could not. The manuscripts were irreplaceable. He felt that the death of one's firstborn child could be no more painfully absolute a diminishment of one's life and measure.

"He wondered, what could he do? Call the gendarmerie? Contact the press? Relate to them the intertwining lines of the sinister plot in which he'd been ensnared, a sad, duped victim? Appeal to the American Embassy? Demand as an American citizen that everything, everything be done immediately toward the apprehension of the criminal and the return of his manuscripts?

"Then, ah, then dawned upon my father, in all its radiant idiocy, an idea only he could have struck upon. Listen to *this*, Sasha! If the thief really was the writer Gogol, Father mused, truly, if it were Gogol *himself* who had just robbed him of all the treasures of his pen; if, as he was so well aware, *only* his manuscripts were missing, then *here* was certainly no crime of avarice in the abstract; the famous Gogol could be nothing more nor less than a literary pirate, a bootlegger!"

Grandfather paused. I smiled encouragingly, afraid that he might have stopped to ask me another question.

"At this juncture, my boy, let me clarify how and why your great-grandfather might have been led to such an astonishing conclusion. You know already that Father was never published. If I may put the finest gloss on the matter, perhaps his work, as Poe might have said it, 'did not permit itself to be read.' But his unpublishing was not for want of trying. In the four or five years preceding his encounter with Nikolai Gogol, his submission of manuscripts to the editors of literary magazines and publishing houses was carried out in the most painstaking and exhaustive fashion. Meticulously and conscientiously, he monitored the rejection of dozens of short stories, each one mailed to dozens of magazines and received home again accompanied by the curt and fateful rejection notice. He filled two whole ledgers with the record of his stories' peregrinations. A manila folder bulged with the slips of paper that were the sole reward for all his labors.

"He fared no better with the book publishers. His novelette landed on the desks of several editors in every publishing house, major and minor, for which he could find an address at the local library. It was as though the desks and not the men who sat in them were responsible for processing his submissions, the notes returned with his clean, unrumpled manuscript seeming hardly more sensitive to his achievement.

"Father made certain that he had retrieved every single one of his own beautifully and painstakingly hand-written pages before leaving for Europe, thinking that editors in the seat of Western culture might be more sympathetic to his achievement. Of course, he never got a chance to find out.

"So, what is the point? As a result of this miserable history, I submit that Father became convinced that he was the unfortunate object of a fiendish conspiracy. Why, he wondered, should Gogol, or any other writer for that matter, become a famous author, when he, regardless of his efforts, could not? Why did every story come back from every editor with the same response almost every time— 'This is not right for us'—unless they were all working together? He didn't quite know where Gogol fit into the hierarchy of what could be nothing less than a cabal of international proportions, but he did have an idea as to Gogol's role in its machinations. *Why else* would Gogol steal Father's manuscripts unless he and the editors intended to publish them under the name, the ludicrous name of Nikolai Gogol!

"Perhaps, my boy, this is not precisely the twisted path my father's thoughts followed when he happened upon a plan of action, standing like some marble tribute in the middle of the Westminster lobby —for who am I to say? —but surely something must account for the folly he was about the commit.

"Even as he stood, the bustling, anonymous patrons of the hotel rushing past, some bumping right into him, Father's plan took on clear and substantial outline.

"A *maître d'hôtel* grabbed him roughly by the arm and said, 'Eh, Guv'nah? You ull right? Yur holdin' up traffic!'

"Startled from his reverie, Father bent close and whispered in the man's ear, 'I need your advice.'

"The two conversed briefly—much gesturing of hands and nodding of heads—to the effect that an hour later, Father sat in the office of 'a barris'er, discree' and trus'worthy.' In no time at all, a fee was negotiated and his plan committed to contractualese. Father left an enormous retainer with the man's secretary, then proceeded straight to book his passage home. After a stay of only three weeks, Father cut short his lifetime dream sojourn to the capitals of culture by eleven months, one week, and two and one-half days.

"*Before* we approach our *denouement,* I supposed I should mention a last, curious, perhaps inconsequential event that took place on Father's departure. Aboard his ship, he had tired quickly of the farewell celebrations on deck; the streamers and noisemakers, and the pretty girls wistfully dangling handkerchiefs from above and below, quite obviously meant nothing to him. Lying on his bed, he stared at the little rectangular ceiling and listened to the sounds—whistles, horns, laughter, and crying—that came in at his open portal. Then he heard a voice above the tintamarre, speaking English with a decidedly Russian accent. The voice said again and again, 'All shordd whos goink ashordd. All ashordd whos goink shordd.' At first, Father thought the voice emanated from the hallway, which was as logic told him only proper. But he couldn't stop believing otherwise. The sound was coming from the portal! Surely the caller was a steward up on deck. The thought did not convince him. Not just the direction, but the tone of the voice—taunting, beckoning—did not seem right. And that damned Russian accent! Finally, he could stand it no longer. He jumped from his bed, leapt to the portal, and poked his face through. He had a clear view of the dock—thronged, colorful, and boisterous. Looking up and down, here and there, Father half expected to see a pair of flashing coattails, to hear a bark-like cough. Then he heard it again. The sound clearly came from the hallway. Without a trace of Russian in his voice, the caller passed his door—'All ashore who's going ashore. All ashore who's going ashore.'—then he went away.

"For the next four years, Father was too preoccupied to write a single word of fiction. His mind, or most of it, as you shall see, was bent on Europe. Once each month he received—having eagerly awaited and anxiously ripped it open—a report, a list of publications that his Paris lawyer had undertaken to peruse on his behalf. Can you guess why? Why, Sasha? To find one of Father's stories published under Gogol's signature, what's why, my boy! Ha! Your great-grandfather was paying a high-toned Parisian barrister enormous sums of money just to read the literary magazines of Europe!"

Grandfather thumped the armrest of the rocker repeatedly with his beefy fists and began to laugh. Tears soon poured from his eyes.

"*And,* to come up with the scratch, your great-grandfather held down the only honest job he ever had—writing copy for an advertising agency in downtown Manhattan! Damned good he was, too," he added, belly-laughing between guffaws. "They doubled his salary after only one year!" He laughed madly.

"To each and every list that Father received," Grandfather continued, having regained some control of himself, "a note was attached. It always said the same thing: 'As you can see, M. Post, the substance of your claim has not been borne out in an actionable manner, as yet.' Now, *that's* a clever lawyer.

"With every check Father mailed in response, he included a note instructing the lawyer to be patient and, above all, diligent on his behalf. Always, he urged, in just a month or two, somewhere, in black and white, his stories would appear, and then they'd have Gogol right where they wanted him.

"Now, Sasha, you may wish to ask a question or two at this point. For instance, how could Father have ever proved his stories had been thus published? Or, why didn't Father find a lawyer in Russia, one that might at least have been capable of taking more precipitous action against the thief? Why did he employ a lawyer to begin with, and not a detective? You might even ask why he simply took it on faith from the tall stranger that Gogol was indeed a published writer, let alone a great and famous one? Or, most sanely, why didn't he just admit a loss on all those damned manuscripts and get on with it? I have no sensible answers for any such questions.

"One day, in the summer of 1852, Father received a wire: 'Gogol is dead,' the lawyer wrote, 'No evidence, your claim, preliminary disposition, his estate. Heard of manuscript burning. Title: *Dead Souls*. Hoax? Will investigate.'

"Minutes later, the noon post arrived. In his shattered condition, Father wouldn't have given it a second glance, except that it included a package of dubious aspect, wrapped in filthy cloth and tied with coarse baling string. He noticed, too, the foreign stamps. Inside, Father found a cheap cigar box full of ashes and a scrap of vellum scribbled with characters he took to be Russian.

"Father ran from the house. Half an hour later, he handed the note to a young lady at the Russian Embassy. She was pretty, with dark hair and a dimple in her right cheek. He looked at her shyly. Totally out of breath, he couldn't say a word. She asked, 'Vot can I do fordddd you?'

"For a brief moment, Father thought she was flirting. 'I want you to tell me what it says,' he replied, gasping for air, pushing the note at her, 'if you don't mind, my dear.' The woman said..."

"Great-grandmother?!" I interrupted excitedly, sitting up quickly, jangling the bedsprings.

"Sasha!" Grandfather said, beaming. "Please! Let me finish. The woman said, brushing her thick curls back from her forehead, smiling as though something in the note amused her, 'Loozely, it says, "I take da frddeedom. Hope you don't mind. It vas the only merciful ting to do. G." ' "

Grandfather stopped talking. He gazed, smiling widely, over my shoulder. He saw that I was about to speak; as though wiping the smile from his face, he brushed his lips with his fingers and continued.

"And that, my boy, is the end of the story. You know how Father spent the rest of his life, toiling fruitlessly in the truck gardens of verbiage. The editors never really convinced him, I supposed, that he couldn't write to save his own life. Yet he died a happy man, convinced that he had at least one time written as well as any man could ever hope to. The memory of those stolen, conflagrant, unrewritable stories stayed with him always, proof intangible that no one had ever written any better. You see, he died certain—having eventually read Gogol's work—that the great, undeniably great writer had, after all, burned his stories out of spite, that the word 'merciful' in that fateful note had been Gogol's confession of envy. The object of Gogol's mercy, your great-grandfather reasoned, was Nikolai Gogol himself!"

Thus Grandfather concluded his story, his grin a thin line, a smile scratched on paper with a pencil.

Having giving up writing for accounting at the age of sixteen, my only reason for setting this story down lies in the knowledge that few people can say his great-grandfather knew Nikolai Gogol. The story is its own justification for being.

August 22, 1939

PEOPLE

I DON'T think any mystery has preoccupied me as much and for as long as that of the endless proliferation of humanity. It's only, in part, a matter of numbers. Seven, eight billion men, women, and children, every one to be fed and clothed, educated, employed, tended and buried—that's all quite unfathomable, of course. Not to mention seemingly impossible.

Or, in our age of communications, only too fathomable if all you care about is statistics.

Look out over a golf course, and there's people everywhere you turn but plenty of room to make sure you don't murder someone if you're the least bit careful and yell "Fore!" when necessary. And what of all the wastelands? The Rockies and the Sahara? I understand in Norway you can walk in the woods and not see another human being for a week. I once drove for two solid hours at night through Montana and didn't see a single light bulb. Between my mid-sized town and Chicago there are dozens of little towns, with not even five thousand inhabitants each, peppered in between the endless corn and soybean fields.

Sure, there's still plenty of room for all those somebodies not yet gleaming in lovers' eyes. That's not what I mean.

It's not people, but *lives,* with all their multifarious and meandering histories, I cannot grasp. I know how much has gone into my own meager existence, and I can't imagine who all these people are and what they do!

What goes on behind all those closed doors? More often than not, when we find out, it isn't good.

What is one to make of such mystery?

One late-winter afternoon, I was sitting in my study drinking beer and reading that weekly attempt at a compendium of life, the Sunday paper. Earlier that afternoon we'd returned from a visit with my wife's parents in Grand Rapids. I was exhausted from the three-hour drive and enjoying (I hate to say it) the absence of my two preteen sons, who were glued to a computer in their bedroom playing ultra-violent games. When the phone rang, my wife yelled up the stairs. I reacted in a way that had become all too familiar since my parents had passed away: Who could be calling me on a Sunday? I supposed all sorts of people might, but none with a happy reason. I had eight siblings, but none of them were close, either geographically or emotionally. I rarely socialized with my friends at the factory. My puzzlement only served to remind me how alone I often felt on Sunday afternoons, even with a house full of kids.

It was Gordon Wilks, a guy I met on the golf course. He laughed when I told him I worked at the Honda plant. I laughed when he told me he was a labor attorney. "Thank God I have nothing to do with the UAW," he said with a big grin, forgiving my association with the enemy, it seems, because at the end of the round he invited me to a poker party. It soon became a monthly ritual: the one occasion when I would let loose, get more than a little drunk and drop twenty or thirty dollars in the spirit of youthful, monogamous abandon, which is the only reason why any married man plays poker anymore.

"I need a favor," he said, skipping the pleasantries.

"Shoot."

"I need you to help me out with something."

He paused as if I knew what he was talking about.

From the tone of his voice, embarrassed but adamant, I wondered if he was about to ask me for money. If so, he could forget it.

"Sure, what is it." I tried not to make it sound like a question.

"I can't explain. You have to come over," he said bluntly.

"You mean now?" I asked, more out of curiosity than exasperation.

"Look, Sam, you won't mind once you see it. It's just too…" He paused, uncharacteristically at a loss for words.

"Give me ten minutes," I said and hung up before he could thank me.

As I drove past the city park that separated his neighborhood from mine, the sun, slanting beneath the visor, created an aura effect with my eyelashes. It was a nice moment, which, while reminding me of the miracle of sight, made the act of looking seem more significant than anything I might see. A squirrel darted across the road. I swerved and missed it, just. In the rearview mirror, I saw the animal stop in the middle of the street and look after my receding vehicle as if I had just performed a miracle. It struck me that the sudden insight I had just experienced would be, for him, either a constant phenomenon, or an impossibility, with nothing in between.

My thoughts still bright with these reveries, I pulled into Gordon's driveway.

He stood at the rear corner of his house, impatiently waving me up. I pulled up beside him and rolled down the window, but he opened the door for me.

"Follow me. You won't believe it," he said and marched away across his back lawn.

I had often admired the perfection of his landscaping, not that he did anything more than pay a professional service for all those trim flowerbeds and clean-edged sidewalks. My yard was a wilderness compared to his, but I was unwilling to pay the price, in dollars or in sweat. Against a cyclone fence, which shut his lawn off from the alley, stood four manicured evergreens. He stepped up to the second tree from the right, leaned over and poked his head into its branches. Somehow this reminded me of a pilloried public offender seen from behind. I stepped up beside him, but before I could follow his example, he straightened up and sighed.

"I still can't believe it," he said, turning to look at me. His eyes, usually red (I assumed he tended toward alcoholism), were as clear as egg whites with dark green yolks. "I would never have seen it, but I was looking for the tree rot I'd been reading about in the paper. See for yourself," he said, backing away and waving me forward.

I shrugged my shoulders at him in innocent bemusement and looked. Hanging from a branch by a Christmas ornament hook tied to a string around its neck was a doll with a ceramic head unmistakably fashioned in a wildly leering likeness of Gordon Wilks. The doll was dressed in a black robe, which was lifted at the knees by the protrusion of an absurdly lengthy dick, tilted priapicly, painted fire-engine red, with a gold women's barrette pinched on its knob.

"Jeeez!" I whispered, backing away.

"Something, isn't it?"

"Has it been there for long?" I asked.

"The string is cotton. It looks brand new to me. It's been raining for weeks. No, it hasn't been there for long."

I was impressed by this Holmesian deduction.

"Do you know who did it?" I asked, certain that he did.

"Yes, I think I do. That's why I need you with me. I don't want to confront him alone."

"Who is it?" I asked, conscious of my own greedy, if not quite prurient, interest.

Ignoring my question, he said, "I don't want to prejudice you any more than I have to. If I'm wrong, who knows what could happen?"

"But you do have reason to suspect this person," I suggested, following him across the lawn.

"I do. But it's all circumstantial stuff, and if I'm wrong, it's better I've told you nothing. I don't want to be sued for libel."

"Then why do you need me?" I asked, perturbed at being thwarted in my curiosity.

"You're my neutral party. A witness. At some point, I'm going to need your opinion."

His self-control was stunning. I knew that I would not have been so close-lipped in the possession of such a juicy secret. It occurred to me, from the direction he was taking, diagonally across his lawn, that we were about to confront one of his neighbors. The thought filled me with muzzy panic. It was one thing to complain to your own neighbor, who could not shock you more than all prior exposure to his or her idiosyncrasies might allow; but I wasn't at all prepared to be confronted by those of another man's neighbor. I had the same uneasiness about distant relatives, and had on more than one occasion declined an invitation to a wedding on that account. Now I was expected to be a witness in a showdown with some kind of pervert. I wished that Gordon had asked me for money instead.

The house we approached, going around to the front, was next door. Without hesitation, Gordon rang the bell. Almost immediately, a tall, thin, rather striking man, vaguely familiar, opened the door and smiled a smile—though with jagged teeth—of perfectly casual welcome, as if the occasion was as normal as the arrival of the newspaper.

"Gordon! Gentlemen!" the man greeted us inclusively. He opened the screen door and looked up at the sky. "What a gorgeous day! I don't know why I'm sitting in front of the tube! Oh, forgive me, please come in!"

We followed our host through a dim foyer into a small den lit by the flickering green light of a golf game on the television.

"I'm afraid I've been vegetating," he confessed, offering me a seat in a plush lounger. "When the girls are out, it's the only time I seem to have to myself. And you are?"

"I'm sorry," interjected Gordon, looking at me. "This is Pete Mains. And this is Sam Engles. I should have introduced you." He dropped into a captain's chair beside me. "Pete ran for mayor several years ago. You might remember."

Now I knew why the man looked familiar.

"Yes," I said to our host, "I had just moved to town. Sorry I didn't have the chance to vote for you."

It was the nicest thing I could think to say, conscious that his teeth alone would have cost him the election.

"You and about ten thousand others," he said and laughed with mild embarrassment. "Not to worry," he added, turning down the volume of the television. "Losing the election was the best thing ever to happen to me. Can I offer you something? Cranberry juice? A club soda? You'd probably like a beer, wouldn't you, Gordon?"

"Yes, that would be fine."

Pete looked at me.

"Sure, fine," I said. "Same for me."

"I think I've got two cold ones left from our party Friday night," said our host, stepping from the room.

Gordon leaned forward to make sure Pete was out of hearing, and said, with level irony, "Just a regular guy, isn't he?"

"Nice enough," I responded, settling back into the chair. "Hardly seems the kind to dabble in voodoo."

"Oh, don't call it that, for Christ's sake!" hissed Gordon. "If we get into it, just keep your mouth shut."

"Sorry," I said, shifting uncomfortably.

He looked into my eyes and squinted. "Forget I said that. This thing's got me so rattled I don't know what I'm saying."

"Well, you seem to know what you're doing, anyway," I said, all conciliation. "Don't worry about me. I'll follow your lead and keep my…"

I paused, hearing footsteps.

Pete Mains entered the room holding a can of beer in each hand. Though the little light there was in the room was fading quickly with the setting sun, I couldn't help noticing a cross, almost an X, of greasy ashes drawn with a finger on his forehead. I winced and clumsily grabbed the offered can. As Gordon took his beer, Pete Mains smiled at both of us; between the skinny height, the teeth and the ashen cross, he had suddenly assumed all the exotic proportions of a converted Fu Manchu. As he turned to take a seat on a long leather couch, Gordon caught my eye, raised his right eyebrow and tilted his head down as if to say, "Now you begin to see!"

Before anyone had a chance to speak, I blurted out the obvious question: "Excuse my mentioning it, Pete, but when is Ash Wednesday this year?"

"I'm sorry?" he responded, more puzzled than offended, which is what I fully expected him to be.

Gordon shot me a withering glare.

"On your forehead," I continued, knowing I'd only make matters worse if I didn't finish my thought. "Isn't that what a Catholic priest does on Ash Wednesday?"

I knew it wasn't my role to be the inquisitor, but my curiosity was pleasantly relieved when our host quickly drew his palm across his forehead, looked at his hand and laughed.

"Oh, my. I must look a sight!"

"Sam was just trying to..."

"Gordon, don't give it another thought!" He laughed again. "I dropped a dirty frying pan looking for the church key." He paused, seeing the pun. "Ha, church key!" We both chuckled politely as he continued, staring at his hand, "I must have touched my forehead before I washed my hands. Excuse me for a minute."

When he was gone, Gordon whispered vehemently, "Can you believe that line of bull? I'm telling you, he's the one! That was vintage Pete Mains! Now leave it to me, will you? I won't get a thing out of him if you don't!"

"I'm sorry," I whispered back, "but it doesn't seem all that incriminating to me. You want me to believe he anointed himself in there?"

"Listen, you and I are outsiders! Sinners! He's nuts on the subject!"

"Boy, that seems a stretch," I said, shaking my head.

"He said, 'church key,' didn't he?"

"Yeah, that's what he said. What of it?"

Gordon held out his can of beer and pointed at the top.

"Church key?" he asked.

I stared at it, but before I could say anything, Pete Mains returned.

"How do I look?" he asked, hands outspread.

"Fine," I said, "Sorry about my remark about the priest. I wasn't trying to be cute."

Gordon began to fidget.

"I thought it was funny, actually," said Peter, "I'm not a Catholic, I'm afraid, but I'm well aware of the ritual. It's rather pa…" He caught himself. "You must be Catholic?"

"Raised one, but not practicing," I assured him.

"Ah, a backslider!"

Though he employed the loaded word, his delivery was remarkably neutral.

"Though not without my principles," I added.

"Glad to hear it. Now Gordon here, he's a man of principle through and through."

"That's enough, Pete. We're well aware of your view of my principles."

"I see you've been talking about me," he accused him, archly.

"Not much," said Gordon. "I just thought Sam should meet you. He's talked of entering politics."

This was an ingenious lie. And a gamble.

"Well, he'll get only one bit of advice from me," said Peter, turning to me. "and that's forget it. It's the coliseum all over again. The lions and the Christians."

"It can't be all that bad," I interjected, playing my assigned role at last. I was determined to restore Gordon's faith in me. "Whatever the costs, you must have had good reasons for running in the first place."

"Reasons, maybe. None of them adequate, as it turned out. When you get down to it, it's all ego gratification. That is, until they start chewing on your face."

I recoiled at the metaphor. At a loss how to respond, I was rescued by the opening of the front door.

"Ah, it's the girls!" said Pete.

Into the room stepped his wife, an attractive bottle blonde with dark eyebrows, wearing tight blue jeans and a designer work shirt, followed by his daughter, taller than her mother, with long, dark, almost purple, tresses that fell in dense curls over both cheeks. She seemed to be wearing a turn-of-the-century bathing suit, form-fitting and sleeveless, or was it some kind of athletic uniform? She hung back when she saw there was company. She was far more attractive than either of her parents—stunning, to be precise—and her shyness suggested that she was only too conscious of the fact.

Pete introduced us. His wife was Sarah. She smiled impatiently, her high cheekbones stretching the skin up from her prim mouth into straight fine lines of weariness.

"And this is Monica, Sam," Pete said proudly, taking his daughter's elbow and drawing her further into the room. "The first young woman ever accepted on the South High School wrestling squad."

"A lot of good it does me," she grumbled, pulling free from her father's grasp.

"Not again!" exclaimed her father with dismay.

"Yes, again!" Sarah complained. "This time it was some little brat from Central. But it was really his parents' fault. He didn't seem all that unwilling to me."

"Well, you're still undefeated, sweetie," Peter consoled his daughter, stroking her hair. He turned to us. "She's had four byes this month because none of the boys will..." he paused, searching for the word, "*compete* with her."

"It's so humiliating," Monica groaned. Then she startled us by crying out: "*Why* are they all such *jerks?*"

It would have been appropriate for her to run from the room after such an outburst, but she dropped onto the sofa instead; she crossed her arms and legs and buried her pointy chin in her breastbone.

It took no imagination whatsoever to understand why any decent teenager would think twice about grappling with this Spandex-clad goddess in front of a hundred screaming parents.

Again, I asked what I thought was the obvious question: "I know I'm ignorant to ask this, but isn't there a girls' squad?"

Monica shook her head in disgust and stared up at her father. Gordon grunted audibly.

"That's hardly the point, don't you think?" Pete dutifully explained. "Monica is a gifted athlete and it's simply not the same thing."

"Not at all!" whined Monica in agreement.

How can you be so dense? her look scolded me.

"And yet," Gordon ventured, "it's not hard to understand the boys' hesitation."

"So what am I to do, Gordo?" asked the young lady, putting an abrasive accent on what was obviously a familiar form of address between them. "You want me just to quit? I could major in home ec! Is that what I should do? You can hire me to cook for you. Would that make you happy?"

Both parents shook their heads, but I wasn't sure at whom.

"Come on, Monica," Gordon answered gently, stressing the formal address along with his eyes' innocent, defensive appeal, which he threw up to Sarah and Pete. "I only meant to suggest that you put yourself through a great deal of unhappiness and frustration, and for what? I'm sure it makes things very difficult for you at school."

"Who gives a damn what people think!" she shouted. "I've never been the slightest..."

Her father's hand on her shoulder made her stop.

"That's enough, Monica," he soothed her, but his eyes quickly searched out mine; it seemed a non sequitur when he said: "I'm sure Gordon is only trying to help."

"Oh, yes. Gordo is sooo helpful," Monica said, shaking her head violently.

Call me stupid, slow on the uptake, but it wasn't until I saw the manner in which the young lady twisted her lush mouth and shook her tresses off her cheeks, suggesting both enticement and frustration, as opposed to disgust or dislike, that I understood what was really going on. Gordon was, after all, a bachelor, and an attractive, available man in his early thirties. The drama before me was laid bare. To whatever extent, and it was too soon to tell, Gordon and Monica had a relationship.

So what was I to do with such an insight? Nothing was any longer what it seemed. Far from being the innocent victim of either a tasteless prank or a malicious curse, Gordon was guilty of an indiscretion falling somewhere in the gap between a stolen kiss and statutory rape (or close to it), and had received a stern warning. Pete, I gathered, was a concerned parent with a talent for vicious symbolism, or he was a nut; regardless, he had been wronged and was deserving of a certain sympathy. The two women were harder to read: Sarah, having demonstrated strength on her daughter's behalf (it had not escaped me that her father hadn't even attended the wrestling meet), might or might not be conscious of the violation that had taken place in her own backyard. And what of Monica? I sensed deep emotions. Had she flirted, succumbed? Were her unguarded feelings toward Gordon those of a woman scorned, or had she learned enough about her lover to feel, like a wife of too many years, that she had the right to be contemptuous? What was I even doing here, I wondered. I no longer wanted to be of help to Gordon. If anything, my allegiance had been shifted to Pete Mains and his daughter.

My sympathy for the former was conditional; if he was the kind of man to anoint himself, as Gordon suggested, against the mere presence of two men such as ourselves, perhaps the daughter's disloyalty to her parents was a form of rebellion, one which I might heartily condone were I in certain possession of the facts. If Pete Mains was what I thought he was at first, an ordinary fellow, no different than myself (who might absolutely need a comfortable Sun-

day afternoon in front of the tube as a reward for the week's labors),
how much of a father had he been to let things come to this pass to
begin with? Of course, Monica was a handful for her father and (I
took some pleasure in the realization) for Gordon. Yet, she was no
more than fifteen, sixteen at the most! I thought of Sue, my twelve-
year-old. Only Sarah—who still troubled me by her obtuseness—
came close to innocence in this tangle of blame.

These reflections, lightning compared to the dim thunder with
which I express them here, left me with one conclusion: I must do
what I can to help.

"I don't mean to intrude on your privacy," I began, addressing
the room generally, "but have you thought of counseling?"

"I'm sorry?" asked Sarah.

"What would I need *that* for!" asked Monica.

Gordon coughed loudly.

"Obviously, I don't mean just you, young lady. The situation is
more complicated than that, I'm sure."

"What are you talking about?" asked Pete.

"I mean this kind of thing happens all the time, and there are professional people who are trained to help. You know, help you steer
a course through all the emotions, find a resolution that will satisfy
everyone involved. Of course, in my family we've always relied upon
our own good sense, and maybe Ann Landers, once in a while," I
admitted, chuckling to let them know I knew no one was perfect.

I took the ensuing silence for encouragement.

"It's important, I think, before things get out of hand. The business of the doll is innocent enough, I suppose." Sensing Gordon's
agitation, I hurried on, hoping to blunt it. "I just hate to see things
go much beyond that. I can see that you're all very good friends after all, and it's better to get it out in the open and talk about it. It
would be a crime to see it deteriorate into open hostility, or worse."

"What in hell are you getting at?" cried Gordon.

I looked at him. I searched his eyes. His previous frustration with me had turned to anger, visible in his squinty eyes, in the odd set of his jaw. Well, I thought, I've been flirting with disaster all afternoon; but there was more at stake than his simple good will toward me; much, much more. I forged ahead.

"Okay, so you're willing to have it said, right out in front of everybody. A good sign actually. Let's go with that."

Pete Mains dropped down next to his daughter, who took his hand. Sarah sat on the arm of the sofa.

They all seemed fascinated that I had figured things out.

"Gordon and Monica's…" I hesitated, "what shall I call it? Their *relationship* has gotten a bit out of hand and it's causing a lot of stress. How's that?"

Then everyone was on their feet!

"Get the hell out of my house!" shouted Pete and Sarah Mains simultaneously.

"Daddy, who is this creep!" cried Monica.

Gordon, grabbing my arm and pushing me toward the front door, yelled in my ear, "You son-of-a-bitch! Get the hell out of here!"

I tried to explain myself, that I was only trying to help, that I hadn't meant to offend anybody, but I wasn't given the chance.

"Really, I thought that's what you wanted, Gordon!" I said as calmly as I could.

Having once gotten me off balance, Gordon could easily horse me all the way to the front door. My worn tennis shoes slid on a throw rug in the foyer. Fighting the pandemonium, I tried to apologize.

"Sorry! Really, there's nothing to be ashamed of!"

Before I could make myself understood to the members of the Mains family, who had stolen my sympathies entirely away from my now former poker partner, I was banging through the screen door and leaping off the front porch. Thank goodness there were only four steps! I landed on all fours in the grass, stood up, and brushed off my knees, then my palms, trying to muster as much dignity as possible under the circumstances. I turned back toward the house.

There the four of them stood, as close together as if I were a photographer about to take their portrait. I had the oddest sense that they were, after all, a family. Perhaps that was it! Some deal had already been struck!

"But what about the obscene doll, the ashes?" I said calmly, though I was breathing heavily.

"That's none of your fucking business!" Monica screamed.

Gordon turned and slapped her, with predictable results.

I ran to the car and got out of there as quickly as I could. What were they to me, after all? Just one more mystery in a world full of them.

PLATO'S KNAVE

*H*AVE you ever met a buffoon? I mean a real one?

I've met only one complete and irredeemable buffoon. Yes, most men have some of it in them, maybe it's just their socks, or things they can't help saying under stress, or how they behave drunk.

But a thoroughgoing buffoon? That's hard to find.

His name was Miles Allbore. Not really. I can't use his real name. But I promise I won't shade the truth a bit. His name is the only protection he gets. Not after what he did to me.

I met him in college, where you meet all the truly interesting people you'll ever know—college having a way, by the time it's over, of stinging most of our obvious flaws into hiding. We were both teaching assistants in our first year of graduate study in philosophy.

Miles lived off campus all four years of his undergraduate career, during which he took two degrees, a bachelor's in psychology and a bachelor's of fine arts in ceramics (with emphasis on the potter's wheel). No one ever said he was stupid, or not hard working. The mangled masses that comprised his "thesis"—color-splashed clay supposedly spun on the kick-wheel—were so ugly and phallic that word got around and dozens of students crowded the gallery for two nights, laughing themselves ill, Miles being nowhere in sight. What else could his teachers do but give him his degree?

My being a philosophy major accounts for our not meeting until grad school. The department accepted him because he'd come only three credit hours shy of a philosophy minor, and his Graduate Record Exam score in philosophy was just enough to get him by. In truth, they were desperate for students.

I lived in a small basement apartment in a Victorian home. Miles lived alone on the third floor. This unfortunate propinquity made it difficult to avoid Miles when walking the six blocks to and from campus.

Picture him from head to foot: first, a dirty blond Prince Valiant haircut; yellowish eyes beneath virtually no eyebrows (which I believed that he shaved); acne scars everywhere, but nothing active; ears too small for his head and so thin that the light shined through them; a mouthful of expensive orthodontia that provided his one truly redeeming feature, his brilliant smile; height, six foot four, all of him thin, but stooped, like a bent metal javelin thrown too many times; yellow button-down shirts and a yellow tie; faded brown corduroy pants, flared and too short that were also yellowish, and mustard yellow cowboy boots with copper tips. To complete whatever effect it was he hoped to make, and in anything less than sixty-five degrees and sunny weather, he wore a cape; not a dramatic, full-length, dark drape, but a waist-length yellow cape reminiscent of the one Robin wore in the Batman comics.

*

I met him during our first training session as teaching assistants. He had come in with the cape on but draped it over the back of his chair. There were seven assistants, and all of us couldn't help taking sidelong glances or just plain staring at him. He seemed to relish the attention and bobbed his head around, smiling at us. The professor in charge of the assistants program came in and asked us to stand and say a few words about ourselves.

When it was his turn, Miles rose, ran his fingers through his hair (his bangs falling perfectly into place) and, seeming to remember something, bent down and pulled a handful of yellow pamphlets from his backpack. Fanning them like playing cards, he said, "Yes, my name is Miles. I'm afraid I don't have quite the qualifications to be here that all of you have, since I don't have a degree in philosophy. I'm sure they are all very impressive, or would be to me. Nonetheless, I aced my GREs and I hope my deep reading of the master philosophers has been equal to yours." Without another word, he walked around the room handing each of us a copy of the pamphlet, which read on the cover, "You and Me: A Philosophical Inquiry by Miles Allbore." Then he sat down.

When the meeting was over, Miles sat at his desk with a pen in his hand, looking around. As people started to leave, he said, "I'd be happy to sign your copy for you." His tone was pure generosity. I was already at the door and left as fast as I could.

When I got home and settled in with a beer and a cigarette, I opened up Miles' pamphlet and was confronted with this epigraph:

The holy black bubonic fuck—
The furthest thing from goddamned luck.
—Anonymous

What followed was twenty pages of virtually unpunctuated (there were empty spaces between sentences) eight-point type so impenetrable they made Immanuel Kant read like Dr. Seuss. I found this on the second page: "And of necessity I intend to prove that my genius consists of sufficient Reason to identify Ideas and their relationship to individual Things in their thing-ness as the subject/object of pure Knowing."

As I put the pamphlet on the shelf, I realized that those words were vaguely familiar. Yes, Nietzsche was always telling us what a genius he was, but I had spent more than the requisite hours with Arthur Schopenhauer and out of suspicion and curiosity pulled down Volume 1 of his most famous book. It took twenty minutes, but I found most of the same words in one sentence, except that Miles had thoroughly rearranged them, twisting their meaning into nonsense.

The next morning, when I left my apartment and got halfway down the block, Miles appeared at my side, took three steps in front of me and turned, holding out his hand.

"Hi, I'm Miles. Shake!" He flashed that smile.

"Shake?" I hadn't heard anyone say that since elementary school. What could I do? I shook his hand and told him my name, avoiding his eyes because he was so intently trying to look into mine.

"Nice to meet you at last," he said, now walking beside me. "I've heard so much about you!"

I didn't turn to him as I asked, "What have you heard?"

"You really want to know? It's a little embarrassing."

Now I turned, even though it meant I couldn't avoid his staring at my eyes. "Yes?"

"I mean it would embarrass me, but," he hurried on, "it's not a bad thing. Just the opposite."

"Okay?"

"Yes. Well, it's just that you're the most brilliant student they've had in the department for years."

"Yes, that is embarrassing, and totally absurd."

"No, really."

"Who said this?"

"Everybody. Really!" "Really" apparently being his favorite word.

"It's bullshit."

"No, really."

"Please stop saying 'really,'" I said, being just a little short with him.

"Um. Sorry." He actually winced.

"Name one person who said it."

He coughed, on purpose.

"I shouldn't tell you names. I don't even know anybody by their names yet anyway."

I stopped and turned to him and said, "Look, maybe you're just trying to be nice. I understand, I suppose, though it's more than a bit weird, Miles. You're telling a bold lie just to make friends. Right?"

He was silent. I continued walking. He now kept half a step behind me. I couldn't resist.

"I read a bit of your pamphlet last night, just the first few pages."

"Wow! That's great! I appreciate it."

"Do you steal *only* from Schopenhauer, or do you crib Husserl and Martin Buber too?"

He crossed behind me and headed across the street.

I shouted after him, "Section 37, first sentence, Volume 1, *The World as Will and Representation!*"

He started running. I remember thinking, no, this won't be the end of it.

✳

Over the course of one week Miles told his Introduction to Philosophy class that he was descended from Bertrand Russell and that Russell wasn't really an atheist, but that he, Miles, was the most committed atheist they'd ever meet. He told Lydia, a plump but engaging and pretty teaching assistant, a few years older than the rest of us, that she shouldn't worry about her weight, that he thought it looked good on her and he wished he could gain weight himself, but his constant "burning the candles" (undefined), kept him slim (yes, he said it), "though graceful." When one of the assistants tried to return his copy of Miles' pamphlet, saying, as politely as he could, "I couldn't catch your drift here, so maybe there's someone else you can give it to," Miles grabbed it, ripped it in two and tossed it in a wastepaper basket. Then he paused, composed himself, and said, with a sneer, dropping his voice, "I'm sure you gave it the old college try," and tried to stare the guy down, then laughed in his face and walked away. Then he asked to escort an adjunct professor in her thirties to an all-Beethoven concert. She agreed because she was already planning to go. The professor later told me that Miles had said, "The Beatles will outlast Beethoven, don't you think? I mean, at least Hegel would have thought so." The woman had replied, "Why do you think that?" but Miles had buried his face in his program and acted like he didn't hear the question. She laughed out loud. Miles stood up and walked out of the concert hall.

Yes, Miles had become the center of attention. He was almost all we talked about, and laughed and laughed about. You'd have thought us (students and faculty both) cruel, but we couldn't help ourselves, because seemingly he couldn't either.

I next encountered Miles as I was leaving a seminar on Existentialism. He was standing in the hall, almost as though he was waiting for me. In that cape he looked like a drowned moth. Apparently he'd forgotten our previous encounter because he smiled broadly with those almost intimidating teeth and invited himself along on the walk to our apartments. I saw that he was limping, but decided not to ask him about it.

He was soon peppering me with questions. As before, the underlying purpose of his inquiries was to be complimentary, and who doesn't respond to that? I told him that I grew up in a small midwestern town, was top of my class in high school, was there on a scholarship, did not have a serious girlfriend, and that Socrates was the reason I got interested in philosophy when I was fourteen.

"Yes, his essays are amazing," said Miles reverentially.

"Essays?"

"Yes, of course, some of the most readable essays in all philosophy."

"Socrates didn't write a word that we know of."

"Very funny," said Miles, chuckling. I noticed that he'd dropped "really" from his vocabulary.

"Ever hear of Plato?"

"What do you think? Come on."

"What did Plato do?"

"He wrote beautiful essays too, some of them almost as good as Socrates', in my humble opinion."

I just couldn't help myself. "Socrates was Plato's teacher."

"I knew that!"

Miles' limp, which had been quite pronounced, had disappeared. I couldn't help wondering if it hadn't been some subconscious plea for sympathy, if not pity.

"Plato wrote every word of what you call Socrates' essays—dialogues, actually, the words of Socrates that Plato remembered, all or in part, and recorded. As I said, Socrates didn't write a word. For all we know, what Plato put in Socrates' mouth could have been Plato's own thoughts and no one else's."

"This splitting of hairs is so dispiriting," Miles whined. "Essays, dialogues, who said what, who wrote what? What difference does it make? I haven't read Socrates since my senior year of high school. I was only fifteen years old, by the way."

We were, to my considerable relief, just arriving home.

"Miles, let me give you some advice. I promise to keep this conversation of ours just between us. But you must never repeat what you've just said to anyone. People will laugh in your face and professors will give you hell."

Then poor Miles did the first reasonable thing I'd seen or heard him do. He stopped, looked me, and said, "I understand. Thank you."

As he began to walk away, I said, "And get yourself a copy of Plato's *Republic* to…," I couldn't help myself, "refresh your memory."

✳

Two weeks later, Miles threw a party. He had invitations printed and handed them out to virtually every grad student and professor in the department. The invitation called it "A Gathering of Intellects" and didn't request an RSVP. He scheduled it for five to seven PM on a Tuesday afternoon, and added at the bottom of the invitation: BYOB.

"You'll come, won't you?" he pressed me after he'd handed me the invitation in the hallway. "I mean, you're just downstairs."

I took pity. "Sure, Miles. I'll be there, but probably not right at five." As he was leaving, I said, "Hey, Miles, why the early hour on a school night?"

He came back, swinging his shoulders, and said softly, "I want to weed out anyone who might be lukewarm about it. Gives them an easy way out." He gave me a not-quite-exaggerated wink and walked away.

✳

Six-pack in hand, I climbed the stairs to Mile's apartment at six-fifteen, giving myself every chance that I wouldn't be the only guest. On the stairs Lydia was coming quickly down and passed me without saying anything. I called after her, "Leaving so soon?" She didn't stop to answer, but the next day she apologized and told me that she'd only stayed for five minutes, and not just because she was the only guest. He had actually complained that she hadn't brought any booze. Her sharing this confidence would lead to our dating, but I'll come to that.

I stood at his door and listened. Miles was playing music from *Saturday Night Fever.* I couldn't hear anything else. I almost turned and left, but then I laughed to myself. What a hoot, I thought, if I really am the only one!

I knocked and it took a full sixty seconds for Miles to answer. I was certain that he'd counted it down. He opened the door in an out-fit just like his usual getup, except everything, including the cape, was lime green.

"Come in, my friend," he said, with an arm-sweeping bow.

I didn't wait, even a second.

"Miles, where is everyone? In the kitchen?"

He took it in stride. "Is that a six-pack? Let me put it in the fridge. I'm still waiting for the others to show."

He gave me one of my own beers and said, "Please, have a seat," motioning toward a futon with a towel-thin yellow pad. His apartment was twice the size of mine, one long rectangular room taking up half the third floor. The windows had blinds, all closed. The only light was from fixtures in the ceiling. His bed and a desk were behind a curtain, now pulled back, at the opposite end of the room from the futon. Closer were two more futons facing each other in the middle of the room, with a glass coffee table between. I counted nine large bookshelves, which were the only adornment of the walls. I saw no TV or radio, just an elaborate and expensive component stereo system from which the Bee Gees worked too hard at "Stayin' Alive." From where I sat I could make out the contents of the closest bookshelf. It had five shelves, four feet wide, the top three filled with phonebook-thick hardcover biographies of philosophers, scientists, novelists, composers, and rulers of ancient Greece and Rome. The fourth shelf down held a uniform slab of yellow—what must have been five or six hundred copies of his pamphlet—so jammed in that I had to assume there were boxes more somewhere. On the bottom row were tooled-leather copies of Homer, Virgil, Dante, Cervantes, Milton, and Shakespeare, the latter in single volumes, each devoted to a different play, and one to the poetry. The contents of that one bookcase—so unlike the usual gallimaufry of bent-cornered paperbacks—must have cost a ton of cash. It struck me, Miles is rich!

Then he came back from the kitchen with one of my beers in hand and I thought, No, he's not. I'm missing something.

Mile sat at the other end of the futon and stared at me over the top of his beer can, from which he sipped.

I felt there was only one obvious item for discussion, at least to start.

"I guess your strategy worked," I said.

"Strategy?"

I winked at him.

"Oh, that."

I was slightly impressed he remembered.

"Yes, maybe too well." He looked around, then at his watch. "Yeah, I don't suppose anyone else will show."

"Lydia?"

"You wouldn't believe it," he said, his eyes widened and he became slightly excited, "she was actually a bit scared to be alone with me. I told her I had no intention of taking advantage of her and offered her a drink. She just turned around and left."

"I'm surprised she came at all."

"Why's that?" A hint of hurt in his question.

"Miles? Her weight?"

"What do you mean?"

"You brought the subject up with her awhile back. You don't think she was offended?"

"Of course she wasn't," he said, straightening up from his slouch, "or why would she mention it to everyone in the department?"

"That's my point."

"Nonsense. I was complimenting her. If I'd insulted her, she wouldn't have told a soul out of pure embarrassment."

"She did tell everyone out of pure embarrassment."

He thought about this for a second.

"Then why did she come to my party?"

"Morbid curiosity?"

"What?" he said, raising his voice and standing up.

"Why do you do it?"

"What?"

"Why do you say such insensitive things?"

"Look who's talking. Three times now you've insulted me. And don't think I forget that easily."

I stood up, sighing.

"Then why did you invite me, Miles? Look, I've got to go. I didn't come here to argue."

I headed toward the door with my beer, half empty.

"Don't leave yet," he said, rather pathetically. "I have something for you. Wait right there."

He almost ran to the opposite end of the room. He plucked a book off the shelf above his desk, pulled it out of a slipcase, opened it and began to write inside, pausing to consider in the midst of the effort. He came back and handed me a slim hardcover copy of his pamphlet.

"I had a special run of 100 printed just for friends," he said, handing it to me.

Just what I need, I thought, taking it.

I opened it. The inscription read, "I appreciate you [sic] thought. Miles."

I closed it and looked into his eyes. He was so moved by his own gesture, he was on the verge of tears.

This would not bear encouragement, I thought, closed the book and left without another word. But I couldn't leave it at that. I shouted through the door, "Thanks, Miles!" and ran down the stairs before he had a chance to say or do anything more.

*

After she told me about Miles' party, I told her his version of the story. We laughed so hard I couldn't resist asking Lydia out, and we began dating.

We were well-matched. I was on the hefty side myself, and we found each other attractive in more ways than that. Her being five years older and much more experienced with men caused her to be gentle and considerate, because that's what she expected in return and had never received. And I (laugh if you like) still believed in the concept of the "gentleman" and acted accordingly. Once we discovered these things about each other, and that we were both nuts about Spinoza, thought Existentialism impossible to live by, loved Mahler and Bruckner, thought Bruce Springsteen overrated, and secretly read horror novels to take a break from the heavy stuff (me, Lovecraft; Lydia, Oates and King), well, we ended up in my bed at least three times a week.

Of course, we couldn't help talking and laughing about Miles. Our stories about his party made us partners in a secret, once we decided that just revealing that we'd gone was likely to make us objects of amusement.

And Miles just kept on being Miles. It was impossible to avoid him walking to or from campus, so I heard things that made me want to run away screaming. For example, he couldn't help sharing with me his suspicion that some people thought he was gay. I told him, truthfully, that I'd never heard that said by anyone and that I considered it none of my business. He proceeded to, in his words, "prove that I'm not," by telling me about a conference with one of our professors who, he said, believed in the, "shall we say, Socratic method" when it came to younger men. This was not news. It was also well known that said professor was considered to behave himself with his students, regardless of age or proclivity. Miles insisted that it wasn't true.

"He'd heard something I'd said to another professor and asked me to sit on his lap so that he could explain Heidegger to me!"

"Miles, if you repeat that, you could get in a hell of a lot of trouble."

"You're always telling me to shut up," he said, "and I take umbrage, if you want to know."

"I'm just trying to keep you from shooting yourself in the brain. The professor is a respected member of the department whose publications have been polishing the department's reputation for a decade. No one has *ever* accused him of inappropriate behavior with his students."

"Well, I'll tell you what he polishes."

"Miles?" I laughed. "You actually made a joke! I didn't think you had it in you, even if it is totally inappropriate!"

"What are you talking about?"

No, he didn't see the joke.

"Sorry, my mistake."

"I was referring to his extremely polished manners, which he uses to ingratiate himself with his victims."

"I don't want to hear another word."

"Fine. But I can assure you I did *not* sit on his lap."

"I'm sure you didn't, Miles."

"And I'm not gay."

"Miles, as far as I know no one thinks you are."

"Well, I heard there were nasty comments about my clothes and haircut."

"So? What do you expect?"

This stumped him, and I was certainly not going to elaborate. We proceeded in blessed silence.

∗

A few weeks later, after vigorous and satisfying sex, Lydia told me this story: "Miles was confronted by one of his students in the teaching assistant offices. Quite loudly, this young woman asked Miles if he graded on the curve, because if he did then his giving her a B on her recent paper was unfair because she'd seen some of the other papers and they weren't half as good as hers. Miles actually blubbered, he was so confused and embarrassed, so unable to control himself; he said, 'I wouldn't grade on your curve, young lady. You don't have any.'" Intense laughter here from both of us. "This got him invited to the chairman's office that afternoon. I heard the initial encounter and asked the chair's secretary if she'd overheard anything. Boy, had she! The chairman started right in shouting. 'What the hell were you thinking, Miles, making fun of a girl's figure?' Miles' excuse was that she was insulting him, challenging his authority and questioning his judgment. 'And what makes your so-called judgment so superior you can use it to insult a student's body? How would you like it if I said your haircut looks like a mop without a handle?'" More intense laughter. "Oh, that hair!" Lydia exclaimed. "Anyway, Miles evidently said, 'I will apologize to her immediately.' 'You damn well better, Miles,' said the chairman, "or I'll fire you as an assistant and have you expelled!'"

I said, "It's hard to believe he didn't fire him that minute."

"Well, there's a reason for that. Afterwards, the chair told his secretary that Miles had fallen to his knees only seconds into the confrontation and held up his hands pleading."

"And the apology?"

"Nobody knows exactly. The student could have pursued the issue, but she let it drop. The only thing anyone's heard her say, and she says it every time she sees him, no matter who's listening, is "Hi, pussy lips."

"Now, c'mon," I said, disbelieving.

"I've heard her say it myself," she said, and, turning over, sighed, "After all that, I need a nap."

*

Things began to deteriorate between Miles and me at a party at our Hume and Kant professor's apartment. Lydia and I were necking in the kitchen. Miles came in weaving and blinking drunk. He looked around and opened the refrigerator to get a beer. Popping it open, he stuck his face in mine and said, "You think you're big shit, don't you?"

(Later, Lydia and I, wondering what set him off, concluded it was the acceptance by *Exegesis,* a small philosophical journal, of my 500-word note on the secular nature of Karl Jaspers' "transcendence.")

I backed away but didn't respond.

"You think you're better than I am, don't you?"

I stayed silent.

He turned to Lydia and said, "Your boyfriend is dumb."

She said nothing.

"That doesn't say much for you, does it?"

I pulled back a fist intended for his jaw, but he backed away with his arms up in mock surrender.

"Well, I want you to know you're an empty nothing! How's that for new philosophical exit Jesus? Ha!" he crowed, "Empty nothing! Exit Jesus!" as he wandered out of the kitchen.

Until we'd had enough and left, every ten or fifteen minutes he'd find us and, regardless of who was around to hear, stick his thumbs in his eyes, wiggle his fingers, and shriek, "Empty nothing!" Later we heard he'd behaved in similarly obnoxious ways to other students until he was told to leave.

✳

Halfway into the semester, Miles walked into my Intro to Philosophy class just as I was getting started. He was carrying a handful of his pamphlets.

"Excuse me," he said to my students, "It's easier to deliver these to your teacher and have him distribute them at the end of the period."

He came forward and laid them on my desk. I was speechless. Having returned to the back of the room, he took a seat.

"Thank you, Miles," I said. "Don't worry. I'll pass them out."

"I'm not worried. I just want to audit for a bit. I hope to pick up a thing or two that will help with my own teaching methods. Is that okay?"

It certainly wasn't, but what could I say? And the students didn't seem to mind.

"Fine," I said.

I looked at my notes on my lectern and said, "Okay, folks. I know our discussion of Plato's Cave last week wasn't on your top ten list, judging by your reactions, or lack thereof, so today let's talk about something you might find a bit more interesting."

I went to the blackboard and wrote the word LOVE. That got them to sit up. Miles, instead, seemed to droop with boredom.

"But this is a trick lecture, so take good notes. I'm not going to attribute anything I'm about to say to any specific work or philosopher. Your assignment is to find the specific works my words come from."

"You're forcing us to read, aren't you?" said one serial smart aleck.

"Ain't I a stinka? As Bugs Bunny used to say."

Laughs all around, except from Miles.

"Now, everything is from three, count 'em, three works you've already read, supposedly, or have been assigned for next week. That's all the hint you get."

I certainly had their attention. Miles, arms and legs crossed, feigned sleep.

"Okay, here goes. What would be the high point of love, the zenith? One potential answer is the concept of 'oneness,' of a person becoming one with something, whatever we might choose most to become one with. But is that possible, short of a Mr. Spock mind-meld?"

Miles sniffed loudly, while everyone chuckled.

"Do lovers ever become one in the sex act, physically or mentally?"

That brought total silence to the room.

"Or is it just an illusion? A very pleasant illusion, yes, but an illusion nonetheless. It's quite possible that men and women, or any individual man or woman, never actually achieves oneness with anything. One plus one never equals one."

Miles put up his hand and said quite loudly, "A Zen master might disagree."

"Please," I insisted, "This is a course in Western not Eastern Philosophy."

"Sorry," Miles said, softly, reluctantly. Whether he agreed with me or out of simple embarrassment at his rudeness, I couldn't tell.

I continued: "Can anyone tell me a word we've discussed before that describes my approach here."

The smart aleck put up his hand. "Skepticism," he hissed.

"Excellent," I said and hurried on, not wanting to encourage him further. "But let's give ourselves a chance. Though we might never attain oneness, we shall grant a definition to this achievement, so we'll know it when we see it, experience it. Let us call it 'Pure Love,' the actual attainment of oneness. Now, Pure Love…"

"What nonsense!" said Miles, standing and backing his way toward the door. "You're making all of this up, and these poor kids are going to read themselves silly trying to find your precious 'attributions.'"

I excused myself and followed Miles out of the room.

"What the hell, Miles?"

Miles fluttered his cape and gathered it at his throat. As he turned to leave, he said, "Exit Jesus."

Later that day, the department chair said, "He got around to your class, did he? You're the fourth one."

"Can't you stop him?"

"I've talked to him, of course, but he insists on a student's right to audit any course at the teacher's discretion. You blew it."

"Me?"

"You didn't ask him to leave."

✳

Three days later I walked into Miles' classroom at five minutes after the hour. Miles had begun his lecture. I took a seat and Miles, mid-sentence—"That's all the hint you…"—stopped for a moment and seemed about to continue, then said, "Can I help you?"

"I just want to audit for a bit," I explained. "I hope to learn a thing or two I can use in my own classroom. Is that okay?"

Before Miles could answer, I added, "Do any of your students object?"

A lot of shaking of heads and a "Let him stay."

"Fine," said Miles.

Miles had written the word MUSIC on the blackboard.

Miles continued: "The philosopher in question connects emotional responses *a priori* to an intellectual, just and benevolent existence. But he has made one fatal mistake in his reasoning. Music is relative in terms of the response it engenders. A song in the Dorian mode may induce a feeling of bravery in a man…"

A young lady with thick glasses interrupted, asking, "What's the Dorian mode?"

"Not now, Kat," said Miles.

"You know I don't like that name," she responded, turning over her notebook in protest.

"I apologize. Kathy. Now, to continue. Such music may induce a feeling of bravery in a man, but the response is not static for all men. Others may feel different emotions altogether, and not elevating or even positive ones. Vanity can easily creep into the courageous heart."

That was my cue. "You can say that again."

He ignored me. "Cruelty, hatred, brutishness, bullying, even megalomania have all been labels placed on men called 'brave.'"

I stood up and, backing toward the door, said, "Awesome exegesis, professor. I plan to use it in my class as soon as I brush up on my Plato."

Miles' not-unhandsome face crumpled with rage.

Needless to say, I got a mild rap on the knuckles from the department chair, but he laughed the whole time we discussed it.

✳

One last dust-up before I get to the final blow. I wasn't the only one who saw odd borrowings in Miles' pamphlet. Those of us who noticed them decided it didn't matter because the pamphlet wasn't part of his required course work, and its vanity press publication was seen by all as an embarrassment. It would certainly never help him get a job as a teacher.

Then Miles made—what, a gaffe, a gross miscalculation? He wrote a paper that was entirely the words of Camus and Sartre. It was actually quite cleverly done, if nuts. He even molded a rather pleasing shape to the ten-page essay, complete with an intro and ending, and a convoluted but not implausible argument. But not a word of it was his own.

In this class, the students read their own papers aloud, having handed out copies to everyone. When it was Miles' turn, and he'd finished reading, his professor said, "Miles, you understand the meaning of the word 'plagiarism,' don't you?"

"Of course," Miles answered, smiling, oblivious.

"Well, I'm damned," continued the professor, "I've seen a hundred plagiarized papers, cribbed from the internet, obscure magazines, monographs, even, believe it or not, love letters."

The class of ten students tittered.

"But I've never seen anyone lift his entire essay from the writings of his assigned subjects. Miles, I recognize every line. They're all from either Camus' or Sartre's works."

"You noticed!" Miles said, "I was afraid you wouldn't get it."

"Get what, Miles?"

"The assignment—and it was very stimulating, thank you—was 'discuss one major aspect of the synthesis of the works of Camus and Sartre in widely accepted existential criticism.'"

"Yes, and you were assigned half a dozen sources to work from."

"I went one better and created my own synthesis, professor. Don't you see that? I think it's brilliant."

"Miles, anyone could have done this cut and paste job in the time it takes to type it up."

"I'm sorry, professor," said Miles, hurt by this, but keeping calm, "This paper took me at least a full Sunday afternoon and evening to write."

"That doesn't excuse the fact that these are not your words."

Miles looked around the room for help. As I was later to learn to my astonishment (but not from Lydia), it was Lydia who spoke up in his defense. She said it was the most original approach to an assignment she'd ever seen and wished she'd thought of it herself; that, if Miles was cheating, he would have tried to cover his tracks somehow, by changing words perhaps, though that would have been an abuse. If in fact it was so obvious what he'd done, how could the professor call it plagiarism? Wasn't plagiarism by definition meant to hide itself? She even said that the paper possessed a kind of hyper-existentialism, which intensified the works of both philosophers by showing how their ideas could so easily blend with and strengthen each other.

By the time she was finished, the professor was knocked speechless and quickly dismissed the class.

Mile's now-famous essay earned a C. When Miles appealed the grade to the department chair, he raised it to a B-minus after reading Lydia's defense, which she was happy to provide in writing.

✳

Not two weeks later, I found Lydia at the back stairs of the apartment building. I was not expecting her, though her absence over the last few days had begun to puzzle me.

"I was hoping we wouldn't meet this way," she said, "I was actually on my way up to Miles' place."

I honestly didn't understand. "Going to study together? That's kind of you, Lydia. Lord knows he needs the help."

"No, that's not it."

Then I realized she was dressed up more fetchingly than I'd ever seen her. I hardly recognized her. Everything she was wearing was brand new. I'd never seen her in a dress before. She looked fabulous. She blushed down to her cleavage as I looked her up and down.

I understood.

"How long?"

She took my meaning.

"Since last week."

"You might have said something."

"I know. He said he would tell you himself, but he obviously hasn't yet."

I wanted to hit her. Not out of anger. I wanted to smack her for her own sake.

"Before you say anything more, I'm going upstairs. I'll have Miles come down and explain everything."

"No way. Lydia! No way. I won't let him in the door. I'll never talk to that fucker, that fuck-up again!"

"No, listen. Don't say that. It hurts."

"Then explain yourself."

"We're engaged. We're leaving after the wedding this Saturday. We're going to Europe for a year, maybe more."

"Very funny. That's the kind of lame, stupid-ass thing Miles would say."

"He's rich."

"Rich?" I asked, remembering his bookshelves.

"Not just rich. Very, very rich."

She turned and headed toward the upper stairway. Then she turned and looked at me.

"I'm sorry, really. I liked you a lot. But I think Miles has gotten a bad deal around here and, and, he's lonely."

I started to laugh. I could see this hurt her too, and stopped.

"What's in it for you, other than all the money you could ever hope for?"

"Don't be insulting. Partly it's that. Sure, why not? But mostly because he's sweet and he loves me."

"You sound like an eight-year-old."

Then she got mad.

"Oh, fuck off. He's the best lover I've ever had. If you must know. The best!"

Then she ran for the stairs.

And that was the last I saw of Lydia or Miles. Yes, there was at least one thing Miles knew how to do. I had to hand it to him. If he really was rich, he sure hadn't paraded the fact. Whatever he was looking for in college, it wasn't a career, but some kind of validation beyond his trust fund, or whatever form his wealth had taken. He might have tried to buy my silence the few times I'd threatened him, but he was apparently above that. And who was I to say he'd bought Lydia? My plump Lydia, as sweet as mown hay and smarter (and hornier) than any girl I'd ever known. Her defense of Miles' paper had actually been quite honorable and was quickly rewarded in a way she'd never dreamed of, and most certainly hadn't angled for. I was sure of that.

✳

I did hear of Lydia and Miles years later. By then I was a tenured professor at Tulane, though twice divorced and childless. My work was all I had at the time. I received this letter from Lydia.

Dear Friend,

It's been eight years, hasn't it? I never got a chance to say goodbye. I don't presume to think that you felt I was "the one," and though I truly enjoyed your companionship, I never felt that we'd be right for each other.

I learned only by accident that you were a professor at Tulane, and tenured to boot! I ran into one of our old classmates and she told me. Two books published too! I'm very proud of you. I hope the other aspects of your life are happy and fulfilling. I haven't enclosed a return address, so I don't expect or desire a response. Perhaps I'm just embarrassed, but I don't want to make things worse by having to interact with you again.

All that aside, I felt I at least owed you this letter and some idea of what happened to Miles and me.

Yes, Miles was rich, but nowhere near as rich as he'd led me to believe. We lived like royalty for almost two years, and Miles gave me anything I'd ever wanted. He really was very sweet, even with his yellow clothes (I got him out of the green ones at least).

What I didn't know until it was too late was that he wasn't THAT rich and we'd been living off the principal of a six-figure stock portfolio, which was his inheritance from his father. It saw more downs than ups because he chose to make all his own investment decisions. He lost a fortune in a venture I won't bore you with.

I know you well enough to believe that none of this will give you any satisfaction. But it gets worse.

Miles passed away just a year ago.

I won't bore you with our attempts to rebuild a life during the five years after we went broke. We had no children. I'm now a legal secretary and doing fine.

Miles died on a fishing trip with his friends from work. At dusk, he got separated from his friends and, trying to find his way back upstream, apparently stepped into a deep pool. His waders had filled up in seconds, they believed, and he drowned.

He had a life insurance policy, which was the one asset he left untouched. It keeps me afloat.

But that's not why I'm writing. I want you of all people to know that, with all of his odd qualities—and you and I laughed long and hard about them, didn't we?—I loved him. I loved him passionately. I have no regrets. Not one.

Take care of yourself.

Sincerely,
Lydia

I can add only that Lydia was wrong. I was very much in love with her, and she broke my heart. My two marriages were empty of what I had imagined my life with Lydia would be. Lying in bed with Lydia, stupid philosopher that I was, I thought I had plenty of time for the phenomenological Dasein, to "be there," to exist with her in the moment, and let our future take care of itself. So I never told her.

It turns out the buffoon was me.

THE
FOOTBRIDGE

*D*URING the summer of 1970, an elderly man walked through a park in a Midwest college town after midnight. The full moon moved above tall oak trees as if being handed from branch to branch. He walked down a long gravel road beside an earthen wall that banked the north side of a river. At one point, the wall gave way to a boating ramp flanked by docks with rotten wooden legs. The river widened as he came to a low dam. The water pooled before it slid across a great concrete chevron, tumbling upon broken concrete blocks and rebar ten feet below. He imagined walking across the top of the dam: the slippery moss that clung to the smooth flat concrete, the water spilling, pushing at his freezing feet.

Below the dam, he walked on sand at the roiled water's edge. Farther out, the river gave back sparks of moonlight. The dim roar of the dam was faintly echoed by the lapping of a frothy wash upon the sand. Then the sand gave way to earth that the recollected river cut into as it continued on its way.

From this grassy bank wishbone-shaped twigs stuck up like fetishes. On other walks he would watch the boys, intent upon their propped fishing rods, hauling out lumbering green-gold carp with cancerous black smears on their bellies, tossed upon the grass to die, gasping, flies at their eyes.

Below the dam it was all sycamores and weeping willows lining both sides of the river. Out of their vaulted architecture thrust the double spires of a suspended footbridge. He slowly mounted two short flights of wrought-iron stairs—for he was beginning to tire (the purpose of this walk)—and reached a lace steel archway. Standing upon thick wooden boards, he saw how they fell off at the first step, curving down to the glimmering darkness where the reflected moon bobbed like the head of a treading swimmer. As he descended, his hands alternately gripped, right and left, the steel cables that were all the bridge offered to a hesitant step or a poor sense of balance, in compensation for its queasy yaw.

He stopped at the bottom of the span. He waited, staring upriver as the swinging slowed.

His name was Alfred Wittman, sixty-two years old, prematurely "retired" professor, disappointed and exhausted researcher. The world didn't know his name. The mistake of his life was his prodigality toward science. He had abandoned the practical fields that had offered solid opportunities for development (and advancement), if not discovery—the computer chip, in particular, had early revealed its potential to him like the wink of a strange woman—to pursue things better left to the cultists and philosophers. Even worse, he had foregone the rigor, if not the spirit, of the scientific method, the empirical test, as he chased discredited chimeras. The man who had once ranted "control is encumbrance" and "experiment is blinding," seemed now like someone who had forgotten how to use his own right eye. His papers describing the qualities of "five o'clock in a clock-less world," or testing the premise, "to foresee a circumstantial detail is to prevent its happening," were never published. Because others had received large grants to study familiar oddities like ESP, and out of amusement on the part of a department faculty that considered it a subtle form of ridicule (the proverbial handing out of rope), he had continued to receive his paltry two thousand for research expenses, right up until the end. That was three years ago. Now, if he was known at all, or remembered by his colleagues, it was as the derided campus nut, an exemplum of tenured obsolescence.

He lived in a seniors' apartment complex, where they brought him meals and took his wash, for which he endorsed his Social Security check. His rooms contained a black-and-white TV, sofa, wooden chairs and a Masonite table, a mattress on a steel frame with wheels (which amused him), a clock radio, sets of plastic dishes and tin pans, toilet articles, discolored linen, and a new word processor that terrified him, bought by a distant, stupidly prospecting nephew and hypothetical heir. His closets were stocked to the ceiling with boxes of books, which he kept (contrary to his own advice to sell the lot for the money), because, he said aloud, "Enthusiasm is fickle. I might reread them all!" He hadn't cracked even one in years.

Each day, he would awake at nine, bathe, and as he ate cereal with milk, watch the morning news and read the newspaper. Then he'd start work. For six hours a day, he peeled address labels and sealed envelopes for four cents a dozen. The clean, sharp papers passed through his hands quickly, each moistened and pounded into finished units, deposited in a tray. The process occupied his hands but required no concentration, leaving him thought without content, only flickering images, like sharp gestures on the periphery of vision, and, most pleasantly, the awareness of being aware, which seemed a delightful consequence that begged further scrutiny. Someday he would write it down, fit it all into a coherent system. In the meantime, he marveled how the trays filled themselves so quickly, faster than he could account for by his efforts.

He was now both a miser and a budding hoarder. He had saved almost half a million dollars in his career, in part because he'd remained a bachelor. His pension was roughly $12,000 a year. He never touched either one. The pension, slightly sweetened from what he'd earned, plus health care, had been the inducements to retire early "in lieu of a protracted administrative process focused on failure to perform required duties as a teacher and researcher."

The books aside, his second bedroom was already filled with newspapers, empty food and drink containers of every description (always rinsed), and plastic bags of every shape, color, and size. The piles had begun to creep into his living room.

Occasionally, with vestigial sadness or longing, Wittman would think of the classroom, his thought experiments, or his elated cries as he sat pounding his typewriter. The intellectual excitement of his academic years seemed as evanescent as what it had replaced— the religious fervor of his childhood: the seven-year old, clutching his missal in bed, mumbling a prayer to alter (people, time, his own thoughts) every circumstance that frightened him, to leave unaltered everything (home, parents, being seven years of age) that enriched his sense of comfort and security.

As he proceeded up the footbridge, he noticed the grinding and pinging of the cables shifting beneath his weight. Deciding that a prolongation of the sound was worse than a brief increase in its volume, he reached the opposite platform with a few brisk steps, with the cables hushing themselves behind him.

But for the height of the angle afforded by the footbridge as he reached the other side, he might never have seen the light from the ice skating house—a cinder block building (in winter flooded with six inches of water) with the character of a bunker: high walls against the wind, no roof. That pale light, flickering against the inner walls, struck him as secret and unsanctioned.

He clambered down the iron stairs and started across the grass toward the skate house.

From up close the building looked dark and empty. He began to hear voices, sibilant as whisperers, but seemingly unconcerned with keeping it down. The sound had that quiet, windy quality of a chant, which has nothing to do with volume, and beneath that sound, an indefinable rumbling.

The wall of the skate house facing him offered only a blank, doorless rectangle. Around to the right, away from the river, Wittman found wide double doors. When his fingers gripped the door handle and his thumb pressed down on the lever, the skate house grew quiet.

Suddenly terrified, he turned and ran around the far corner. The rear wall of the building abutted a hill from which grew tall spruces, throwing shadows upon the grass and the wall. He heard a forceful voice, rhythmically accented, like a sergeant calling a cadence. Then the rumbling and the chanting resumed.

Out of the corner of his eye, Wittman saw something move. In a wind-nudged branch of the nearest spruce hovered two figures of light, which were (he understood, after a moment of delicious wonder) thrown by the light inside the building through holes in the cinder block wall.

He stepped silently up to the lower hole and, rising to his toes, peered into the skate house. His eyes (still strong) adjusted quickly to the dim light. What he saw seemed to taunt explanation: men and women, arms straight up, hands flat, palms up, floating (as if in flight), chanting "Time is God, Think God, God is Time, Thank God, Time is God" as in a round—each and every one of them goose-pimple-naked.

Because of the width of the cinder blocks and the smallness of the hole, he could only see the farthest of them down to mid-calf—closer, only floating heads. He had an idea what was going on.

Frustrated by the restriction of his vision, he backed away, looked around. He noticed other holes, beginning near the ground, that didn't go through, as though a sledgehammer had broken the first of the blocks' double walls. Studying the holes, he realized that they offered a series of hand-holds rising to the top of the wall.

Soon, he had his right foot in the peephole, his right hand clutching the broken rim of a high hole. Having mounted thus far as quickly as a young goat, he now felt winded, his age looming above him like an overhang. Only two more steps and he'd reach the top. Heart thumping, the chant a dim wash of sound beyond the cold stone, he considered backing down and going home the intelligent choice, but before a conscious decision had been made, with a single burst of energy, he mounted the wall and peeked over the top.

As he had suspected, the feet of the naked chanters were shod in roller skates. He almost laughed, but the solemn fervor of the chant imposed a dignity upon the absurdity of the rite that stripped derision of its meaning. He saw now that all of the men had erections. His initial reaction of shame vanished seeing them thrusting forth their chests, making bold, swooping passes at the women, who in turn slowed to allow the briefest, delicate contact, hip to member.

The room was lit by four gas lanterns placed in the middle of each wall on the long benches surrounding the floor. Clothing lay folded in neat piles on the benches; in a corner stood a small cooler and stacks of used plastic glasses spotted with a red drink. From that same corner issued a loud, wordless cry, and the chanting stopped. A man in a black jumpsuit and cap stood and turned, swinging his arm up and around until it pointed directly at Wittman's blinking, unbelieving face.

The lights went out. Wittman heard nothing as he negotiated the first few steps down, then fell on his back into the grass. Breathless but unhurt, angry but hopelessly curious, he stumbled around to the doors, which opened immediately. There, a silent crowd issued forth, everyone dressed or buttoning a last button, tucking in a shirt or blouse, four carrying lanterns, one, the cooler. They calmly scattered into the night without a single word of consternation or parting, or a glance his way—as though Wittman wasn't there.

The last to come out was the man in overalls, who turned to him and smiled, extending his hand, saying in a sweet voice that belied his advanced years, "Greetings, my name is Dead."

Wittman saw what seemed to be his own reaction mirrored in the man's face—Dead went white, lips taut and trembling —which engendered a spark of pity in his own breast. They shook hands. Dead slapped his head with childlike exasperation.

"Of course, I'm sorry," he whispered conspiratorially, thick white brows bobbing, "I forget. It's supposed to have that effect. A contraction of David Edward 'Ed' Dodd, you see? I find my people relax about the going over when they spend a few hours with a man with a name like that. You'll get used to it. Anyquestion?" he concluded, speaking the last two words louder as one.

Wittman found himself remarkably composed. His heart no longer fluttered like a large fin in his chest.

"No, no. I'm just sorry, too. I didn't mean to interrupt. I happened to see your light and curiosity got the better of me. I'm sure it looked very bad. I mean, like I was...."

Wittman broke off voluntarily. He'd found himself speaking rapidly, as though he had much to get off his chest, while Dead tilted back his head and brought it forth and down upon the gentlest smile in a supreme gesture of understanding and forgiveness.

"Anyquestion?"

Embarrassed now, but in spite of himself, Wittman looked into the man's face. He saw, beneath moonlit brows, intelligent eyes, old beyond brilliance, that seemed to mark and catalog his own every gesture with recognition and self-reassurance. Wittman had the rather exalted sense, which he once felt quite often, of confronting additional evidence for the proof of a grand new theory.

"Anyquestion?" he repeated.

"Well, yes, if you don't mind. It isn't my business, and the last thing I'd do is tell. I'm the liberal type when it comes to consenting adults, rest assured. I'd just like to know what...."

"Call it therapy. We do other things. There's a nice quarry for swimming. I even tried basketball once, without the ball, but their sense of it as a game kept interfering. Yes, this is the best I've hit upon so far. You're welcome to join us. We'll be back on Tuesday."

Fleetingly, Wittman saw himself buck-naked on skates and blushed.

"No, I don't think so," he said, trying not to smile.

"If you change your mind, just join us," Dead said with singsong nonchalance, "but don't forget your feet!"

"Feet?"

Dead slapped his forehead again. "Oh, I almost forgot!"

He turned on his heel and pulled the skate house doors closed, then locked them with a key he took from his pocket.

"I've got to return this in the morning," he said to himself, returning the key to his pocket.

"Pleasure meeting you. Hope to see you again," he said, grabbing Wittman's hand, squeezing it briefly. "Now, I must run. Take care."

A blur of black, like an animated hole in the night, Dead hurried off as though some crucial matter required his attention.

"Feet," Wittman said to himself, "he means skates!"

The evening's adventure seemed neither a dream nor a memory as Wittman sat staring at the stacks of envelopes on his kitchen table after a restless night. Improbable, ludicrous, yes, but nonetheless real and present: those naked bodies floating in a rhythmic pattern as formal as a waltz, the women slowing, offering that little bump from the hips as the men passed by. There was about it all something at once distant and lofty, a religious radiance explicit and inexplicable, as well as an attraction purely sexual, a revivifying distortion of the fantasies his brain had ridden like a downward spiral over the decades. But not because of what those bodies did. He remembered (what he hadn't understood at the time) the tension rising like heat from the skaters, rippling with the drone of the chant which both cut and intensified the sensuality of the dance, holding it in a state of perfectly undiminished and incomplete excitement.

He tried to envision himself, his torso, that rumpled pillow of flesh mounted on dwindling legs, hairless, all of him pale but for the skates' black boots. His organ, long a bachelor, a shadow between his thighs, at the first brush with a (pretty?) young woman, draining blood from his body for the renewal of its own life, arching upward like a third arm of triumph. And what if he failed? The community strove for more than what was, perhaps, only an incidental pleasure: the soul through the body, and through other bodies, seeking other souls, and through them something greater than themselves. And no one was alone.

That afternoon Wittman bought beautiful shiny black skates with red wheels.

He had no precise idea what time to arrive that Tuesday night, fearing to be first, obliged to make dozens of awkward introductions, the center of curiosity perhaps delaying the proceedings. He decided on the same hour as before.

As Wittman lumbered across the footbridge, his breath quickened as he saw the light from the skate house. Descending to the grass, he remembered Mollock, the shapeless black creature of tentacles and a toothy grin that once had haunted his dreams: each morning, he'd said to his mother, "Today, I am Mollock!" and growled, dissolving the dream's terror in their laughter.

This errant memory faded, vaguely troubling and unexplained, as he stood, knuckles poised before the skate house doors, listening, hearing nothing within. He knocked. The door opened quickly. There stood Dead, dressed as before, arms opened wide in welcome.

"The next *IS* joins us!" he shouted, stepping back as Wittman followed him into the room. Dead scanned the room, sweeping it with his arms, his voice growing even louder: "Welcome *IS*, friends. IS that is is without boundaries. I have told you, without boundaries, each day we grow!"

There was a brief applause as Wittman walked sheepishly into the light, followed by an amazed hubbub clearly not directed at himself. It occurred to him that they had been waiting for him. They were all seated on the benches against the walls, naked, but for skates, black or white, everyone clutching bits of clothing. The room was pleasantly warm, and the now-gibbous moon sat up in one corner like a lone spectator. As Dead escorted Wittman to a space near the cooler, the faces smiled with genuine kindness and welcome. One—a pretty brunette, perhaps twenty-five years old, whispering to another as he passed—seemed familiar. He glanced at her several times, but she did not turn to him.

He sat and looked up at Dead. There was an awkward pause

during which Wittman did nothing (waiting for instruction), broken when Dead said, "Please proceed!" Of course, he thought, putting his skates down, and beginning to undress. He felt himself going red. Soon he was down to his shorts. Committed thus far, he leaned slightly from the bench and slid them off, lifted his feet from them and sat back, clutching the white clothing in his lap. Dead looked at him expectantly. Wittman laid his shorts on the bench and smiled. Dead pointed at his feet. "Of course!" Wittman whispered and bent over, reaching for his skates. He righted the heavy, stiff leather boots, pulled out the tongues lined with red felt, tugged the long black laces. The boots slid on easily. His thick fingers fumbled with the laces, tying them off finally with a double knot. He gave the dull red hard rubber wheels a spin.

"Now, now, NOW, *IS* begins!" Dead's voice rose to a triumphant call. He backed away and turned to address the assembly. "As then, as now, as when, we are all *IS!* And we are moving, moving toward…." He pointed at the sky. "My friends. Listen. As you have listened before, not with your ears, but with your listening!" he shouted, "*IS!*" he shouted, offering the word to them with both arms.

Everyone applauded.

"*IS!*" Dead repeated.

Shouts and laughter.

"All right," Dead answered, letting his voice taper down. Starting low: "*IS* was first only was. Remember? Then *IS* was we, *IS* we! Now!" Voice rising: "All of us *IS*, and we're moving toward what?"

"Over!" everyone sang, the second syllable rising in unison.

"Are we afraid?"

"No!"

"Why not?"

"Over *IS* too!"

"What will get us there?"

"We will!"

"What will we find there?"

"IS!"

"All right!" answered Dead, bringing the volume down again.

Wittman only half listened, vaguely recognizing the manner, if not the vocabulary of this catechism. It didn't seem important that he understand, and if later it became so, someone would explain. He fidgeted with his shorts, wondering when the dance would begin. He leaned forward to peek at the young brunette. She sat, astonishingly naked, on the edge of her bench, her face flushed, eyes wide and unblinking—she seemed to glory in every word. Unlike the others, she did not laugh or smile; as though any moment might reveal to her the mystery of her own life and death. Her brow furrowed before the impact, her chin trembled on the verge of her crying out. As his shock at her beauty dissolved into envy of her rapture, he realized that she, alone among her fellow novitiates, was quiet in response to Dead's formulas.

Then he remembered—it might have been during his final year as a teacher—an incident that had catalyzed his daydreams for weeks. He was in the middle of conducting one of his thought experiments, posing to his class the question of whether or not morality could be verified, quantified, and categorized scientifically. Then the pretty, troubled junior, drawing a rosary from her penny purse, chin trembling, began to cry, her protestations of her genuine effort for a good grade disintegrating into an abject confession (before twelve fellow students) that her sexual practices, abhorrent to "My God, my Father," as they were, were innocent in their essence, because the underlying intent (she said), lascivious, procreative, or scientific (she said), did not alter for good or evil the neutral animality of the act; nonetheless (now crying abjectly), she was trying to be a good girl, trying as hard as anyone, but we are all so frail, so mysterious, and while she sought forgiveness and understanding, her outburst (she said) shouldn't necessarily suggest to those present, of either sex, young or old, that she was not still theirs for the asking. "It's just what I am!" she wailed. He never was able to understand why he hadn't stopped her in the middle of this emotional breakdown. Only when she had stopped talking did he escort her, sobbing, from the room. In the hallway, he'd tried to give her a comforting hug but she pulled away violently. He told her to go home to her parents for a few weeks. He never saw her again. Until now? he wondered.

The catechism ended. There was a pause. Wittman leaned farther forward and raised his hand to attract the young woman's attention. She smiled perfunctorily, with neither recognition nor avoidance.

Dead held up his arms like a conductor, turning on his heel, catching every eye. He turned up his palms. The congregation stood.

That Wittman, standing, immediately fell on his backside, surprised him less than that no one appeared to notice, let alone laugh. He rolled onto his knees and stood, hands flailing more for a steadying hand (which wasn't offered) than for balance. Too preoccupied to long regret overlooking this minor detail—that he hadn't been on skates (roller or ice) in fifty years and might have practiced before coming here—he shuffled his feet, content with jerky forward progress, as the others swirled around him, perfect swans to his graceless coot.

The chant had begun: "Time Is God, Think God, God Is Time, Thank God, Time is God...." Dead had taken his seat near the cooler and, to Wittman's puzzlement, seemed quite detached and unconcerned with the proceedings. He stared blankly, a bit wearily, at the sky—the virtuoso, bored and undistracted by his pupils' exercises.

Wittman joined the chant, mumbling when his concentration allowed of any division. Inching across the smooth concrete, he felt a growing confidence that he could at least prevent the humiliation of falling. His greatest difficulty rested in his arms: he needed them loose and flailing for balance and felt his feet begin to shoot the moment he thrust his arms up like the others did. He compromised on an unsteady two and ten o'clock attitude, hoping to earn some credit for trying.

The dance began to impose its rhythm upon his body. Expectant and fearful, he felt for the surge of feeling he remembered from his perch upon the wall, watching with lust (as yet abstract) the forms and provocative gestures of the unembarrassed bodies as they passed. He felt no immediate erotic connection to the pert breasts, splayed thighs, and rigid members of the crowd swirling around him. Only when the young brunette twice brushed past him did his heart turn over. Yet nothing stirred below. Instead, vaguely at first, but soon palpably, unmistakably, he felt an immense sadness, a sense of abject supplication deliberately hindering sensuality, which he located in the expression on each face (he hadn't had the angle to read from above), which seemed to regret with resignation (as if it were an ineluctable barrier) the inflammation of the flesh. And yet, all was not disappointment; though he felt thwarted in his inability to reach the physical condition of the others, he glimpsed in his own lightheartedness a horizon of bliss attainable in the eventual sur-mounting of his own (very different) barrier to their suffused state. Beyond that, he had no aspirations.

He shuffled a bit, then rolled, crossing and re-crossing the room, careful not to run into the others as they circled and eddied about him—always a new face passing, eyes heavenward, lips churning out the chant faster and faster. He shivered, as a cool wind dipped down through the room. The moon had fallen beyond the concrete walls. Hoping yet to achieve some valence of intensity, Wittman closed his eyes; uncannily, all grew quiet. He waited, feeling for the change. Was this some new level reached, some heightened phase of the rite? Something thrilled inside him. With delicious terror, he opened his eyes.

Everyone was by the benches, pulling off skates, quickly dressing. It was over. He'd heard no signal from Dead, but he wouldn't have seen a gesture to desist. Alone in the middle of the room, feeling silly and alien, he shuffled back to his clothes and sat down. Anger mounting in his chest, he tore at his laces. A cool hand fell on his shoulder.

"Wait. After the others," Dead whispered, "Anyquestion?"

As Wittman looked up, the other sauntered away, laying his hands on various shoulders, squeezing, patting as he went. The young brunette greeted Dead with a questioning smile; he bent toward her, whispered something, then he kissed her lips. She bowed her head as if in assent. Dead's hand caressed her cheek, her chin, then absently passed across her right breast, as he stepped away from her.

This cooled Wittman's anger. Having cursed himself for having come here, he now saw, in Dead's familiar, casual caress, the level of connection that he, a mere novice, a stranger, could hardly have expected to reach on the first night.

The skate house was soon empty but for Dead, and, to Wittman's delight, the young brunette, who sat near the door in a summer dress patterned with purple flowers, her feet bare, her fine long legs crossed at the ankles. One of the lanterns had been left in the corner nearest the doors, and the moon had reappeared above the cinder block walls. Wittman approached them, buttoning his shirt.

Arms crossed on his chest, his white brows bobbing, Dead said, "Not very satisfactory, was it?"

Wittman smiled, hunched his shoulders. The young woman seemed preoccupied with something only she could see through the darkness of the double doors.

"Well, friend, don't worry. It takes time. It's apparent that certain things our little society takes for granted have grown for you somewhat, shall we say, sleepy?"

Wittman would not look at him.

The question of why no one ejaculated occurred to him, but he kept quiet.

"Charlotte, come here, sweetheart."

Yes, that was her name. Was she the one? She stood, looking down, hands clasped below her waist. Dead took Wittman's elbow and drew him to her.

"I've asked my assistant to take care of that problem." Again, he caressed her cheek. She turned and looked up at Wittman boldly, without curiosity. "She's had some training in this area. I trust her completely and so shall you. Any question?"

She reached for Wittman's hand. He grabbed the top of her hand, then turned his own up; her splayed fingers drummed across his palm.

"I'll leave now," said Dead, "lock you in for a while. Take a turn around the park. When I return, we'll talk about your contribution to our little ministry, Mister...?"

"Albert Wittman," he replied, squeezing the cool, smooth fingers.

The black jumpsuit winked out behind the doors. The key turned with two brief metallic notes.

"Over here," she said, pulling him toward the lantern. She dropped his hand and stepped away from him. "Take off your pants." He quickly obeyed as she looked for something in her purse.

"Here, put this on," she said, holding out to him a condom packet.

As he did so, he found he no longer had any difficulty with rigidity. She grabbed the pants and laid them on the concrete, tugging the legs, smoothing the cloth out to the shape of a man below the waist. With one quick, continuous motion, she hiked her dress and pulled white cotton panties down and stepped out. Her cool, expressionless purple eyes reassured him that she didn't know who he was. She stepped up to him and kissed his cheek. Her left hand brushed his thigh, then closed around him.

"Why, you're ready!" she said, backing away, surprised.

She turned with a questioning glance at the locked doors. Then she sighed, stooped and sat back on his pants, hiking up her dress, bunched in her fist at her belly. She drew her knees up and let them fall open. Breath short, Wittman knelt down, pulling his shirt up, glimpsing the furred flesh that was thrust up between her pale thighs by the hard floor. He pressed himself in. She gripped his upper arms. Leaning on one arm, he reached to guide himself, encountering a soft dry wall.

"Wait," she said, tonguing her fingers. She reached between her thighs.

A wettening, then a loosening, permitted entry. He pushed, found a halting way into her. And, as he began to move, Charlotte moving against him, it was—when she whispered hotly in his ear, what he knew wasn't true, what he knew was true because he was here with her—it was indeed a going over.

THE STORY
OF MY UNIVERSE

*O*NE morning, about a week ago, I woke up and realized that I wasn't innocent any more. I looked in the mirror, and I looked as I've always looked, but I realized that inside I was not like other people.

I used the word "realized," but what I really mean is that I "remembered." The longer I looked at myself, the more I recalled a life that wasn't mine, or at least not the one I'd known for years.

I don't mean that I remembered that I was an alien from another planet, or a victim of amnesia just coming out of it, or recovering from brainwashing, or experiencing a drug-induced flashback, or any of that nonsense.

The feeling I experienced as the memories increased in number and detail was both exhilarating and, as you'll soon see, horrifying. Also, underlying everything, these memories didn't seem entirely new, nor even forgotten, but more akin to dreams coming alive. I could not question the truth and accuracy of them.

My wife was still asleep, but I was scared to go back to the bedroom. I was reminded of the old LSD joke. A couple of stoned kids are sitting in a bedroom and one kid is watching as the walls melt. He says, "Gee, I sure hope Mom doesn't come in and see all this."

I suppose, and I say this reluctantly, the closest I can come to describing it is that tired and suspect sanctuary of victimized innocence, "recovered memory." But, as I understand the experience, it's

239

supposed to come almost as a surprise or shock. But there was no sense that I was finding something lost, at least, not at first.

Then, of a sudden, I felt dizzy. I grabbed the sink and held on or I would have fallen. A moment of almost blinding confusion took over, leaving a simple, vivid realization: three years ago I murdered someone I didn't even know.

As I said, this experience took place about a week ago. Over the next few days, I managed to continue to function in my role as a surveyor for the county. My wife asked me only once if something was troubling me, and I said I had a bad migraine, to which I'm prone. She left me alone.

What follows is the product of many hours staring into the TV pretending to watch, or staring at the sky as I held my surveyor's optical level. Gradually, I was able to organize what were jumbled fragments and flashes of visualization into the following narrative.

I'd been walking in the country after a fight with my wife. We were visiting her parents and I couldn't stand another second in that house, so I just started walking. It was a small town, Belvidere, Illinois, and I was soon alone on a country road. As it was getting dark, a young man in overalls approached me and asked for my wallet. I laughed at him and he shoved me, knocking me down by the side of the road. I picked up a rock, stood and hit him with it so hard I could hear his skull crack. He fell on his back. I checked for a pulse and, finding none, quickly grabbed his feet and dragged him into the tall grass between the road and a white fence. Not knowing what else to do, I started walking back to the house, surprised by how calm I seemed to be. With absolute clarity, I considered my options. I had used lethal force and hidden a body. I couldn't claim self-defense because he hadn't done more than push me and ask for my wallet. Hiding the body and not immediately calling 9-1-1 was a crime, even if the actual killing could be said to be in self-defense.

But I'd read enough about cases of self-defense leading to charges to know that I had not reacted proportionally and could well be indicted for manslaughter.

Even if I wasn't, my career would likely be over, and my marriage, already in jeopardy, as well.

Of course, I hadn't actually hidden the body. It would be found in the tall grass soon enough. It was nearly dark and the road rarely traveled even in daylight. I made up my mind and returned to the body. You have to really hide it, I thought to myself. But how?

On the other side of the fence was a hundred feet of pasture and the river that ran through town, the Kishwaukee. If I could get the body into the water and it floated a couple of miles downstream, it would hang up on a concrete dam, and that would be so far away that no one could determine where the body had come from. In fact, the likeliest determination would be that he fell off the dam, hit his head and drowned. But how could I manage it? Then I remembered that somewhere nearby there was a stile over the fence. I found it less than fifty feet up the road.

The body had been remarkably light, just skin and bones. I hadn't seen and couldn't see now how old the man was. I touched his face and there was significant stubble, so at least I hadn't killed a boy. I felt his head where I'd struck him and there didn't seem to be any blood, though my fingers sank in slightly as if the skull had shattered.

I'm six-two and 250 pounds, so picking him up and shouldering him toward the stile was hardly a challenge. I didn't even break a sweat. Although blood wasn't apparent, I still kept his head away from my clothing. I climbed three steps and laid him on the platform in the middle of the stile. I stepped over him onto the back steps and picked him up again.

It was getting darker, but a half-moon hung on the other side of the river. I wasn't blind. The pasture was dry and full of hoof prints. I couldn't be sure, but the ground seemed hard and just grassy enough that I didn't believe that I could be leaving much of a trail.

I reached the river and dropped the body in, not wanting its weight to disturb the grass more than I already had. I had hoped that it would quickly begin to float away, but it just lay there, face-down, half-submerged. What should I do? I knew that my arriving home wet was going to be questioned and remembered.

Then, a stroke of luck—in the moon's reflection on the water, I could see, hung up on the bank, a reasonably stout branch about ten feet long. It was soaked through, but not so heavy I couldn't use it to push the body into the current where it began to slowly float away. Then I replaced the branch in the muddy groove it had left and pushed it down until it seemed to be firmly stuck. I walked to the stile, taking a slightly bowed path back, careful not to step in my own prints. Just to be sure, I passed my hands over all the steps and the top platform and found nothing wet. In seconds I was back on the road. The only thing that made me uneasy was the grass I'd pulled the body into at first. I couldn't tell if it was noticeably flattened, but there was nothing I could do about that.

I returned to the house as quickly as I could without getting winded, so that I wouldn't be questioned for staying out too long after dark.

I remained just a bit grumpy with my wife, not that I could remember what our argument had been about, and went to bed as quickly as I could get away.

By breakfast we'd made it up, me apologizing as usual. I proposed we take a nice walk that afternoon, before setting off for home.

Holding hands for much of the way, we wandered, or I let her feel like we were wandering, but in half an hour we were coming up on the stile. I scanned the grass leading up to it and saw only a shallow depression that didn't seem large enough to have been made by a man's body. I considered asking her if she'd like to go over the stile to the riverbank, but I remembered how fastidious she was about her clothes and knew she'd decline. As we passed the stile, I could tell it was spotless. And that was that. Everything else was up to luck.

Once home, I checked the regional newspaper online, the Rockford *Register,* and found no mention of a death. The next day there was a story at the top of the news. It said a man estimated to be in his early thirties was found dead just upstream of a flood control dam on the Kishwaukee River in Belvidere. As yet unidentified, he was dressed in faded denim overalls and black work boots. His hair and skin color were both fair. Height and weight both medium. Cause of death was pending a coroner's report, but police said that evidence of a severe blow to the head, while potentially the result of an act of violence, could as easily be attributed to the man's falling and striking his head on the dam.

A policeman said something about the dam being a dangerous nuisance for decades. Many people, kids mostly, had tried walking across it, slipped and fell, hurting themselves, sometimes fatally.

The officer expressed his hope that friends or family would come forward to identify the body.

Of course, I couldn't have been more relieved. The next day, the verdict was in, the coroner having determined "death by misadventure." Most likely, the man had fallen, striking his head on the dam, and drowned. No one had come forward to claim the body.

Over the next few weeks, there was only one further mention of the fatality, including the fact that no one had yet reported him missing.

I was home free, or so I thought. The story went on to quote a detective who said there was one thing that bothered him. In virtually every other accident on the dam, the injured party had fallen downstream, sliding down the sloped dam and landing among large blocks of concrete and rebar meant to slow and smooth out the downrush of water. In this case, the dead man had fallen into the upstream side of the dam.

I continued to check the paper for another month until I could hardly remember why. Then it was all gone from my mind.

I'll come back to what might have caused me to remember, but as for forgetting so completely?

I was a pretty rowdy kid, always running into trouble and fights, doing daredevil stunts, and, as a result, I have a number of noticeable scars—on my forehead, my right earlobe, the top of my head, and both of my knees. I remember each injury vividly, all except one. I have a scar on the bridge of my nose. At the age of five, I'd been hanging onto the outside of the back porch rail above an uncovered garbage can. I managed to fall head first, and my nose struck the edge of the can. The cut was deep, and my parents couldn't understand why I didn't cry. They only told me about this years later when I confessed to them, in some other context I can't remember, that I had absolutely no recollection of how I got that particular scar. I have always suspected that the trauma of pain and blood was so great that I simply pushed it out of my mind, and to this day I still don't have any idea what happened. Was I pushed by a friend, did I slip? I don't know.

How does this relate? That remains the mystery, except to say that that is at least one traumatic event in my past that I have totally forgotten. Perhaps that trash can caused some kind of permanent damage that left me prone to forget other traumatic events. Killing a man certainly qualifies. (And who knows how many other memories I may have lost? Again, I don't know.)

Perhaps it was my disintegrating marriage and eventual, humiliating divorce, which was complicated by the discovery of an adulterous affair with the woman who is now my wife, that caused me to relegate the incident of the man in overalls to the very back of my mind until it took on a dreamlike unreality and virtually disappeared.

And now I know why the memory of the dead man returned. I hate to use the cliché "triggered," which seems too much like the mind is a puzzle box and pressing just the right spot opens it up, though the metaphor is more related to firing a gun. In this case, it was like a gun was fired right into my brain.

The big news nationally the day before my "recalling" (as if my brain was defective like a Toyota seat belt and was recalled, and replaced), was of a tornado that hit Belvidere, killing fourteen people when the twister leveled a shopping center on the west edge of town. Because I had once had a personal connection to that little town, I went online to follow the story, and one of the links that popped up was the Rockford newspaper I've already mentioned. The article was long and detailed and mentioned that the tornado had caused a minor tsunami in the river running through town, which demolished a portion of a flood control dam. The Kishwaukee River being otherwise at low crest at the time, the onrush of water through a seven foot gap in the dam was so far doing only minor damage downstream, mostly to crops close to what was now a flooding river. The Army Corps of Engineers was already onsite working for a temporary solution to the problem. One official was quoted as saying the dam should have been torn out long ago.

Four days after my "recalling," I bought an online subscription to the Rockford paper, which allowed me to scour its database all the way back to the day after I killed a man. The simple search word "overalls" brought those early articles up, but, then, I found this:

BELVIDERE, IL—After three months, the mystery of the identity of a man in denim overalls who was found dead above the city's flood control dam has been solved. His name was Edward Pratt, twenty-six years of age, and a resident of Garden Prairie, six miles west of Belvidere. It was originally thought that he'd slipped while walking on the Belvidere dam and fallen, hitting his head on the concrete and drowning. The coroner's report called it "death by misadventure."

His estranged wife, Martha Pratt, a resident of Marengo, some ten miles away, has identified the body by photograph. Her reasons for not coming forward earlier appear to have been her estrangement from her husband and the fact that she didn't follow local news. She said, "I hadn't missed him. Not at all."

To this reporter, she explained that she hadn't seen her husband for weeks prior to his death. She knew he was living in a small boarding house in Garden Prairie. She testified that he didn't have a job or a car to her knowledge, and that he was living on his half of their mutual savings, which they'd divided when he moved out of the house. She said he had owned a bicycle for years.

When asked by the authorities if she thought it possible that he had died by falling on the dam, she replied, "Not unless you found his bicycle nearby."

Belvidere's Chief of Police Robert Cavanaugh has declared that what had been a closed case has been reopened for investigation.

Using the search word "Pratt," I learned from ensuing reports that a bicycle fitting the wife's description as a "beat-up green Schwinn ten-speed" had been found in tall weeds on the east end of Belvidere near the Kishwaukee River. A high school senior named Claude Bowers had found the bicycle and turned it over to the police two days after the man was found dead. The bicycle had been in a lost and found compound ever since, until it was shown to the dead man's wife, who said, "It sure looks like his."

The teenager showed the police the location of the bicycle when he found it, which was roughly one half-mile from the edge of Belvidere, next to a road that ran along the Kishwaukee River.

I also learned that inhabitants of Garden Prairie knew Edward Pratt as an irritable loner who drank to excess in the town's two bars and occasionally started fights, which, because of his slight body, he usually lost. The owner of the boarding house Pratt lived in said he had people skip out on him all the time. He also confirmed the description of the bicycle.

One resident said that he'd often seen Pratt riding his bicycle around the countryside.

The police had searched the area in all directions from the location of the found bicycle to the edge of town, and, by boat, had inspected every inch of the riverbank on both sides. All for nothing. The fact that the river had flooded twice in the last three months made the riverbank search particularly unrewarding. One officer was overheard to say, "A damned waste of time."

So now I knew. Pratt had been on one of his aimless wanderings when he saw me walking toward him. He must have dismounted, rolled the bike into the weeds, and come forward to accost me. Why he would try, unarmed, to rob someone practically twice his size and weight was a mystery.

And then I remembered—the last two things in the puzzle box— his drinking in bars, getting into fights. He was drunk. He stank of whiskey as I carried him to the river. I smelled it, that sharp tang, as I stared at the computer.

It's an hour later, staring into space in my home office, and I recalled that I too had been drunk—gin and tonic before dinner and all of a bottle of cabernet.

Why hadn't the newspaper said anything about alcohol in his blood?

Had there been a bicycle? Had he been the first to speak? Had I knocked him off the bike? Had I said something to make him push me? Had he asked for my wallet? Had striking him jolted me sober —enough to make my careful maneuvers in disposing of his body possible? Was it all my fault?

I do not know.

This brings this account up to the present date. This morning I exhausted every last possible means of searching the newspaper database and found nothing more about Edward Pratt. The last entry had been more than thirty months ago. It was largely a rehash with the headline, "Investigation Continues in Death of Garden Prairie Man". The story concluded, quoting the police chief: "We now have to assume the worst. As far as I'm concerned, this case will remain open as long as it takes to find the murderer."

Given the amount of time that has passed since it happened, the whole thing grows grayer and more faded every moment. Almost as though I'm beginning to forget it all over again.

✳

It's been more than a week since I finished writing the account of my "recalling." I have stayed away from my computer, and I pull up this file now with some trepidation. I haven't reread what's written on the previous pages. Perhaps I should have started a new document to say what I have to say to myself in cold, clear words, but it's bad enough to have even one such document in existence.

Actually, I'm scared to death of what I think is in the previous pages. You see, I remember more than the mere gist, but I doubt I do with the clarity I possessed when I wrote them. I say "doubt" because I am not only uncertain about what they say, but about what they describe—about what actually happened to me. I think I am guilty of murdering someone, but that knowledge is tinged with questions and evasions, like an old, scarred table that's been heavily shellacked. Will I even believe what I've written?

Memory is a stupid thing.

Yes, I could have just deleted the file and gone on with my life, same as before. I've gotten sufficiently comfortable (terrible word under the circumstances) with my memories that I can usually push them so far in the background that they don't really matter.

What a thing to say—"don't really matter."

Dreams don't matter, of that I'm certain. The difference between these pages and a dream is only a matter of semantics. I'm talking about the words that describe, either with clarity or badly blurred, a memory. (We wake with memories of dreams, but they disappear unless we quickly write them down.) But there's one big difference between what I've written and a dream. How many times have I listened, without boredom, to someone tell me about a dream they'd had the night before? Dreams are boring as hell, except to the persons who have them, and usually boring even to them.

I'm pretty sure, though, that there are people in my ex-wife's hometown that would not find this file, this dream of mine, in the least bit boring. In fact, it would electrify them, if I've said what I think I've said.

My real purpose in coming back to all this is to put in writing my options. I have already mentioned one. Hit delete and move on.

I could get in my car and drive to the Belvidere police department and tell them I might have, no, did kill a man three years ago. And what could I expect? Incarceration and acquittal, because I can't prove anything, except that I was in the town that day. Psychiatric evaluation and dismissal because I honestly don't remember all that much, except that I hit some guy with a rock and probably dropped him in their river?

Maybe under questioning I'd remember things more clearly, enough to convince a jury. But why would I do that? Do I want to go to prison?

Or, last option, send them this file and let things take their course. Maybe they'll find me as a result. If not, then at least they have one plausible solution to the crime.

But in order to do that I'd have to read it all over again. I'd have to decide to leave in or out certain details, either to make finding me more easy, or more difficult, or impossible.

Do I want to be the perpetrator of an unsolved crime, forever waiting for the moment when I can't stand it anymore, either the undeserved freedom I now enjoy, or someone someday knocking on my door and putting me in a police car? And who's to say they won't find me if I don't do anything? I suspect it will go worse for me if they do. The fugitive is never given much of a break.

Those are my options. Now I plan to read this entire document and make a decision. Or not. Maybe I'll just flip a coin. Either way, unless a veil of forgetting drops over me, which will never be total, I'll have to do something.

Here's me talking to myself: What would you do?

Wait. There's one last option. I'm going to print it out and give it to my lovely wife. She is part of this. It's time she knew. I will give it to her and say, should I send it to them? I'll let her decide.

*

After dinner last night, I put the document in front of Helene and asked her to read it while I cleaned away the dishes. She's a very quick reader, something I admire in her, since I'm slow.

Her response was: "I didn't know you'd taken up writing short fiction. That's an interesting twist at the end."

When I told her it was all real, she laughed and said, "Well, of course. It's meant to be. You should send it out. I'd love to see you in print."

No, I insisted, it was true. It all really happened and I couldn't live with the uncertainty any more.

Helene is beautiful and sexy and we love each other very much. She is also seven months pregnant with our first child. She picked up the sheets of paper.

"Very funny," she said, angrily, and ripped the pages in two and handed them across the table. "I don't want to hear another word of this nonsense ever again."

ABOUT
THE AUTHOR

CHRISTOPHER GUERIN has two degrees in English Literature from Northern Illinois University. He worked in the symphony orchestra business for twenty-five years, twenty as the President of the Fort Wayne Philharmonic. His stories, poems, essays, and book reviews have appeared in numerous publications. His work was anthologized in 2017 in *A Gathering of World Poets* (Nibir Ghosh, Phd. ed.). His book of 200 sonnets, the first volume of a projected 600 sonnets entitled *My Human Disguise,* was published in 2018 and is available on Amazon. He has written a dozen children's stories, four volumes of short stories, and three books of poetry. His one act play, "Quartet," received a staged reading with Actors Equity actors in 1998 by the Open Door Theater, and will be fully staged in 2020.

www.ingramcontent.com/pod-product-compliance
Lightning Source LLC
Chambersburg PA
CBHW071252250626
47159CB00004B/1143